The most diffic[...]
first novel publis[...]
matter what writi[...] the writer may have,
most publishers simply do not want to take the risk of
putting out a novel by an "unknown."

Hence, *Ben Bova's Discoveries*. There's a wealth of
talent in the science fiction field waiting for the
chance to get their first novels to you, the reader. The
*Discoveries* series will present novels by such writers:
many of them experienced authors of short fiction or
nonfiction, others brand-new writers who have never
published anything before.

As editor of the *Discoveries* series, I promise you
the same high standards I insisted on when I edited
*Analog* and *Omni* magazines: science fiction that
entertains you with bold new ideas and high-quality
writing.

H. C. Turk has created an unforgettable character in
Melody Preece, and a whacky universe where Erth
and Marz are almost—but happily not quite—like
our own Earth and Mars. ETHER ORE is wildly
original, and Turk is a writer who can make you laugh
and shudder with apprehension at the same time.

—Ben Bova

# BEN BOVA'S DISCOVERIES

## H.C. TURK

# ETHER ORE

A TOM DOHERTY ASSOCIATES BOOK

ETHER ORE

First printing: November 1987

A TOR Book

Published by Tom Doherty Associates, Inc.
49 West 24 Street
New York, N.Y. 10010

Cover art by Boris Vallejo

ISBN: 0-812-55635-6
CAN. ED.: 0-812-55636-4

Printed in the United States of America

0  9  8  7  6  5  4  3  2  1

# CHAPTER 1:
## Spare Artists and Sweetbread

Melody had heard of the ghosts of Marz, but was not terrified of these spectres until she became one.

Settlements for mining the planet's unique ore crop began when Melody Preece was seventeen. Immediately thereafter Marz became her ultimate goal. As was normal for youths of UR nation members, Melody at this age was already ten years into her program for earning adulthood by working, employment in various areas of the world's work force of children. Although thirteen years of normal service remained before Melody could legally be considered adult, her professional intent was to retire before thirty by gaining abnormally great credits, such as Marz, a stint on the Tan Planet.

In this era, the greatest influence on world politics and society was the pacifist Adele Hidler. Führher Hidler had gained her greatest fame by virtually preventing World War II using the force of her personality, overcoming her demokraptic nemesis, Wynton Churchell, via heated and well-publicized debates. Hidler convinced the world to reject Churchell's ideas, his militarism, and especially the Briticher's

unfortunate desire to force Yurope's Hebish popula-
tions into a separate state instead of integrating them
with the societies of their home nations. Hidler's
insistence was to accept Jewbrews as people instead of
segregating them as a religious cult.

Churchell had long before succumbed to lung cancer caused by smoking Kuban cigars, but in 1978,
Hidler still led the Wienar Republik. Twenty years
before, in tribute to her respected but deceased nemesis, Hidler had initiated a UR-wide ban of tobacco
usage except for medicinal purposes as prescribed by
a physician. As an economic move, this legislation
was most distressing for Melody's people, her family
being sixth-generation Kubanas. As the last of the
original fourteen colonies and the only one to retain a
semi-independent affiliation with Ingland, naturally
the state was intensely Britch as a matter of heritage;
and though Churchell in the thirties was less than the
consummate statesman, he was still Monarch. His
regal position as well as Hidler's Nicotine Edict
caused understandable nationalistic animosity; but
eventually even the Kubans came to realize that
Hidler was correct, and Churchell was just another
queen. Since one of Churchell's last acts was to
permanently transfer the throne's governmental control to Parlyment and state ministers, his successor
was far easier to love, for Henry VIII was a jovial man
with no power.

Promoting worldwide peace was scarcely less difficult after Churchell's demise, for then Hidler had to
deal with the United Separate States of Ameriga's
imperialistic president, Lynda Buns Jonestown. Perhaps Hidler's most controversial decision was to
subsidize Howaye in its efforts to avoid becoming the

137th state. The upcry arising from the East Atlantic Treaty Organization was over the possibility of their having to literally buy future independence for the nations of the world now that a precedent had been established. The Cave-In Theory thus arose, EATO's fear being that once a crack formed in the surface of socialism, would not every clod drop away? Those most absurdly paranoid believed that falling interest rates near a border would cause Calizonia, for example, to plummet into Ameriga's jaws.

Marz, at least, would certainly remain under the jurisdiction of the United Republik Nations, and no individual country could compete in power or influence with the United Rations. Here as well Hidler was a great factor, her complete revamping of Doitchland's educational system having been adopted by the UR, Kuba a charter member. Uniquely, Melody conjoined these areas of outer space and education, for the Marzian ore farms would be the subject of her mistress' task, if only she could find her away across those desired millions of miles.

Although a broad range of technologies fascinated her, Melody was still young enough to be thrilled by new experience before being moved by new ideas. Regarding Marz, she was not looking forward to being involved with the new organic minerals allowing pulse fusion which made travel between planets feasible: Melody was looking forward to looking. During her career, she had often flown by plane, her consistently greatest pleasure in flight not the travel itself, but the phenomenon of looking down to a world left behind. When Marz was made available as a possible job site for the rare stu'ent, Melody knew no greater thrill could exist for her than to look down and see

Erth left behind, to look below to Marz from a position of superiority. Her goal was set at seventeen, but not until seven years later was it achieved.

Melody's mother was on the board of directors of Kuba Gazelleschaft, the governing body of their small nation. Her father built replica eighteenth-century Frensh toilets. Of course these endeavors were hobbies, not professions. With Hidler's changes in the world's educational system, vocational and avocational roles became modified. The basic definitions remained the same: a hobby satisfies; whereas a profession pays. The difference was that the drudgery of work became an educational accomplishment ending with maturity so that one could reasonably devote her energies to a beloved hobby. Youthful work paid didactic credits, a sufficient quantity providing the child with legal adulthood. Then a hobby was chosen (exchangeable under certain conditions) which supplied the retiree not only with an emotional income, but with the satisfaction of swap stipends according to a set scale. With this barter, one could save to buy spouse or child privileges and begin a family. (Melody's parents had been able to afford only one child, though an illegal pregnancy mandated an abortion. As her mother noted, "You'd think if they could travel to Marz, they could build a decent condominimum.")

Melody's was the second generation to work at education, becoming familiar with as many areas of world life and production as possible so that eventual adulthood might be lived properly, fully. This was the basic principle of education as established by Hidler's ministers, that a person could best select a lifelong endeavor by sampling all those appearing to be of interest during youth. Congressional practices first learned by being hired as a page at the age of eight would likely require a refresher course in later years, but experienced events are more memorable than rote data. Melody's had been an average education, beginning at home and extending all over the world as subsidized by Kuba and the UR, covering areas chosen by the individual and her parents, but including state-mandated activities from refuse collection to assembling calculors, from health to mental and manual labor with all the accompanying theory and physical participation. Melody was on a concrete crew in Perjia troweling roadwalks smooth by the age of twelve. At fifteen she was in the purchasing department of the North Koran Air Force, small-arms division, and had authorized a multi-million-pound order for sawed-off shotguns and phlegm throwers; for children were encouraged to participate in decision-making processes whenever their talents allowed. Grand decisions had always been one of Melody's fortes. She heard of people living on Marz, learned of plans for accepting stu'ents two years later, but had set her goal from the first.

Marz was no abstract objective for Erth —conquering the universe and so on—after the discovery of a remarkable semi-organic plant form which adsorbed and "refined" a mineral from the soil that allowed pulse fusion to become a practical source of power. Although the mineral could be physically removed from the Marzian soil, the unternuclear rearrangement which transpired within the plant body was all-important and not duplicable artificially. Thus the value of the plant was its ore, and the crop was mined. Specifically, the mineral was a radioactive isotope of the common element saturnium, though some scientists insisted that in itself the ore was a new element. The difference, however, was profound; for whereas saturnium made excellent bullets, the Marzian ore had a unique sub-atomic structure whose surplus middling force bonds temporarily could be made to retain vast quantities of electrons, forming super-electrically charged supra-nuclei. The affected moo-masons were "charged" via unchecked thermonuclear fusion, this explosive force to be released thereafter under magnetic control as an electronic plasmic beam. Potential for electric power production was unlimited, but unnecessary; for cheaper, simpler, and safer salar power had been perfected decades before. The ore crop did, however, allow an excellent propulsion system for moderate interplanetary travel. Detractors of the Marzian enterprise pointed out that the only value of the ore was to allow travel to Marz for what end purpose? But since no expensive wars were likely to occur on an Erth whose people were well off due to prevalent salar energy, what better way to spend the excess resources? True, the poorer, unaffiliated nations of the world were still embroiled in living and warring and starving, but this would not be cured by eliminating any sort of transportation.

Marz was only a beginning, however, greater ventures planned, the outer planets being examined to no profound conclusion as Melody planned Marz as an end for herself, an end to her childhood. The average age for gaining adult status was thirty, if sufficient credits could be earned. By twenty-four, Melody was well on her way to an early retirement, perhaps as soon as 1981, when she would be twenty-seven. As an adult she would be free to choose an appealing, productive avocation as supported by unlimited free labor from the world's children.

Marz would be a huge credit for her, but some unique problems were involved. First, Erth-Marz voyages were 291 days apart in order to take advantage of orbit relations. Since service stints on the planet were therefore ten Erth months, those few stu'ents accepted would have to be truly dedicated, as the average Erth profession was rarely longer than a half year. Furthermore, on Erth one could visit home for the hollydays, but there would be no family on Marz for the duration. Parents were encouraged to hire their children occasionally, but Marz was so desirable an occupation that this practice would not be allowed, lest nepotism sully the reputation of the UR and its most distant enterprise. And here was the greatest problem for Melody: exclusivity of personnel. There were no clear guidelines available for selecting stu'ents for Marzian duty, the incomplete section listing in the *UR Encyclopedic Dictionary of Employ by Pre-Adults* still marked "Provisional."

Any job could be gained on Erth, but to retain the occupation long enough to earn credits, a child must demonstrate an aptitude for the required tasks, or evident potential for attaining same. Regarding Marz, the order was reversed; for the stu'ents had to prove themselves in advance—but how? The work itself required no special abilities, and the conditions were no worse than a steal mill. As on Erth, exceptional merit was no factor, to obviate prejudice against the average lass. One rumor said final selection was determined by shortest straw, but Melody preferred another pointing out that Marz was a good place to dump someone you didn't want on Erth for a near-year. Pinky Lingerton got to go after flooding half the Naptha Valley, didn't he? But of course Melody knew those negligent or intentionally destructive would not get past the stratosphere. Her career goal, then, was to be good, but not too good, and to promote herself so that UR Education's upper echelon would have to take direct action with her, Melody planning to beg and bat her blue eyes until they got sick of hearing her whine and shipped her off to the Brown Planet.

Not too much pleading, however, and no teasing. Wiggling around men would lead to sex incrimination charges, but a bit of smiling never hurt. Besides, Melody was short and on the slim side, more impressive for her neat teeth than massive body lumps. Current fashion for women was the broad hip/thin waist/narrow shoulder/evident breast look. Melody was two out of four here, but by batting .500 was she major league or half-fast? Still, Melody knew she was not unattractive, one of her most satisfying recent thrills overhearing two handsome boys—real sweethards—agree that although liddle, Melody was "kind-acute": high praise in current terminalogy. They made no mention of her hair, however, which was a color Melody could only consider hair brown, for nothing else was quite that hue. Perhaps pampus grass . . . But being smart and a hard worker were more important than appearance, these traits valuable to Melody in her twenty-fifth year when a simple story made her desperate.

She was working for a newspaper. Her special love was composing headlines, but writing two paragraphs about an eighteen-year-old on the latest translation to Marz gave her chills. Lucky Lad to Space was her headline, though she thought: Sucker Lucks Out. Soon thereafter, frustrated Melody stopped dreaming and began implementing plans, plans which would lead either to Marz . . . or to reform school.

Her base for attacking outer space was a bread factory. She remained in this Awstralian plant for eight months. Such a lengthy stay was unusual, but Melody needed time to gain a position of power. A fine record led her to Research. Since the current fad in nutrition was bulk, bulk in bread and bier and candy, Melody's intent was to ease the resulting diarrhea by producing a new dessert bread containing refined sucrose—an unheard-of ingredient for a human foodstuff, though legal. Her months-long plan led next to Marketing where Melody initiated an abnormally large trial run of the new product. Soon complaints of insipient dental cavities and internal blockages reached the factory, and the breadsweet was threatened with termination. Having some influence in the consumer welfare department, however, Melody was able to release a compatible fluoride-based prune spread to counteract her dessert. Then the UR's data integrators put two and two together and arrived at a certain clashing Melody.

Before the UR took notice, the bread factory discovered Melody's work, suggesting that she had learned enough of their business. The board of directors personally spoke with her, their manner polite, for they were uncertain of her exact effects, her specific methodology. The latter was not easily explained, for when dealing with people, personalities are often more decisive than positions. Therein Melody's almost ignorant innocence was beneficial in her manipulating adults and other children. To succeed, Melody had to convince people of her views, about the value of sugar bread, for example. As in any venture dependent upon the acceptance of interpreted data for success, Melody's machinations were convincing as ideas only when she seemed genuine as a person. Her own honest responses were an unintended aid here, Melody's opinions made acceptable because few people wanted to hurt her feelings. She was the type who became depressed upon failing, Melody unable to play the role of brave girl and hide her reaction, though she wanted to be tough. So upon asking kindly but professionally for someone to support her position, her small smile unintentionally revealed that, yes, I'll be hurt if you don't agree. Not much, but some. Intelligent Melody was not so smart as to be aware of this influence. And though few people wanted to sadden Melody, to hurt her, Plant Manager Josef Hagen was not among them.

Unlike the board, Hagen had determined for himself Melody's devices, and if not the worldwide, then the personal consequences. Hagen knew. He knew more than Melody could bear.

Not only the world's parts but the world's people Melody tended to characterize with headlines. Efficient Manager Remains Reserved was Hagen's. But he was not reserved Melody's last day at the plant, and she had no words for his actions. No words, only terror.

She had been cleaning out her desk when Manager Hagen entered her tiny office and firmly closed the door behind. Before, Hagen had always seemed average, another nondescript superior. But now he was intense, filling the room with his presence.

He was red. Blood was pushing at his face, and his eyes seemed ready to tear. His teeth were so tightly clenched that he could barely speak, but Melody understood every word, and she felt them, felt his voice cut in a manner she never wanted to hear again.

"What are you trying to do?" he hissed in a tone that frightened and silenced her instantly. "I might lose my hobby because of you—are you out of your mind?"

With each word, his breathing became louder, and Melody was amazed. She could not move. She could only stare at his trembling lips and feel the consequences she had never predicted, consequences which had turned a quiet man into an animal.

"You do this on purpose?" he screeched, and stepped one pace closer, Melody wanting to back away, but there was no place to go. "Just because you're a woman you think you can scroo every man? I ought to break your back," he told her. "I ought to break your *goddamn* back." And Melody believed him. "Get out of this plant right now so that I will *never* see you again. Do you understand? Do you understand to get away from me before I knock you out?!"

Melody understood. While Hagen still spoke, she ran from the office, not fearing embarrassment from being seen running like a child. She was a child. And she never wanted to be an adult if it meant facing a person who wanted to strike her, to break her. Never before had she experienced such genuine violence; and though Hagen had not touched her, nothing could have been more real than his opinion, the honesty of his idea.

* * *

Her parents were requested to be present at the interview in the UR Ed Center in Lucksemburg. Melody was ordered to attend. And though Missus and Misser Preece were sure to accompany their only child, Melody was nevertheless prepared to genuinely beg them to help her; for when the letter arrived stating that her childhood was under review, Melody in a flash was struck with the fact of her foolishness, that perhaps she had jeopardized her entire career for a goal with no clear path for success. And yet she had achieved the first part of her plan, for she was being interviewed by the Ed Center's hierarch, was she not? But Melody knew the connotation was difficulty, not gain; and as she flew with her parents to Yurope, Melody felt more the little girl than ever she had since first releasing her mother's hand that day at the age of seven, watching as her mother smiled and walked away from the assembly line where Melody began learning about the world of business which would lead her not to Marz, but to a man who wanted to break her back.

None of the several conversations with her parents on the subject had been even remotely terrifying. Melody's explanation was always the same.

"Marz is the most wonderful enterprise I can imagine, and I've wanted to go there forever."

The three Preeces were in Father's hobbyshop. Mother sat at her husband's desk, an unfamiliar, somewhat distressing site, Mrs. Preece trying to ignore the jumbled abacusser printons as she —typically—used the fone and factingrate simultaneously. Melody's father, tall and graceful with hands like a lumberjill, applied tank escutcheons as Melody watched him bleed. He had a nick on his forearm, another near his elbow, for it seemed a brush with even a smooth object could make her thin-skinned daddy bleed. As the three conversed, Melody followed her father with a roll of sinus paper, snubbing his wounds with tiny pieces, Melody surreptitious in her moves so that Father would not be embarrassed by the attention.

"Mel, what about the proper channels for something of this nature?" Mrs. Preece offered.

"Mom, you know I've been making applications for a million years. But applications are just talk; Marz is special and requires action."

"But, Mel, what about all the bad things they're always saying about Marz?" her father added with some concern. "I've heard of experiments with the ore crop that are illegal on Erth, and radiation sickness, and, and . . ."

"Ghosts," Mrs. Preece concluded with a superior expression.

"I scoff at this silliness," haughty Melody returned, exaggerating her mother's exaggerated bearing. "Look at all the terrible things they used to say about the Knotzis years and years ago."

With the fone to her ear, Mrs. Preece then demanded, "Why would you want to go to Marz, anyway? The whole project is just what you'd expect from the Doitch. A Wienar can't wait to find something growing so she can cut it down, or dig a hole just so she can fill it with garbage."

Melody then gave her standard explanation of Marz' unique credit opportunities, memories to last a lifetime, et cetera, as her mother confirmed their reservations in Lucksemburg.

Melody went to bed. She had enough of the world; so Melody retired from it. Between jobs, UR children were allowed to return home to recover from the last and prepare for their next employment. Melody's refuge was her mattress. Whatever the problem to face or forget, Melody would ultimately lie on her counterpane and let the difficulty pass through her and away. Situated emotionally between the bread factory and Yurope, pressured Melody thought of neither, stared at the ceiling she did not see, and let the knots in her nervous system dissolve. Her typical process was to relax, think only of nothing, and never, never cry in bed. That pillow was for peace. The sleeping quarters on business trips were different, and Melody would bawl all over their impermanent support. But this bed was home. If tears were necessary here, Melody would leap up and stomp about the room or slump in her armchair. But as long as she had that ceiling to ignore, Melody would not cry on her bed. Not in the single place she had established as sanctuary. So Melody reclined, relaxed, and nullified those areas of anxiety and fear within her. But since they were the only emotions she had, Melody lost consciousness along with these feelings. Held safely for a time by the haven of her bed, she felt only the blissful void called nothing.

He was diminutive with a head shaped like a pear. Mr. Glieson's title was Second Executive Vice President of Exceptions, suitably impressive to Melody, who was not breathing. Not much. Certainly that tiny intake of air would support no living creature. Her parents were all encouragement and support—"You haven't done anything evil, dear"—but Melody felt half of her 5'1" ninety-eight pounds. As she waited, mindless Melody could think of no preparation, no further delay. Before she could begin thinking again, she was in Glieson's office.

He fit in his chair like a fist against a pillow, the leather quilts surrounding him like a pigskin shawl. A cordial secretary led them into his large office; and after the shaking of hands and giving of names, the four began, Melody trying to seem composed but feeling horrid; for after the polite and nonchalant greetings, the only one of power—headman Glieson —became all sternness, as friendly as the fist he resembled.

But not in the least did he remind her of Hagen.

"I first thought this was one of the most imaginative comic ploys I've run across recently," Glieson told Melody clearly as he glanced at her folder. "But then I realized two areas of concern. First, there was no entertainment occupation on your immediate schedule that you could have been preparing for; and second, it wasn't funny."

Melody said nothing. She was flushed and could form no immediate reply. With Glieson's final phrase, Melody knew her childhood would last a long, long time, that she would be scrubbing testical tubes and welding into her sixties. Minimal Man Punishes Hugely.

"It of course was too contrived, too artificial to be humorous. And the elaborate planning," Glieson continued, checking his notes. "The paperwork involved and all the personnel you connived. At least you didn't scroo with anybody. You would have lost your future infant privileges for that."

The senior Preeces glared at Glieson after his last remark, but he was looking only to Melody. And since Melody's morals were being questioned—an unexpected turn—she found herself speaking.

"I barely winked or anything, Mr. Glieson. It was all . . . intellectual. I'm too plain to be wiggling about."

"On the contrary, Miss Preece," he stated, "your appearance is perfectly adequate for genderexing. I've seen worse do more. And as for intellectualism, what you are is a human bullshid artist."

After Glieson's claim, Melody's parents began nodding their heads in unavoidable agreement. Melody looked to them, astonished at their following comments.

"Our daughter has been rather subdued these past few days, Mr. Glieson," Father began, "but it is not untrue that she rambles on a bit. I know for certain, however, that a great deal of this is due to her vast supply of fine ideas. But as well, some portion may simply be . . ."

"Krap," his wife concluded.

Melody now looked to her parents and found treachery. Though no one was utterly lying here, Melody did not approve of the connotation. But she was not so guilty as to be without pride, and not for long would she remain subdued.

"What was the point, Miss Preece?" Glieson next asked. "Our only guess was that you planned some grand practical joke to determine whether the UR's data integrators actually processed stu'ent information. Now that we've established that our factingrates do function, and that you children are not set loose on a hapless world without supervision, perhaps you might explain. What were you trying to do, Melody, trick us into sending you to Marz?"

Until that question, Melody had been prepared to reveal her plans, to speak without shame of her great goal. And though she did so regardless, Glieson's awareness made her prideful truth seem foolish.

"Since I learned that stu'ents were being optioned to the ore farms, I saw no use in being a child without being on Marz. As for the 'humor,' I wanted to promote a situation that the public might find interesting, though certainly something harmless—and potentially valuable. I intended to thereby achieve the Ed Center's attention and be deemed worthy of selecting as my next occupation the ore crop of Marz. I wanted to gain this interview wherein I could describe the truth of my plans, and my ultimate, honest goals."

"Very well, do so," Glieson replied quickly.

Melody's response was not immediate, for again Glieson had surprised her. But when she spoke, she spoke with certainty.

"I've done all the explaining possible. I am a person, not a fool, and have done nothing destructive nor worthy of ridicule."

Glieson looked firmly to her a moment, but she did not avert her eyes. And though all her shame had been removed, Melody was obviously affected.

"You're not going to cry, are you, Melody?" Glieson asked seconds later with no sarcasm.

"No thank you, sir," she replied graciously.

"Good," he declared. "Marz could stand a few

good children, but they don't need babies. They might, however, have room for a spare human bullshid artist. Do you know of any available?"

"Only the one, sir," she replied, managing not to weep for joy until leaving his office, for then Melody was on her way to Marz.

# CHAPTER 2:
## Meat Machine

She wanted to drag her heels through the iron oxide mud, but in a .6 g field, one tends to have a spritely bounce regardless of depression. After eighty-nine Marzian days, Melody was unimpressed by the vista about her: a dull grey sky with a brownish tinge of stratospheric dust whose swirling clouds were no longer exotic, but irritating. Marae Planitia's low hills made a swamp seem exciting, but the endless head-sized rocks and larger boulders and gullies and waved ridges were not so boring. The local surface was of true interest—because the miners had to walk it. Only the harvested plants returned in electric karts because—hey, in a six-tenths field you can walk forever, boot plastick much cheaper than transporting superfluous vehicles forty million miles.

Dull Planet Scores Low on Stu'ent Test, Melody thought. Nearby were adults—Melody the only child in the quadrasphere—all of whom seemed constantly satisfied; but this was due to their finances, for the stipend scale on Marz was astronomical—triple time for interplanetary work—whereas stu'ents received only heuristic credits. Never before had Melody been around so many hobbyists: they seemed so reserved and humorless. But though she knew every miner about her; still they were no more than acquaintances, Melody with one close friend in the compound, and he was not on this shift, only acquaintances who seemed strangers.

They all wore UR regulation coveralls, baby blue beneath the sticky, brown dust-mud which caked the fabric. Melody recognized the individuals gathering around her even though a catalytic, invert oxydyzer was strapped across each face, a device necessary to extract breathable air from the thin Marzian atmosphere. Melody hated these things because they generated heat, and Marz was a hotplate in the day. She hated them because the inner-nostril tubes made her sneeze, and sneezing while wearing air tubes was no joke. You had to rip them away immediately or pinch your sneeze nerve or pull out a nose hair or *anything*, because if you sneezed with the tubes on they would either collapse or be filled with mucus, and then you were really in trouble, having to clear them while holding your breath and trying not to sneeze again. They can send a girl to Marz but not let her breathe?

The pee-on miners could only dream of the pressurized face masks worn by Management. Melody would have preferred a mask if only because speaking was then accomplished via radio, and you can always turn a radio off or pretend it doesn't work. But with the tubes you had to talk in order to remain courteous, especially at dusk, the shift's end when all the strange acquaintances you hadn't seen all day collected on the main trail back to the compound and asked how your day had been. Then you had to talk Marzian: breathing in through your nose and exhaling through your mouth to speak. Melody was sure these people enjoyed speaking outdoors just because of their pride in having mastered the process; whereas Melody knew she would *never* be fluent. Worse, when she became agitated and her human bullshid words tried to leave too quickly, Melody tended to gasp, all the experienced miners recognizing the Marzian choke at once, turning away so they could shake their heads and mutter, "A flipping stu'ent when we have hobbies to do . . ."

"Hi," Melody smiled to old Randy, that ancient miner so long on Marz he seemed part of the topography, endless bending to harvest the ore crop having shaped his back to match the horizon line. Marjorie and Suzannanna received only nods, no words, Melody waving to other folks. A few of these began choking themselves for another reason, shocked to see polite, petite Melody flip the universal crossed-fingers obscenity to a young adult named Seitz who no longer *accidentally* brushed against her backside with his grabby hands. Not after that day last week when Melody had enough of fingerprints beneath the coccyx and heaved a handful of Marzian mud up his nose, necessitating his buddy breathing with his contracted girlfriend all the way back to the compound while she demanded to know the cause, Seitz nearly suffocating on rust-dust and unsatisfactory explanations.

Old lady Nuri stood by the entrance to inflatable dorm B, the bunk balloon housing four dozen miners in individual cubicles. Nuri made certain all her people cleaned their feet by stepping on the flush shake-grating which vibrated the greasy dust loose as aided by magnets below the floor. Nuri could seldom adjust the duster properly; consequently, the routine included holding on to belt buckles and equipment lest they be vibed loose magnetically and shaken to destruction against the grating, leaving the miners semi-nude and indebted for destroyed UR property. Melody lost her personal rad measure the first day which cost her an extra week on the planet. Never again could she approach Nuri at the door or in the cafe without reacting by grabbing for all the metal on her person. And still she had nightmares due to losing a week of freedom because of one mistake.

Above the air room entrance someone had applied neat plastick letters denoting "Hotel Hot Air." Since neither Nuri nor her superior, Dorm Director Telak, had ordered the name removed, levity was evidently not prohibited. Most people were boring on their own. Equally unofficial was a flag flying limply outside one of the sealed cubicle windows, a red-wide-and-blue USSA checkerboard hung by a typical Amerigan perpetuating the demokraptic myth that her flag came *before* chess, that fella countryfems invented baysball, apple pot, and probably Marz itself.

"How's your crotch, Preece?" Nuri asked as Melody rattled, tooth and bone, on the shake-grate. Her reference was to a bout of Marzian itch skin Melody had contracted weeks before. Mumbling nothing in reply, Melody only thought, Shakin' Nuri After Others' Affairs.

She entered the balloon to complete her day's routine, activity less interesting than her stint in the army at age thirteen. At least the army's regimentation gave one something to focus on. But on Marz, everything seemed slack. Here the miners worked hard on their own accord, their reward being monetary; but the few stu'ents present were just common laborers. To Melody's great disappointment, the worst part seemed that she would be stuck in the fields for the entire duration, never reaching a higher level in the ore mining process—tech or administration or herbal refining—so she could spend her time in Management Center, a solid wall building where the VIPs worked and lived. If unspectacular by Erth standards, the flat edifice seemed paradise compared to the Marzian labor balloons. But Melody had been inside Management only once, after her arrival when she received an official welcome. Then they kicked her out into the dust, and there she remained.

Upon applying for a superior position, Melody had learned that "this sort of job-jumping won't do on Marz." She thus pictured herself as never receiving any training or having any fun: never learning of ore force theory by mapping nuclear bonds in Management's labs, never tearing about the sticky dunes in an administrator's treadkar. All Melody would learn, so it seemed, was monumental boredom. In some cultures there were laws against boredom, but not on the Backward Planet.

She had to bathe. This was a post-entry requirement for all workers, primarily to keep Nuri's balloon undamaged, in that the mediocre Marzian atmosphere was rife with a bacterium whose by-product attacked inorganics. A secondary problem was caused by another buggy fiend. The most significant creature on the planet—the ubiquitous Marzian mole —housed a parasite willing to move in on the nearest Erthette without invitation. These mites, which could penetrate the semi-sealed UR suits, were of no great concern to Management because they ate only human skin which the miners could replace on their own. But since water on Marz was scarce, the dust was removed with a smelly salve applied by hand, then removed with disposable sponges which were conveniently dissolved hours later by the absorbed bacteria. A quantity of steam for final rinsing and facial cleansing was standard issue, drying via spiral tongue towel. Lazy laborers were no problem; for the salve, if not completely removed, would dry into a powder which shrank and cracked the skin, removable only with an extra ration of water sold to the miners for an exorbitant fee, extra time on the planet for stu'ents. After one raw patch of buttock cost her two additional days on the Bum Planet, tearful Melody remained scrupulously desalved. The itch skin she contracted days later came from overzealous scrubbing. Though becoming familiar with the vagaries of this planet, Melody unfortunately was learning by attrition.

Body odor was no problem with the bacteria eliminators, but Melody had few friends to offend —exactly one, she realized, huge Chas Chaeung and his body of slab muscles. He had a friend superior to Melody, his fiancée, Nan Flamini. Melody had no jealousy here, for they made an excellent couple, regardless of dissimilar sizes. Her jealousy was due to Flamini's being a factingrate technician. She lived in Management.

In her cubicle, Melody was pleased to be alone for a time. She had a plastick bed and desk with vid viewer, standard issue capillary pen, and *Marz Instruction Book on Off-World Living* (including chapters on "Wilderness Eating," "Surviving the Dust," "Emergency Breathing," "Applied Loneliness," et cetera). Bad Book Bites Butt, Melody sneered to herself.

Another available publication was the *Marzian Ex-Press,* the local newspaper published by some administrators as a secondary hobby, just for fun. Despite her newspaper experience, Melody could not participate here, because she was not allowed to have fun. In the *Ex-Press* were announcements of the latest births, rare deaths, ore production figures, Marzian Miner League wallball scores, but no mention of Erth. No mention of the only true world in this stellar system so as to avoid tormenting miners and stu'ents pining for home, certain of whom knew they would be stranded on this greasy rock till the onset of senility or suicide, whichever came first.

On the wall above her desk, Melody had attached her one souvenir of the journey: a postcard of Erth, a genuine photographic print taken at 100K miles into the translation, for Melody had never seen Erth. She had not been able to look down or look back, for they were in a space vehicle, not a tour bus. Neither had she seen Marz when approaching. As though a foreboding, since Melody never saw herself in the position of superiority she had imagined, as soon as she left home her position became inferior, not changing after eighty-nine days on Marz. Three weeks under plus-g loads from the pulse fusion drive had been a vacation considering the null-consciousness chems supplied, but here Melody had to stay awake, stay awake on the Dead Planet.

She wrote a letter to her parents, the same content as always: I hate this place. Get me out if it means your hobbies. I'll die here or kill myself. If you had reared me properly, I'd still be home. Melody then destroyed the paper, for it was no communiqué, but a catharsis. Her real letters said little more than: Hi

MomDad, love you, still here, two million days left, love, Mel. These were sent by radio for free. Those her parents returned had a greater content, but they made Melody lonely; so she packed the factingrate prints away in the bottom of her desk. Melody had enough loneliness on Marz; she didn't need any imported from Erth.

While writing, Melody unavoidably heard the strains of a classical horn sonata played on a piccolo trombone cubicles removed. The player was no expert, and the composer . . . regardless of his reputation for architectural excellence, Mostart didn't swing.

Apart from these live performances, entertainment on the Dull Planet was minimal. The UR supplied dimensional music (mostly from past centuries), solid-state visuals (mostly government erotica), and recreational dregs (mostly chewable opium). Nothing here for a girl of Melody's sensibilities. She wasn't onto dregging off, or after genderexing, and her ears were best fit for words, human artist words. Where was the high lye, the cladaks, the conchfights? But the miners, not being sensible girls, needed little of even their own entertainment, for generally they worked themselves into a stupor. The porn was rarely used, so Melody understood, because the genuine activity was secretly encouraged by Management. Not regarding stu'ents, of course, Melody the exception; for she had demanded that Seitz be executed; yet still he lived —was his continued existence not virtual encouragement?

Melody tried to watch a movey, an Amerigan Eastern, but determined that the primitive life of horseboys and their greenjeans was too close to her own currently meager existence: different-colored apparel, but similar dust. After blanking the vid's see-screen, Melody left her cube, needing to get away.

She checked the shift schedule in the corridor. By eating early, she could catch Chaeung in the diner. To do so, Melody would have to accomplish some maneuvering, for her eat card showed her third meal due at 1800 hours Marzian mean. On Erth, she would have simply arranged for a new card to be printed. But forgery was difficult on Marz, Melody having access to little equipment besides her semi-liquid pen. She felt especially primitive because such sophisticated social devices were unavailable to her. She would thus have to resort to the most primitive social device of all: lying. She was not, however, without guilt, an unfortunate headline coming to her: Melody Misuses Mundane Marz.

She had to stand in queue fifteen minutes just to eat veggies: Marzian greens were especially nutritious, and of course virtually free, but Melody missed frozen tofuel. Peanut butter was available as a condiment, but it got stuck in her cavities, Melody avoiding the product regardless of Seitz' claim that it would make hair grow on her ... As for dessert, why were they always out of dognuts? Stand around a lifetime to eat this?

While waiting, silent Melody had to listen to the conversations about her. A requirement for Marzian duty was familiarity with two of the three UR languages (Doitch, Inglich, and Check), but Melody had found that the miners did not need to speak these languages, merely pass a test. Learning of this, it seemed to Melody that her entire life had been wasted; for if success only meant passing tests, she

could have replaced Hidler by now. Worse, since
Melody was fluent in all three languages, she could
not help but hear all the nearby babble. Average
miners talking about work and monies and not getting ahead. Average men talking about blondes and
redheads then looking at hair-brown Melody, then
looking away.

One conversation that did not register was a woman's mentioning ghosts. This one Melody had first
heard on Erth, frightening her but mildly when en-
countered on the more tan of the two planets. The
story was the same whenever told on Marz: at dusk
just now, something I could see right through, looked
like an ore plant. Oh? her companion replied, and the
conversation ended. Even those with the stories
seemed uninterested in the topic, mirages of plants so
typically Marzian boring that no one cared. Where
were the haunting princes from ancient races? Not on
this planet. Dull Spooks No Scare.

After average miners and unspectacular ghosts,
Melody had to fight the server. And Melody lost.

The man asked for her card, and Melody provided
her false story. "Lost it, sorry," she smiled. He told
her to apply to the dorm leader for a new card, and
Melody pleasantly replied she would do so as soon as
possible. But this man she had never spoken with
before looked at Melody and knew he was receiving
her artistry.

"Just because you're a stu'ent," he told her quietly,
"doesn't mean you can't follow the rules. They're not
that hard."

He hurt her feelings. Images of Hagen immediately
came to mind, but what was the comparison? Melody
took her veggies and moved away, feeling bad because
the server had been correct, though not criminal in

telling her, and Melody felt the creep. She sat at a table by herself, looking down to her meal. She did not want to eat. She did not want to move. Not until a deep voice called out loudly did she recall her purpose.

"Mel, here."

Looking up, she saw massive Chaeung seated tables away motioning for her to join him. His neck was as wide as his head. Chas was a pale-skinned Neegore with hair too short, making his head seem like a blunt object for purposes of demolition. Chaeung had the lips of a baby, mean eyes, and a lode of kindness in his geology. He gestured as though ordering Melody, Chaeung too big to be moving about needlessly. Melody joined him. Curt Bruiser Found Soft in Best Places.

"You got lost," he stated with typical firmness, typical brevity. He had two trays heaped with greens and was plowing through the crop. No meat on this planet—no animals. Even the Marzian moles were bugs. "You look flat," Chas added.

"Well," she sighed, "the server got onto me for cheating with my card, and I don't feel so good now."

Instead of encouraging words, Chaeung replied with brutality. After a brief look to Melody, he stood like an explosion, his body an erthquake.

"I'll kill the son of a bitch!" he wheezed, looking over to the food line as he began relentlessly moving away.

Chas was serious, and Melody was frightened. She had never seen him outraged, and it had come at once. His face was rock and his eyes were now evil. Melody was shocked, but not so much that she could not leap to her feet and grasp his arm, moving into his path to stare upward and squeeze him until Chaeung looked to her and not the doomed server.

"Please, Chas, he didn't do anything wrong—I did."

Chaeung turned to her, blinked, and slowly returned to his seat, looking between Melody and the server with an expression that seemed deadly. In a moment he was eating again, but the other twenty people in the room were still buzzing and staring, the oblivious server heaping greens once more. Melody pretended to be eating just so she could have an excuse to look down. Her guilt and embarrassment at being chastised had been magnified by Chaeung's reaction. Now as she sat across from her bulky friend, Melody found herself glancing about, wondering whether the other people in the room were still glancing back. And her breathing was strange, short exhalations signifying an upset condition. Chas' odd breathing only seemed unusual, but with that body, a locomotive huffing was required for his aerobic sustenance. Melody was merely hurt. Chas, however, appeared normal again when next he spoke.

"You need God," he told her.

"I believe in God," Melody replied as though uncertain.

"You need more of It in your system," he offered in his stately voice. "An Xian, right?"

"Yeah, I'm pretty plain," Melody admitted. "Your beliefs are, uh, sort of . . ."

"Weird."

"Well, I wasn't going to say that. I meant . . . technical. What do you call it?"

"Creatism. Based on the discipline of Actal Manifestics."

"But that's a theoretical science, isn't it? Particle physics, right?"

"Sub-material physics," Chaeung corrected her. "AM posits that matter is not composed of smaller and smaller discrete entities, but of ideas. Matter is made of manifested concepts, ideas made actual by God, via creation. The idea of movement made real is light, and 'c' is the speed of stillness. The idea of attraction made physical is gravity. Position is manifested in the real as matter. Space is separation. AM is the key between creation and physics."

"Not all AM physicists are members of your religion, are they?" Melody asked.

"No, but scientists can be dumb."

"They haven't come up with any practical, er, manifestation of AM yet, have they?" she wondered.

"No, but they're working on it. They can't be that dumb."

"More studies and number jockeying, I suppose."

"The ore might be the core," Chaeung replied with inferred mystery.

"How so?"

"Revelatory inverting middling force bond. May be the key to the ether."

"The ether is a fairy tale, Chas," Melody asserted. "It's not orthodox doctrine with you, is it?"

"Yes."

"Oh, sorry . . .," she muttered, looking to her greens again.

"Ether is the conceptual medium, the matrix reality coalesces from. Vacuums are made of ether."

"What scientists are working on this—U Ration?"

"May be nearby. May be why no one goes to Management."

Now Melody was interested. New religions and/or scientific disciplines were impressive, but secrets were her forte.

"You know the Sueedish?" Chaeung asked.

"Sort of. They're supposed to be feuding with us because the miners are tearing up the ore crop before the Sueede geologists can study it."

"The conflict is true," Chaeung described. "May be between the UR and outsiders re secretive data, creation basis science, the revealing ether ore, is the rumor."

Before Melody could pant in anticipation of hearing more of a subject which had captured her, she saw a woman in Management green overalls approaching Chas from behind to fling her hands roughly over his eyes.

"Identify at will," the newcomer ordered as she winked at Melody, who smiled brightly in return.

"Nan, my Nan," Chas answered correctly.

"Hi, Nan," a pleased Melody responded as Flamini sat beside her own best friend. "What are you doing with us pee-ons?"

"Oh, I had to realign the proceed-leads in the oven factingrate, and was just lucky to catch you two. What occurs here profound?"

"The ether is amongst us," Chas pronounced.

Nan nodded. Sitting beside imposing Chaeung, average Nan seemed more a satellite than a partner. Her skin was less of a contrast, mid-thirties Flamini a dark-skinned Cockassion from the Muditerranean. As usual for Marzian longhairs, Nan wore a bandana to exclude the pervasive exterior dusts. This covering was satisfying to mid-coiffed Melody as well, for

Nan's gorgeous auburn follicles were thus not available for comparison, just the face, Nan's large mouth and active expression. To Melody, Nan looked like no dumby. This was more important to her than Nan's perhaps handsome aesthetics, her semi-bounteous chest.

"Profound, that's us," Melody declared. "Chas here was just proselytizing me toward the ways of AM."

Nan was at once into the subject, Melody recognizing the enthusiasm of a true believer.

"Then you've heard the Beginning: the fact of any existential property's having an inherent nature is due to its being comprised of concepts."

"I was thinking of something more . . . tangible, perhaps," Melody replied. "Chas here says Management is working with AM and the ether ore. What can you say, Nan?"

"Well, Mel, you know there's practical Management and experimental," Nan responded. "We of the former just arrange things and keep them working."

"Experimental," Melody crooned, "I love it—what do they do there?"

"Rumors abound," Nan announced with imitation sagacity. "Potentially we're talking about a physical power literally beyond nuclear forces. If anything, I hope the experimenters are working on control; for, of course, the greatest aspect of any power is its potential for misuse, for destruction." And Chas added:

"Beyond control, the need re power is for survival."

"Gee," Melody professed, "I never got to philosophy. I was still working on bread."

"With us, you learn," Chas stated through his meal

as Nan leaned against him. "We know; you know."

"Yeah, a little ignorance goes a long way," Melody mused, Chas returning with:

"I thought you didn't know philosophy."

"I'm better with rumors," she mentioned, then turned to Flamini. "Come on, Nan, what about more destruction? Are you talking about radiation from the ore crop? Are we all dissolving slowly?"

"No, no, Melody," Nan explained. "If the ore were being used for generating Manifestic power, the danger in exposure would not be from tissue damage but from psichosis."

"How's that?"

"You see, the power of AM is idea, literally the nature of things. When applied, concept power changes the norm. With matter, you can imagine changes such as something massive becoming smaller, or something fast becoming slow. With people, since sanity is normal, exposure to an uncoalesced AM field would render people psichotic."

"Oh, that's nasty," Melody uttered distastefully. "I don't like destruction after all. But they're not going the classic route, are they, Nan? I mean, usually a new power is first harnessed as a weapon. They're not making bombs or anything, are they? We fems don't like no bombs."

"I hear they are."

Becoming totally humorless, Melody told Flamini, "I was only kidding at you, Nan. What kind of bomb can you make with ideas?"

"Not *with* ideas, but *about* ideas. Theory describes a concept bomb."

"Oh, no—blowing someone's hopes and dreams apart? That makes me sick."

"But it could be made more immediately physical than just modifying emotions," Flamini described. "Use, uh, a fusion bomb as a comparison. An N-bomb releases a field of heat and radiation which physically alters matter. A concept bomb would release a field to change the nature of things as I said before."

"You mean big to little, fast to slow?"

"This is all only theoretical," Nan offered, "but the effect of a concept bomb might be general for an area as well as individualistic for included members. That is, not only might specific entities be individually altered, but their habitat or locale might also be modified. For example, carnivores might turn omnivorous in a fertile area which becomes barren."

"Modern change to archaic," Chas said.

"Unfortunately," Nan advised, "because such tampering with nature is inherently destructive, characteristics theoretically tend to change from good to bad, from bad to worse. Even in nature, improving things is more difficult than letting them rot."

"Fee-cees," Melody whispered.

"Don't curse," Chaeung ordered. "Bad for nice girl to be vulgo."

"I never swore before Marz," she sighed.

"You need God."

"More of It in my system, right?"

"Pray to the ether for guidance," he suggested, a phrase followed in his mouth by a mass of dull greenery.

Melody had not touched a rowbutt in weeks. These electrical, automated harvesting appliances were used only where the ore plants grew in abundance on open land, but such growth was a rarity. Most of the crop was found in gullies and on rugged hillsides where harvesting could only be feasibly accomplished by the ultra-versatile machines that are people. Melody's compound was situated in an area rife with small patches scattered within walking distance. Similar in appearance to a sonflower with petalless blossom, the ore crop was valuable for its upper root system and lower trunk, the only portions of the organism where the middling force mineral collected. No more efficient method had been devised for attaining the mineral from the Marzian soil, and growing the plants from seeds had so far proven impossible. Thus, the Marzian miners worked the land, going forth on foot trailed by small electric sleds which held the ore plants uprooted with tined implements: two-pronged ore forks. The workers ventured in small groups, supplied with maps which supervisors had coordinated from data gathered by surveyors.

The latter was Melody's latest desire, to scout around in a real kar instead of towing a toy one. She wanted to be on a local surveying team, not to find new, exciting areas—for none existed on thoroughly explored Marz—but simply to get away from the harvesting. She was tired of the work. The hydraulic ore forks numbed her hands, and the environ numbed her mind, her spirit. She was sick of the ugly Marzian moles, misnamed insects which dug treacherous tunnels about the ore plants and caused her to stumble. She was tired of the dust and bacteria, the lice and the lousy company, the natural food and the artificial housing. Melody wanted out. And Melody was planning.

Join a survey team, she thought. That would lead to

Management Center where the surveyors were based. Once there, become involved with the sub-material physics research mentioned by Chaeung and Flamini. Then she could be part of a significant theoretical discovery that would bring her fame—and more important—a ride home!

There was no ride that day, only exhausting hours of work and a long walk to the balloon. Melody had no decent company at dinner, for Chaeung ate third shift, and she was lying to no more cruel servers. But at night, sitting at her plastick desk writing terrible letters to her parents, listening to an amateurish reading of a juvenile horn concerto, Melody found she had to do something. She had to leave—but could not—so at least she had to talk to someone; and, as though stricken, leapt to her feet and walked to Chaeung's cubicle.

The semi-rigid doors were poor for knocking. Since the hour was late, Melody could not call loudly outside his cubicle without disturbing the sleeping miners and being fined an extra decade on the Debilitating Planet. But since there was no reply as she spoke Chas' name outside his door, and because she *had* to talk with someone, carefully Melody tried the latch—unlocked—and pushed the door open, prepared to call for him through the crack.

She thought he might be sleeping, but that was not the purpose being put to his bed. She saw this kinetic high contrast of skin against bedding, and an old thought returned to her as she stared within the room. Melody had never been jealous of Chaeung's engagement, a practical reason being that making babies with Chas would squash her. But Nan Flamini was not much bigger—would she have this problem? Of course not, Melody learned, for this more mature woman was familiar with proper technique: the girl goes on top, exactly Flamini's position as she sat with spread legs on Chaeung with no clothes, no clothes on either, and they rocked together like some meat machine.

She looked a moment and was not seen. So surprised and embarrassed that she could barely breathe, Melody closed the door quietly and backed away. Still without jealousy, she now felt fear, having clearly seen Flamini's too long, rude nails scraping, gouging Chas' chest, his hair in this area the same as his head, short and curly, extrablack; Melody only thinking that you better not, you better not hurt him, Flamini, because he's the only friend I have. And when she returned to her cubicle and retired for the night, Melody was no longer in need of company, for how can mere friends affect a woman so completely taken by her tears?

# CHAPTER 3:
## *Phantoms Religiously Held*

"Melody? You need to help us with this ore."

Four in the group that day plus the senior leader asking why Melody was moving away from the hillside where already the miners had begun uprooting the ore crop.

"I'm sure I saw a great patch past this rise, Tabio," Melody answered with perhaps insufficient concern in her manner.

"But Melody, nothing corresponds on our map to your sighting. Come back and work with us now. You don't want to be fined more working days on Marz, do you?"

"Tabio."

"Yes, Melody?"

"How can they keep me here longer when the ships only come every three hundred days? They either keep me ten months extra or nothing extra, right?"

"Well . . ."

"I just thought of that last night, Tabio. It just came to me. All these 'fines' I've been incurring—it's called bullshid, isn't it?"

"Now, Melody, do not curse at work or you might be fined . . . er . . ."

**39**

She stood with her arms akimbo as the miners about her bent to their tasks, looking between Melody and Tabio, who slumped before her. He was just a miner, after all, not an expert in stu'ents, in human depression artists.

"Tabio, I'm looking over here for a patch that perhaps I may see. Just let me check this curiosity, and I can be right with you."

"But Melody . . ."

He did not see her again that day. Amongst the countless rocks of Marae Planitia's low hills Melody walked, having procured a personal map, a personal plan. Two and a half hours away was the Sueedish settlement, a brief walk for a girl with no friends within forty million miles, no friends at all. Finding her way was of some concern, but Melody had attained an electronic palm projector that would display the region on her hand. This of course was not procurement, she thought, this was stealing. She cared about the immorality involved, but not enough. What could they do, keep her on Marz an extra ten months —for what, taking a walk? for desertion?

Between the hills and over Marae's waffle ridge area Melody walked, passing rowbutt forces and hand-picking teams. Everyone noticed her, but Melody did not approach near enough for speech; she merely waved in a pseudo-friendly manner as though she had some business traipsing across the alien wilderness. Melody's attitude was that this must be business, for there was no pleasure on Marz, not on any Marz she knew.

Once past Marae's most significant peak—Montei Unverit, a genuine mountain in some past, primeval era—the remaining journey would be across Skopein

Planum. No ore plants grew there, much to the miners' remorse, for the plain was largely flat, and would have allowed total rowbutt harvesting. As she walked, Melody felt a sense of unique antiquity; for although the surface of Marz was no mystery, perhaps no human had ever stepped on the exact path she traversed, not near that rock nor over that hole, Melody feeling that the solidified drifts she crossed of a once flowing material belonged to her in some manner, that the rare outcropping of bedrock was a personal discovery. But even these vital impressions and a point-six g field were not enough to prevent Melody's exhaustion after nearly three hours of constant walking in the heat.

With her first sight of the geologists' buildings, Melody had to sit. Only two hundred yards farther; yet she could not make it. Her air tubes seemed too small for the oxygen intake she required, Melody having to consciously force herself to breathe in an uncomfortably slow manner, for she wanted to pant. Her feet were so coated with dust that her shoe snaps were buried. She was sweating what seemed to be clammy grease. When finally recovered enough to continue, Melody still remained; for next she had to wait: for a plan, for a lie—for some procedure. She looked at the three surprisingly small plastick buildings, and hoped she had the right compound; but with only two settlements on the continent, how could she go wrong? Did the people and vehicles seen beyond appear Sueedish? Then she thought that perhaps it best they not be Sueedish, for she could not speak the language, Melody aware of the nationalistic bent of these people, their Scandinative pride.

She waited, for a plan, for a breath—both provided

by the passage of a UR vehicle, Melody inhaling sharply with the sight. The treadkar was enclosed —Management! Too far away to intercept; nevertheless the vehicle was something to follow.

This walk was easy. But by the time Melody arrived, Management had already disappeared. Whatever their purpose here, certainly they could not have gotten far. With no additional planning needed, Melody approached the building nearest their kar, and tried to enter.

Of course the unit was sealed to retain its air supply, Melody looking at the entrance instructions she could not read. So she pounded on the door. A tall, youngish, handsome, virile man enough to make her giggle opened the door; but Melody did not smile, because she knew it looked stupid with tubes in the nose.

"Hi, I'm with the United Rations. Could you tell me where our party is? I seem to have misplaced them."

Holding a temporary breather against his face, the man looked at her quizzically and spoke not a word she could understand. Trying sign language, Melody pointed to the unmistakable UR insignia on her chest. The man replied, one word, in Inglich.

"Tid," he said with perfect clarity.

"No, no," Melody moaned, and pulled at the insignia until the staring, incomprehending man understood, looking away to roll his eyes, stepping back to motion for Melody to enter.

He pointed to a dirty floor grille in the large atmosphere lock and stared at her feet, then looked up to wink, a hint of a smile. Melody stepped aboard with but the single heart throb, a blow enough to bruise her ribs from within. The Sueedish device had brushes as well as magnets and vibes, the force the man applied nearly vibrating Melody from her feet as he turned the intense wheel while shaking his head unseriously at her filth. Soon the room was air-equalized, the man leading buzzing but immaculate Melody into the building, a final, moderate smile, but no further intriguing comments.

As Melody removed her tube set, the man walked ahead until reaching a woman, the Sueedes talking funny for a moment. The woman smiled and said nothing understandable to Melody, but led her away, the man returning to his post. He was missed. Immediately the woman revealed a comforting friendliness; and though the man with his size and dramatic eyes and masculinity intimidated Melody, this was an influence she was willing to confront. But he was gone, Melody fighting not to glance back, to get a look at those shoulders or . . . something. At once she decided to apply for a boyfriend her first day home despite the hassles of analyses and gender lectures. Maybe she'd get over this. Maybe implies maybe not.

With no peeking behind, she continued with the woman, who chatted along, Melody smiling, understanding her personality if not her words. They moved to an office, Melody told with a gesture to enter alone. Therein were people from Management, none of whom she recalled having met. No stu'ents present, but four adults who looked at her as though she were a Marzian, the woman with the firmest gaze speaking.

"Who are you?" she demanded, staring at this worker-blue uniform.

This was easy for Melody to understand, but she

was in her element now, the artist responding as though disappointed, looking away and shaking her head.

"Have you forgotten me already?" she returned with annoyance to a person she had never seen before. "This is who I am," Melody insisted, and briefly displayed her confiscated palm projector.

"Oh . . . in case we get lost . . . ," the UR woman answered, the authority gone from her voice and expression, her uncertainty inspired by Melody's confidence. But as presumed by the artist, Management was too busy to be worrying about a smooth-talking spare.

They were about to do some serious looking to one another regarding Melody; but a second door in the room then opened, the speaking fem quickly whispering to her people as the Sueedes entered.

"Remember, everyone," she ordered firmly, "we have done nothing wrong; so be neutral, but let's not be bullied by these krapitalists," and she turned with her group to the Sueedes.

"Good afternoon," a heavyset elder man greeted them with average Inglich and an excellent smile. "I would like to thank you very much for joining at us here, and now to greet you and introduce our personnels."

"All right, enough small talk," the Management woman snapped with a rancor surprising to Melody. "What's your problem and why have you dragged us here?"

"Yes!" a second UR person called out loudly. "This planet must be big enough so you geologists don't have to force us away from areas vital to your own concern—your literal transportation to Erth."

"You want us to stop?" the third miner proclaimed with astonishment.

The Sueedish speaker turned away, looking to his dumbfounded fellows, a few foreign words exchanged, then back to the miners.

"But friends, Dr. Deign," he offered to the lead woman, "we have never more than asked you to please talk about allowing you to study an area before you take the crop. But a day or so we require, and will in all ways cooperate with arrangements. But your electrics and personnel's bio elements interfere—"

"This crop doesn't last forever," the fourth UR member stated as though speaking to fools. "We have to get it in the can before it's ruined. We can't be waiting for your vague studies."

Melody knew this man made her look like an amateur when it came to creative conversation. No, the ore crop would not last forever—but neither would the sun. Melody could not understand her associates' coarse attitude. But the scene ended quickly, and there was no time for contemplation.

"That's it, we've had enough of this abuse," Dr. Deign retorted. "My people are leaving. The next time you want to communicate with us, I suggest you contact UR Central on Erth, because our work here is too important to suffer more of your nationalistic prejudice."

Deign stomped through the door, followed by her companions, all of them offended and displeased. All but Melody. Melody remained. She was going to apologize. But before Melody could speak, Dr. Deign pushed the door open again and snapped, "Are you coming or not?"

She was. With a final glance to the shocked Sueedes,

Melody stepped into the hall, Dr. Deign forcefully closing the door behind, leading her group down the corridor.

"I guess we showed that selfish lot," one of them said, the five moving briskly.

"That's the only way to handle their shauvinism —before it occurs," Deign described harshly.

This sort of decisive boasting continued until they left the building, Management a storm through the Sueedish corridors. Melody alone had a smile for the woman seen before who waved as the UR bevy flew past, and outside.

Melody was not so swept up herself that she failed to recognize her own position; for as Management moved to their kar, Melody saw it was a four-seater. Not even a group still tense from verbal battle would overlook a surplus body, its improper color. But Melody admitted she was extra.

"Very well, see you back at the compound, then," she stated briskly, and turned to walk off while donning her breather.

She planned on remaining out of Management's sight until they left. But before Melody could move around the building, Dr. Deign choked to her people, "Who the blue was that?" but they had no answer, the Marzian air breathable only for queries, not conversations.

Seconds in this poor air was long enough for unprotected Management. After delaying for but the single muttered question, the four entered their kar, and left. Melody stood behind the nearest plastick wall until Management's electric whir was no longer heard. Then she began walking back. The situation was now both the best and the worst possible for her to contact the Sueedes; for Melody could truly admit that she had never been part of the group, and had been stunned by their disagreeable position. But Melody knew that in a way she *was* part of the group, that their position was official UR policy; and she was too ashamed to try to rectify the damaged communications caused by her superiors. Melody felt bad about the whole affair, and could no longer face the Sueedes. She did not have the nerve. Perhaps later she could think of some acceptable method for approaching them again, but not that day. At least she had found their settlement, the proper building, and knew a friendly face or two. Maybe tomorrow, Melody having reached her limits in assertiveness and deceit, having been proven the mild child compared to Management.

Then she realized what should have been the worst part of the situation: she had to walk back. Another two and a half hours. But her body felt much less tired than her mind. Then she thought of Chaeung and Flamini, and her heart seemed to collapse. Melody plodded on. Tomorrow she'd steal a bleeding kar.

After an hour of walking, Melody found the Sueedish base again—or her own—*something;* for entering the tepid shadow of a remnant mountain ridge, Unverit's eroded peripheral, Melody caught sight of flat plastick amongst the huge rocks. Low in the sky now, Sal provided light at just the right angle to glare off a building's roof—but what building could be in the middle of Marzian nowhere?

Presuming that something here was intentionally hidden—a reasonable thought considering the locale —Melody decided to carefully approach. After several minutes of cautious crawling, her idea of concealment was reinforced. Beyond, in a naturally enclosed gully, was a small rigid building like those of the UR or Sueedish settlements; but this one was sloppily painted a variegated grey-brown, obviously camouflaged. Without the low-angled sunlight on the roof's edge, Melody would have never seen it.

Recalling her army training, Melody circled the building, moving so as to observe to the maximum while presenting very little of herself, making no sound, quick glimpses about her to make certain that she as well was not the center of someone's surveillance.

No markings on the walls. Outside, an open kar that could have been anyone's, a narrow path through the mountain range's far side. Melody was looking for identification, but found none: the building and kar could have been Sueedish or UR. To her knowledge, no other settlement was near, the palm projector displaying only bare terrain as she studied the map on her hand. Since nothing was to be learned there but a memorized lifeline, Melody continued moving about the structure. After more stealthy slips behind boulders, she finally came to a sight which caught all her attention—men! Two men walking outside, along one length of the building, the north side. Two adults with uniforms sloppily dyed brown-grey. After searching carefully for identification on them, Melody found only exasperation. Two men with no insignias, their faces telling her only that they were male. They spoke, but removed Melody could not discern their words.

She followed them, peering down from her position fifty meters away. Fulfilled by this self-appointed task, Melody no longer plodded, her movements and mentality once again satisfyingly precise. She wanted to hum, but this old soldier was not about to make noise. Melody had found excitement here, enough fun to make her forget her interplanetary problems. But as she moved farther, Melody discovered the two men's goal, and then her thrill turned major.

The roof continued behind the building, covering an area with two unfinished walls. Melody could not tell whether the constructors had run short of materials or wanted exposure to the atmosphere for their work. And here was the fascination, Melody looking down, no longer paying heed to the people beyond —several now—nor the indiscernible machinery and peripheral pipes and wiring about them. Now her attention was focused on this cryptic group's results, Melody staring at their product, their power.

Emanating from the unfamiliar equipment was a, a sight. Bluish, but not really blue. Not a light nor gas, something transparent in the air, seemingly flowing, but wasn't it stationary? Like a thick block of amorphous glass; but, no, certainly the vision had no such solidity. But it was real, like heat waves on a hot road, a cool blue that—stranger yet—did not seem truly blue, but negative yellow, a negative-yellow refraction. Yes, this was the best description for Melody. But whatever the transparent emanation might have been, its effects were even more intriguing, and initially unbelievable; for the negative yellow was "projected" against the Marzian sand which was no longer Marzian. White and dry, Melody knew it was salty. A few square meters of sand white and pure only beneath the neg-yellow refraction, a blue which did not make the sand blue as a true light would have. It did not make the water blue, either, Melody certain this color was natural. At the edge of the sand was a puddle, a great rarity on this planet. An artificial puddle gravity-fed by a water tank. Dull, mud-colored water outside the neg-yellow area, but under its influence—where the non-blue "shone" on the puddle—the water was blue-green and moving. Not still as the unaffected portion, but lapping gently on the white, white sand.

An Erth beach. Just as terran as the shores of Florada. Sufficiently flabbergasted, Melody moved quietly away. Not rendered entirely senseless by the sight, Melody decided she had seen enough, and knew she must return to her base by nightfall. Travel at night was feasible with the palm projector, but Melody had no intention of being alone on Marz at night in the wilderness, especially after that negative-yellow spectacle, a vision Melody felt she should understand.

Moving on Skopein's plain once more, Melody looked behind, seeing that she was not followed. Although proceeding systematically on her reversed route, all the while Melody was thinking elsewhere, thinking of a meal, a discussion, Nan and Chas telling her of concepts religiously held. Somewhere in that conversation, Melody was sure an answer lay for the negative yellow. Something about a conceptual force to change the nature of things, to make pleasant people boring, florescent plants grasslike . . . How about, Marzian sand and mud modified into an Erth beach?

Having approached mind-boggling inferences, Melody at once began plotting again. Tomorrow, not to the Sueedes, but to this hidden building to discover the truth of the ideas involved: the exact nature of the research being performed and the experimenters' identity: UR, Sueedish, or . . . ? But now a more immediate problem was before her: nightfall. Solitude. The combination.

Halfway to the balloon, Melody noticed the sun was setting, the small sun of Marz, a dull tan in this atmosphere. As though inspired by the change from light to dark, tired Melody's thoughts became as tactile as the dust clogging her steps, and she was struck with a feeling that both chilled and exhilarated her; for Melody realized she was walking alone across the face of an alien planet so far from home that even the sun was smaller, having receded from her as though never again to be available. All the homesickness and loneliness she had felt before were incomparable to the unique impressions which came over her, Melody certain that the planet she now traversed was more alien than even the Marz she knew, and that on this world she was completely alone, the only person, the only life, having come from no human settlement, with no living goal ahead, and Melody was suddenly cold. Then her thoughts were proven exactly proper yet totally incorrect; for although she was no longer alone, how real are people who only partially exist?

She was near Skopein Planum's exact center according to her palm projector, a path taken previously, Melody following her own footprints. Yet on this journey she saw organisms not there before, Melody going completely still to stare at the largest growth of ore crop she had ever seen, countless neat rows barely visible in the fading light. Rows as though planted —but the ore crop could not be planted, and nothing of the kind had existed that very morning. Looking about more carefully, Melody nearly understood why she had not seen the plants before—because she was barely seeing them now. The problem with her sight was not the weak illumination, but the patch's inexplicable transparency; for Melody could see the smooth soil beyond by looking through the ore crop. She did not understand, and continued walking, directly to the nearest plant, which became no more clearly visible as she approached, and gained no solidity as she walked through it.

Walked through it.

Ghosts. She recalled the stories of phantoms seen by miners. Melody knew she had found a ghost ore crop, and thought of optical illusions because of the alien atmosphere, and Chaeung and his creation basis concepts here not fully manifested, ideas made real but only partially. She thought of the negative-yellow experiments as she continued to stare, continued to walk through the neat rows with a feeling more profound than her previous loneliness, Melody becoming fearful but not having to run away, not even after seeing ghost shapes in the distance which resembled in form and movement people. Melody did not have to flee until something more threatening occurred, until a ghost came after her. But this was no supposed person or evident plant—this was a huge, squarish machine with legs and feet that appeared directly before her and neared, an animal that silently, relentlessly stalked her.

Melody ran. She ran until there were no ghosts about her, and she was left only with fear. But no loneliness, for she knew that people—her people

—were ahead, and that they were solid and real and all she had to do was continue, nothing more, though she could not help but look back, look back often, though she only needed to walk and breathe and move until gaining strangers who with their first sight became permanent friends.

# CHAPTER 4:
## Abject Ghost Tracks

"You're seeing the doktor in the morning," Niklas Telak ordered. "I've heard of miners seeing ghosts, but never so many she had to run through the night to get away from them."

Melody was surrounded. The compound knew of her bizarre behavior—walking about as though an unleashed pet. There was no mention of Management, and Melody said nothing of them, of Sueedes, of inversely colored experiments. Ghosts were her support now, her justification; because upon approaching her balloon, Melody had been met by a search party led by Dorm Director Telak, a calm-voiced, calm-faced authority who only now was appreciated by her. Not exactly a father substitute, but close enough for Marz. Melody was in trouble with Telak and his people—until they saw her face, until she told them of the ghosts, until she ran on and on with minute detail about ore rows and organic machines and half-real people. Then they understood her tardiness, having received sufficient cause, for Melody was not alone in having seen ghosts.

No long, hot shower was available on this Marz, not

even after occult dilemmas. Melody had to settle for a salve job and change of clothes before meeting with Telak and certain miners in the cafeteria for debriefing. Certain miners with stories of their own. They were all no more than acquaintances, but no longer were they strangers.

"I saw ghosts," a terse Yuropean named Kalamaras told the group as they sat with cups of herb coffee. "I saw clear through ore plants, but I didn't look no closer. I just thought I was seeing things," he added.

"I also," young Su Soichinada told her fellow miners. "Near Skopein Plain, but I looked closer, seeing many, many plants, at dusk one day, out too late we were. I looked closer, but with the sun's setting, they disappeared, seen no more."

Then an older miner, Eve Bonfante, one of the most experienced, whispered her story.

"I saw faces," she said, "at the same locale, but near the foothills. I saw faces at dusk—and I swear they saw me."

"What did you do?" Melody asked, nearly whispering in her renewed fear.

"I blinked hard enough, long enough, and they were gone," Bonfante described. "I looked away, shook my head, and they were gone."

"This cannot be coincidence," Soichinada told Telak, who had been listening without comment. "Not similar sights at not a different area."

"I agree," he replied, "and I think it best we learn more. I'll speak with Management and get some equipment. We can establish observation parties and supply them with data enhancers. Any volunteers?"

"I ain't got time for that krap," Kalamaras scoffed.

"Is the pay the same?" Bonfante asked her dorm

director, who replied after a moment's thought.

"Yes, of course it would have to be."

"I can handle it," Bonfante then returned.

"Too many responsibilities for me," Soichinada responded, "though I still have great interest."

"I still ain't got time for it," Kalamaras repeated.

"I'm going," Melody stated plainly, but Telak disagreed.

"I don't think so, Preece. You were too upset."

"I defy you to keep me away," she asserted, staring into Telak's eyes. "You can't fire me, dock my pay, and God knows you can't send me home. I'll run off unless you tie me down, and I'll never—"

"Very well, Melody," Telak stated clearly. "I'll make a schedule and you'll be included. As for now, I'm hitting the cube. I suggest you all do the same. Regardless, Melody, you see the doktor in the morning so he can quantify your psicho—understand?"

She had to think about it, Melody finding it virtually unnatural to be cooperative, but finally she agreed. But since she also found it easier and easier to lie, would she keep the appointment? Seeing a physician was sensible, however; for in fact, Melody felt terrible. Ever since running from the ghosts, she had been weak and shaky as though she had vomited out half her insides. Obviously she was exhausted from both the running and the anxiety; but although explicable, the illness was discomforting and she wanted it cured.

Although the miners were prepared to leave, Melody was not finished with these people. Soon after her return, Melody had found something wrong with the search party, with the miners who stayed to tell stories: Chaeung was not among them. Believing that

Soichinada knew him, Melody took this fem aside as the miners dispersed.

"Su, do you know Chas Chaeung? Have you seen him?"

"I know him somewhat, but know that you with him are friends, do I not so understand?" she answered.

Unable to hide the truth, and unafraid of embarrassment, Melody had to say, "I thought he would be here . . ."

"Oh, but how is it you do not know?" Soichinada replied. "Chaeung has been restructured to Management. A superior made the arrangement. A Flamini, I believe her name."

"Thank you," Melody said, no longer able to speak or look to Soichinada.

She returned to her cubicle without a thought in her mind, only depression and vertigo. That night she slept poorly, no dreams, but too many thoughts of alien landscapes and established ghosts for her to rest.

In the morning, having to choose between the ore fields and the doktor—since the ghost watch would not begin until that evening—Melody decided to keep her appointment, not because of the psicho tests, but due to physiological problems; for Melody still felt imperfect, as though she had contracted some new type of influenza. She had been eating adequately, but still seemed weak, as though nothing were within her to provide energy. After meal one, Melody walked to the medikal balloon.

In the doktor's antechambers waited typical cases, men and women in moderate discomfort from minor damage: contusions from bucking ore karts, the characteristic lumpy rash of Marzian mites, the bloated skin from unchecked alien bacteria. Melody had to wait so long she feared contamination, feared these ailments would translate through the air to her person. She nearly wished she were in the ore fields instead.

The doktor saw her personally, no internurse. He knew little of her case—though Telak had notified him—so they began with an interview, Melody uncomfortable with him because his shinyblack moustache was not very neat and he smelled like chewing tobacco—a terrible medicine. The typical, blood-red clothing worn by meds Melody had always found unpleasant, for did they not wear this color to hide sloppy workmanship? Unkempt Doktor Spurs Faint Confidence.

"You're here because you saw a ghost?" Dr. Searle asked. "And for this you need a doktor? I'm no medium, girl, perhaps talk to a rubbi."

"I feel bad, Dok," she told him, "forget the ghosts. I'm weak but eat sometimes, good stool, no chemicals for fun—for any reason. I think it's radiation," she concluded seriously.

"In your brilliance you think this?" Searle replied.

"Aren't those symptoms of overdosing on ore crop radiation?"

"I could not know," he said, "because there is no such thing. Ore crop radiation has no effect on organic tissue—completely harmless."

"Doktor, that's what they used to say about X rays—right until the day they outlawed the process. Are you hiding something I don't know?"

"I should know what you don't know?" he replied.

"Let's try some tests," Melody suggested.

Searle agreed. With the internurse aiding him, he inserted the oral, anal, cranial, and vaginal probes which Melody had always considered vulgar in no particular order. The nurse left to investigate some unconvincing screams as Melody dressed and the doktor interpreted the factingrate readings.

"Normal enough," he told her while examining the stats. "On Marz, with your nerves I can see, you need more food for energy, such a skinny thing. You say you've been eating your veggies?"

"Affirmative," Melody sighed.

"So you're losing weight, need more peenut butter —just watch for hair where you're not wanting it. And now we weigh you."

Unimpressed with his medikal expertise, his hirsute allusions, Melody stepped against the scales.

"Ah, but not working here," he scolded the machine. "What your normal weight?"

"Ninety-eight Erth."

"Sixty-seven, then, is not right, surely. Here, let me try," he instructed, and Melody stood aside as Searle weighed himself.

"Funny, it tells me one seventy-five which is close enough. Maybe below a hundred pounds it doesn't work, but I don't know this. Hmmm, let me think . . . ," he intoned, and looked down to Melody's torso. "Sure, you seem a good ninety-five, ninety-seven pounds, and your clothes are fitting. Let me try," he said, and reached to grasp her waist, lifting. His dull expression then changed to surprise.

"My God, girl, you weigh nothing."

He held her in mid-air, twenty inches from the floor, effortlessly.

"I'm only fifty-eight Marz, Doktor," Melody said as she looked down from the ceiling, Searle's touch and response less than reassuring. "Maybe the scale was reading Marzian weight," she suggested.

"Girl, I can count, you might know—and also I can read the machine. But I am holding no fifty-eight pounds Marzian—I have books that weigh more than this."

He was lifting her up and down, up and down, with no effort, as though lifting a book, or a . . .

"Please put me down, Doktor," she stated sharply, and reached for his hands.

He complied, giving her a strange expression as though she were insane. Searle then offered his diagnosis.

"Eat more, I don't know this," he replied with evident concern, staring at Melody as though she were a freak. "I process all the probe readings again, get this Flamini to realign the data integrator first. Maybe I can fix the scale—or my hands. I don't know. Come back tomorrow. For now, I have to deal with sick people whose sickness makes sense."

Melody left. The nurse was trying to calm a man whose field bandage had begun leaking blood. This seemed so clean to Melody: when you're hurt, you bleed, a simple, demonstrable process. The injured man was upset, justifiably, but Melody did not care. She was justifiably selfish. She was only concerned with her own, improper illness, for the doktor had been right: it made no sense. Melody's thoughts were that no disease, no cancer existed which involved one's equally dissolving throughout the corpus. Then, upon stepping into the corridor away from common, clean illness, she had a thought that for a moment was literally blinding, Melody blacking out and having to stop until her senses cleared. Connotation struck her, the idea coming that she was not dissolving, she was fading away—she was becoming a ghost. The process would continue until she became a transparent object like the faded ore crop—or that machine creature —visible only in the dim Marzian light.

In a moment she was Melody again, realizing she was still this person, still alive and able to plan. And she decided not to become a ghost so easily. She would not be like that man, screaming over a drop of blood. Her decision was knowledge, that an understanding of the ghosts she and the other miners had seen was necessary for her illness to be cured. And Melody wanted to be well. Now it seemed simplicity was an idea beyond her; for just the day before, Melody had been so lonely in the empty Marzian dusk that nothing seemed more important than being home. But now her only problem was survival, the basis of one's human life more important than loneliness: alien, average, or abject.

Theirs would not be the most dedicated evening of ghost hunting. Led by Telak, the miners arrived late in the afternoon. All had worked hard the entire day, including Melody, who had been searching behind rocks for hours, checking the plain's edges for hidden translucent plants ready to sift out at day's end, examining the plain's floor for ghost tracks—however they might appear—but none were found. Apart from her own footprints of the day before, Melody found only anxiety, from her past experiences and present condition.

She had been uncomfortable the day, but not fatal.

Earlier, Melody had tried jumping about, thinking that if she were so light, a mere flexing of her legs would launch her into the atmosphere. But this did not work. Her leaping abilities were found to be Marzian average, Melody deducing that if less of her were extant, there would be less to push and less to be pushed; thus, a neutral state. But this was silly, wasn't it? For although she felt somewhat weak, and as far as lifting was concerned she was unable to exert a normal force; still, no physical change was evident which corresponded to her supposedly lost mass —did it? But then she discovered another depressing notion. Melody had always wanted to weigh at least one hundred pounds—the figure seemed so adult —but now she was certain she would never make it.

At least she had the ghosts sussed. Partially. Perhaps. Ghosts were not seen more often because people were seldom outside during the hours of their appearance. The environment of this planet was not exactly conducive to moonlight strolls. Not with those piddly moons. Perhaps more ghosts were being seen lately because they were becoming more active, more perceptually real. These were Melody's deductions, ideas to be proven or refuted not by further judgment, but by a forthcoming scientific study.

When her friends arrived with data analyzers— spectrum enhancers and recorders, vibe/shift detectors, et cetera—Melody felt more confident; for here were instruments to aid in her diagnosis, her understanding. But her friends were tired and uncertain, Telak believing the phenomenon a psichological manifestation of some unique Marzian stress. Kalamaras, who surprisingly had joined the expedition, evinced perhaps the most revealing attitude, the most telling contradiction.

"I still ain't got time for this shid," he insisted; yet he was present.

They did not talk much. Telak preferred to sit on one of the karts they had brought and watch his people ready equipment. Apart from these instruments, Management had offered no interest, no aid. Non-ebullient Melody, however, was eager for evening, trying to guess how the group would behave when together they found a Marzian ghost; and instead of fearing, ignoring, or running from the phenomenon, they could remain controlled and begin an examination, a scientific study to reveal. But when the ghosts appeared, the miners were not together, and some could not see at all.

Having been standing and nervously chatting with Bonfante for too long, Melody moved out onto the plain, twenty yards from the nearest miner. Marz was so dull, hardly a breeze to stir the rare bush, the scarce grass, the sand too greasy to be shifted about regardless. The sun was so low that no shadows existed, the soft light of dusk about them, and Melody was seeing something. At first she thought her imagination was too energetic, for she was certain the ore plants were appearing before her, as though inversely fading into existence. But upon closing her eyes and shaking her head, the vision seemed to end. Turning from the plain and walking back to Bonfante, however, Melody saw the older woman looking past her and shaking her head as well—but to no avail, for the ghosts were visible again.

Telak was off his kart, barking for Kalamaras and

the three remaining miners to get that gear cracking. By the time Melody and Bonfante met at the plain's edge, the translucent ore crop was all around them, the same neat rows seen before. The two fems said nothing, only stared, as behind them Telak received acknowledgments, but only from Kalamaras and one other woman handling data enhancers, the other two studying their instruments with confusion.

"What am I supposed to be reading?" one miner asked Telak with her hands outspread.

"Right here!" Melody shouted, and walked through a ghost plant.

"You're nuts; I don't see anything," the same woman replied, and the other agreed.

"I swear, Director Telak, I don't see a thing, and I'm getting no reading on any band."

"Well, goddamn, I see," Kalamaras growled, but when he manipulated the instruments before him, his voice returned to normal. "I see, but I register nothing."

"I don't care what you don't see," Telak declared to the two confused miners, "keep those machines going and sweep every spectrum and each pressure vibe."

Telak then walked out to stand with Melody and Bonfante. No talking, just looking for a long moment, Melody uncomfortable despite her company; for she was waiting for further sights, further organisms.

"It must be some individual perceptive ability," Telak offered. "I can barely see them myself, and only with peripheral vision."

"Really?" Melody declared. "I can see them with perfect clarity, every striation and that light fuzz on the stems. Can you, Bonfante?"

"Yes, everything."

"Can you count the buds on this one, Director?" Melody asked, but Telak shook his head.

"Definitely not. I can distinguish it as an ore plant, but can't see such fine detail."

Bonfante could, and Melody, Kalamaras seeing less than these women, but more than Telak.

Kalamaras had a handlight out. Where it shone, the ghost plants were not seen. Only the bare Marzian soil was illuminated.

"It's not light that's letting us see them," Melody determined. "Not that kind of light. After nightfall I don't think any of us will see them, and that's in a few minutes."

But the remnants of this day brought new sights, new people.

"Haysus!" Kalamaras called out from one side. "Look!" and he pointed beyond. Melody had already seen them, for they were expected. People, two translucent people with indistinguishable clothes drawing near, moving between the ore plants as though hiding.

Bonfante turned to move away.

"Don't go," Telak ordered. "Those are not bodies, just perceptions. Since you can see so well, you have to stay—and watch everything. Preece?"

"I'm not going anywhere," she whispered, not having looked away from those people since the first view.

They neared. They looked to one another furtively and approached the trio of miners. And when they were within ten yards, the two bent to the ground, then rose to move their arms forward quickly—and Melody ducked.

"What was that motion?" Telak asked her.

"They're throwing rocks at us."

"I couldn't tell," Bonfante said anxiously. "Now

you're seeing better than I."

"I'm going to try something," Melody told her companions, then ran toward the two phantoms, screaming wordlessly. Desperately and immediately the spectres fled. Then Melody's further expectation was fulfilled, for she saw the machine, the animal machine.

She returned to Telak and Bonfante and told the director, "This one I may have to run from myself. I don't like it. I really don't like it."

"I never saw that before," pale Bonfante whispered, "and I don't like it either."

"It's getting too dark," Melody pointed out. "We won't be able to see it much longer—but does that mean it won't be there?"

Kalamaras shone his light toward the thing, revealing nothing. Waving his hand through the nearest plant, Telak replied as though to himself, "No substance at all. It's just a perception. I'm going to have our people set the gear for auto, and we'll leave."

Melody turned to watch him move away, but unexpectedly had to grab for her coverall, because it had ripped at the seams and was slipping off—but when she reached for it, there were no rents, and she could barely hold it, the fabric attempting to slip through her fingers like water, Melody able to retain the clothing with difficulty, her tubes dropping as Bonfante screamed.

"Telak! Telak! I can see through her!"

Melody looked up at Bonfante, who was a terror before her, eyes horrified as she stumbled backward from Melody; and Telak looked on, dumbfounded; while behind the stricken girl, the soundless machine animal neared, now a sight less impressive than Melody.

As an automatic response, Melody was trying to hold her slipping clothes on, to retain her breather —until she looked down to see the fabric fall through her hands. Not between her fingers, but through her hands. Her transparent hands.

The clothing fell away, but Melody was not nude —she was nothing, looking up to her friends with a final word before her voice became unhearable and Melody was lost.

"Please . . . ," she cried, the miners now transparent to her as the animal behind turned solid.

# CHAPTER 5:
## *A Killer for Company*

She was inundated by the rattling vibration and growling din of the creature as it engulfed her, Melody with no opportunity to run or dodge or understand, as solid as ever in a different world ruled by a towering fiend which ate her, drowned her with its noise and metal smell, then surrounded her with its light-killing, life-killing jaws. As soon as the miners turned invisible, the creature behind was completely real, completely on her, Melody literally lost within its maw as her nude body was dragged toward chopping metal teeth heard gnashing each other, and then gnashing her, scraping her skin; and she could feel the hot, hard surfaces against her, ready to penetrate, Melody unable to fight a metal force whose rumbling teeth were eating her. And the last bit of learning for the dying girl was that the greatest aspect of death is waiting, that one's imminent demise requires forever to come, as though the soon-to-be-dead one so clings to life that the final experience is intentionally stretched, foolishly relished as though a new birth; but Melody was dying, waiting for the hot metallic teeth which now pulled her body flat and scraped her hair and head to finally bite into skin and bone and eat the girl so frightened she was not expecting pain, but darkness, utter darkness, forever, forever. And then the light from her eyes was gone, Melody consumed by the creature.

Then dropped on her face in freshly turned soil, Melody looking up with her mouth in the dirt to see a huge machine on wheels move away from her, its path never changing, never having changed, Melody in a broad row of naked soil, a cleared path in a perfect field of ore crop.

A threshing machine. Rather, a harvesting machine with thick, articulated struts—like legs—ending in large rubber wheels. Most astounding was the clanking, grating, gnashing, which became quieter as the thresher continued away. Stretched out in the dirt, Melody looked up to see the high, complex surfaces of the machine, see neat piles of ore crop dropped precisely upon a center segment after being uprooted in front. And there, a large rock dropped through a conveying channel in the machine's rear, spit out like refuse. Like Melody.

She collapsed in the dirt like a worm. Having learned enough, Melody had to return to normalcy, return to life. Sprawled as though lifeless, she sought nothing but life, nothing but breathing; and there was no trouble here, even without a convertor, for she was not being eaten, and the air was clean and dense, Melody needing nothing but the life that was inhalation. And for minutes she did nothing but breathe, had no other sensations, feeling each manner, every change of respiration. She felt those first, racking sucks turn to gasps, tearless gasps, felt them change to panting, finally to concentrated breaths that were intended, Melody consciously thinking: Breathe deeply, girl, just breathe . . .

When breathing—when life—seemed nearly normal again, Melody could accept further perceptions, though she was not moving, not thinking of her naked body spread for the taking. No one was around, the machine nearly gone. All this good air; and now, the smell of soil right next to her nose. Some in her nose. Not the sticky Marzian sand, but rich, black soil damp with inner moisture and with dew. And this smell was unmistakable: the scent not of some soil, but of Erth. Melody was too recently resurrected to be overpowered by this sensation, but the power was there. More perceptions now: the unmistakable taste of the nasty stuff in her mouth as she tried to spit it out; and, yes, it tasted like dirt—who cares what kind?

Slowly raising her head, Melody saw to either side tall, dense rows of perfect ore plants: clearly a cultivated crop. Carefully rolling onto her back, then sitting, deep-breathing Melody looked behind to see that her row was hundreds of meters long. Immediately she was struck with conflicting impressions. First, the fact of the dirt's smell being Erth-identical. But then the realization of her sitting, the feel: this was no full g field, but a partial. This was Marz—but what Marz?

All of this as she sat, inhaled, and looked around. Still dazed, but calming, eventually to regain good thinking. Was that a bird chirping in the distance? No birds on her Marz. Trees here, too, and wildflowers. Too cool for her Marz, but not uncomfortable. No sky like this, either, a rich violet lightening with the rising sun. A small rising sun, Melody noticed as she stood, seeing the lovely lines of a mountain range that was recognized; for, yes, that peak in the soft Marzian light was a geologically young Montei Unverit. And this seemed an especial shock, the rounded-off form she knew now tall and crisp, impressive in its clear greyish colors and impassive outline. But Unverit had not been such a mountain for millions of years—had Melody traveled in time?

Since time travel was the dumbest thing she could think of, Melody forgot it. Automatically as she looked about, Melody began brushing the dirt from her body—and face and legs. Good soil, a bit unclean, but no sticky mess, her naked body not smeared with filth.

Naked body could be problematic, she thought, but there was no one to hide from. All her parts exposed in the air, however—any air—was most uncomfortable, but her clothes were not present. Her clothes had been left behind when . . . When . . .

Thereafter she lost some of her regained calm. Blinking and looking about, she was trying to think, trying to make sense of this nonsense. Her mouth was open and she was panting once more, Melody numbed dumb at being God-knows-where, amazed at being alive, and still beaten by the machine's consumption. As she mindlessly continued to semi-effectively run her hands, unlooking, up and down her body, sloppy Melody was without decent posture or poise, trying to recover, too shaken to be joyful at the simple fact of her reestablished life.

Bruises might later show, but no blood was found, only scrapes and aches. Able to contemplate further, Melody thought of dying, not the machine's unreal eating, but her having turned into a ghost. Although wandering uncertainly from side to side, small shuffles across the soil, Melody was thinking more clearly now, and determined that somehow she had literally faded away from Marz and appeared here. But where was here? Clearly the planet was Marz, but a modified Marz. Was this the Dull Planet of the ancient past, of some distant future?

Better in the mind but still woozy in the body, Melody heard a sound, saw a movement, and looked about to find no further improvement, but a new troublesome thrill. Two men. Two men running toward her from the ore crop's midst. Two men she recognized: not their faces, but their bent running, their bodily outlines. Weren't these the ghost forms heaving stones at her? Two ghost men now as solid as Melody running at her with some kind of tools. These as well she recognized. Not the identical shape as hers, but they were still ore forks. Even dull ore forks with men leaning on them were sharp enough to puncture solid Melody.

In the cleared row and running toward her, the men lacked a certain friendly demeanor with their implements before them brandished like brooms after mice. Looking to all sides, Melody considered running into the shoulder-high crop, but she could barely move, much less move quickly. Melody was going nowhere on her own. She had to stay. But there was no boldness in her, no firm resolve to confront these strangers. She was too weak and upset to move, only turning sideways to present less of her unclad form to the male adults rapidly nearing, Melody fortunate only in that her poor state precluded her suffering the tremendous embarrassment this social situation should have delivered. Too beaten to panic, she could only think: Here comes death again.

No matter. They ran to her and slowed, not attacking immediately. One of the men walked completely around her, looking up and down, fore and aft. The other seemed almost ashamed, but nevertheless he looked. Both were oldish adults with greying hair, dressed in coarse, well-worn pant/shirt combos, dark but not dirty, their boots plastick, slick and modern. Melody could not place the era or area responsible for the stiff onion rings dangling from their necks; but before the first word, she could tell the talker, the staring man more active in his expression and moves, walking around her with energetic eyes and a mouth about to speak. The second man had quieter eyes and lips, facial muscles not accustomed to excess speech. Melody could see this in his face, his static face. Both men seemed average, non-brilliant Cockassions to her, and each brandished an ore fork at her defenseless body.

"Gahd in the sky!" the talker exclaimed as he leered at helpless Melody, "that's the acutest witch I ever had to kill!"

By now Melody was perceiving better; yet before she could be chilled by the coolish morning air of this Marz, she was frozen by the man's words. Frozen inside, but hot even deeper, affronted Melody had to speak.

"That's not funny," she admonished clearly, and pressed her arms tightly against her sides, finding it useless to try covering all that skin, front and rear, with only two hands. "You find me in a horrible strait; yet you offer no aid. Have you never heard of gentlemanship?"

"We've heard of witches," the talker sneered with a nasty mouth, nasty tone, the man standing still now to stare scrupulously up and down Melody's front.

"We've heard of ghosts, too, and seen a few. Just seen one that resembles you," he noted with a trace of enlightenment in his sneer. "One screaming curses at us, and now turned into a solid witch to curse our crop in person. My brother and uncle both have found witchghosts in this very valley. I've heard of others, and now I find one myself."

Melody would have preferred to be merely perturbed at his rudeness, but this was not her position, not their relation. She was being attacked, and felt it. Even to Melody, however, her voice sounded remarkably strong considering her increasing fear, an effect which should have been choking.

"You're looking at a person who's just been run over and is standing here freezing and wounded, and all you can do is call her a witch?" she declared with genuine amazement. "What kind of people are you?"

"Just farmers," the other man said with a crisp tone, his voice not hinting of ugliness—ugly thoughts —as did his partner's. "Just farmers, but even farmers know a witch."

"Of course," the talker sneered, "her hair is that brown. No one is hair brown but a witch—everyone knows that. And look, Bishup, it's real—she's got a hair-brown crotch!" he hissed, and pointed below Melody's waist.

Bishup did not want to look—he did not want to stare—but as though fulfilling a duty, this quiet farmer lowered his head toward Melody's most private aspects, and had to nod in agreement.

"Yes," he decided reluctantly, "only witches are hair brown." Then he jerked a look to his partner, changing his tone as he scowled, "Told you these wouldn't work, Jid," and harshly tapped his onion ring. "Never kept a witch away yet."

Melody was now too astonished for words, an emotion unfortunately not alleviating her fear. Jid's following words seemed somehow predictably perverse.

"I bet her boo-obs are cold, too," he said slowly, looking only to his friend. "Gahd knows there's no better proof of a witch than cold boo-obs."

Unavoidably, foolish Melody had to ask, "What's a boo-ob?"

"Tid," the tacit farmer replied.

"How vulgo!" Melody admonished, and finally covered her own.

"Better check her," Jid advised, quickly dropping his fork to lunge at Melody, pressing her small hands away with his farmer's paws to fully engulf one breast.

His touch was such an affront to Melody that for an instant she forgot her fear, leaping backward as she slapped the man's hand away. Regardless of her active, quivering mouth, Melody was speechless.

As he rubbed the bruised hand, Jid looked to his partner as though Melody were not present in their world, saying, "No, it's warm, good and warm," surprised from either the blow or the temperature. "What does that mean?"

"*Alien* witches have warm boo-obs," Bishup replied, talking too much now for anyone's good.

After no thought whatsoever, Jid declared, "Yeah, and they're small, anyway. That's near as bad as being cold. And she acts like a crone." Then he concluded, "Come on, let's go burn her," and raised his ore fork toward Melody, pressing it too near as he ordered, "Walk, witch."

No more arguing. No more conversation. Only

numb procedure as Melody followed instructions —to the row's end, turn right. Only mindless walking as she stared at the lightening sky—less pink now —and thought nothing of the rich organic smells, of life and colors foreign to her Marz. Thought nothing of the eyes behind she could sense on her common buttocks not small or still enough to be ignored. When thinking finally returned to Melody, her heart a sunken gland in her torso, the only ideas which came were vengeful: I'll get you for this, farmers. I will get you back.

Turning at the row's end as ordered, now-decisive Melody gave a bit of a hip twitch, not at all ashamed of her femininity. In the throats behind, lumps were heard forming. Again Melody was thinking, thinking of the Marz before her: the trees she had noticed above the ore crop, sweet flowers smelled, the dirt road they now traveled, a rural area reminiscent of Erth, but not quite like Erth. To her side, she saw that part of the ore crop filling Skopein's plain was being irrigated with non-bluish water. As they continued, Melody glimpsed buildings through the trees— small but modern, artificial structures—where the residual boulders of Montei Unverit should have been. But Unverit was proud and tall in the near distance, the range's rolling foothills beginning just beyond the buildings, green hills where the forest continued.

The settlement they approached was of a style Melody had not seen since she worked on a medikal dispersal unit supplying the hillfolk of Northern Ajia with vaccines. Those people lived in wonderful plastick huts which were permanent and impervious, houses supplied by the local government to replace their grass shacks. The Ajians kept their new homes immaculate, kept them free of insects by defecating on their perimeters. These Marzian farmers, however, being of a more sophisticated society, were messy, their buildings in a landscape of rusty buckets, broken machine pieces, and discarded household items scattered amidst the weeds.

They turned onto a second dirt road which angled out of sight, the thresher chomping somewhere behind. Unusual here was a companion to this road, a pipeline along the wayside, pale blue and nearly three feet in diameter. Melody knew UR blue when she saw it. Across from the farmstead they neared, fittings were rigged on the line, smaller pipes disappearing into the ground, evidently leading to the buildings. Looking closer, Melody discerned a small insignia on the main piping: not the UR's, but an underhand knot of steel cable, the familiar Iron Knot. She had no idea what the pipes carried, but at least the controlling organization was unimpeachable; for who were more responsible than the Knotzis?

As they approached the nearest structure—trok tires and other mechanicals visible within—Melody realized that other people would be present in the house just beyond, and she would have to suffer additional bouts of leering, shame to reach an ungodly degree. And, yes, sounds ahead, screeching children beating on something with sticks, so it seemed. Guided by simple orders from the men behind, Melody walked toward these sounds; but before the small people were seen, Bishup stopped her.

"Hold it, girl."

She turned only her head, not wanting to show the men behind more of her body than they were now certainly more familiar with than herself. Melody partially turned to see Bishup removing his shirt.

"Cover yourself with this," he said, handing her the apparel.

As she took the shirt, Melody looked directly at him, his face, but Bishup would not return her gaze, his eyes averted as though ashamed. And of course, he was the one partially nude now, the long-tailed shirt covering Melody to her upper thighs, Bishup's pale skin no more accustomed to the sun than his eyes were to leering.

"Thank you," she told him.

Jid was staring at his partner now, amazed, staring at Bishup's paunch, that scar near his non-muscular chest, beside his failed onion ring.

"What are you doing, person, going around naked yourself?" Jid demanded. Bishup answered clearly:

"I don't want my kids seeing no naked woman, witch or not."

Becoming even less pleasant than before, Jid snapped, "Well, why are we going to your place, anyway?"

"It's closer," Bishup told him.

"But I know how to take care of witches," Jid insisted, but Bishup concluded:

"What you know is shid."

Jid's jaw dropped as he stared at Bishup. Then his ore fork dropped also, Jid pointing a stiff finger at his partner and shouting:

"Well, I'll be gahddamned if I won't take care of her anyway!" and he turned to stalk down the road.

Bishup had her continue. A moment later, Melody was surrounded by a pair of young children. They did not look like workers to her, but playthings for each other. Melody wanted to wonder deeply about the local society, but instead she had to absorb more annoyance, more pain. The children were amazed by the semi-clad lady, their semi-clad father. They squealed, and Melody wanted to ignore them. But Bishup chased them away before their lax existence and immature excitement drove Melody insane.

He chased them away without mentioning anything about a witch, perturbed himself by his children's laughing at his situation, his companion, his bare belly. Then, to Melody's virtual relief, she was locked in the mechanical shed instead of being taken to the house.

Within the building were parts for threshers (she presumed), small hand tools, recognized and unknown pieces of metal and plastick, everything she needed to escape. And there were windows which even if unbreakable could be opened by a handy, knowledgeable girl with a roomful of implements. Unfortunately, through one of these windows Melody saw the farmer return with a shirt on his back and a dog at his side, a lovely Lotsa Hopso.

They entered. With its first sight of Melody the dog ran to her, hopping on its hind legs for her to commence petting. A sweet dog with a gorgeous, golden coat that made lovely, growly sounds in a most friendly manner and simply could not get close enough to the immediately liked stranger. The farmer stayed only long enough to give the dog its orders.

"If she tries to leave," he said, "eat her," and Bishup left.

Piece of pie, Melody thought. Piece of pie. Seconds after the farmer locked the side door behind, Melody stepped to it, reaching for the handle. She never touched it, though, for the dog instantly turned into a snarling, frothing creature, snapping teeth inches from Melody's unclad leg.

She jumped away from both the dog and the door. At once the former calmed, settling on its haunches with a pleasant expression, staring up to Melody.

"Talk about witches," she muttered, and the dog wagged its tail.

She proceeded to examine the interior, keeping well away from the three doors found. Before she could formulate any plan, however, a sound from outside caught her attention, Melody moving to a window to see Bishup back a large, elderly trok to the front door of his house. She then watched a procession. The farmer, a woman his age with delicate limbs and a dress, the two children seen before plus one boy much larger, and a quite old man began loading the trok with appliances, clothing, all the belongings which constitute a household. Melody heard arguments about, Yes, we *need* that; No, we don't. She saw certain toys, one table, and many other articles left in the yard or tossed back inside. This hardly seemed to be well planned; certainly the family was improvising. Most interesting was another argument, one not about necessities, but witches.

"The Powerhouse leaking ideas is bringing them ghosts," the woman insisted as she saved a special blanket from Bishup's discarding grasp.

"That don't leak enough to hurt nothing," he retorted, "at least not this far," and he tossed a lamp behind the bushes.

Staring after her lost light, the woman blithely dropped a quitar to the grass, kicking it aside. Bishup eyed it like his own.

"Well, our farm will be Ideatown if they don't stop the seepage," she declared.

"The Chairhuman knows what he's doing," Bishup

concluded, and there went the sewing machine.

Although the costly argument was soon over, the greater function continued for an hour, but Melody returned to her own activity, her own plans—for escape. By now the dog was sleeping—Melody refusing to pet the thing after its vicious commentary —but at least one eye followed the prisoner's every move. Getting through a door or window would be a no-sweat deal—getting past the dog was her problem. Melody had thoughts of smashing the Hopso with an axle or something, but certainly no intent. She would rot in that shed before maiming a loyal puppy, even a two-faced Lotsa.

Too late, Melody realized, for the door soon opened. The farmer entered. The dog hopped merrily against his lower body, the man having to pet the creature (with some perturbance) before he could proceed with business, with his captive.

"Come on," he ordered, and gestured for Melody to follow.

They were waiting for her. Stationed at the trok's far side, the remaining family members peered around to stare at Melody. This attention was beginning to make her ill. Only the older boy spoke, a loud whisper.

"If that's what a witch looks like, I want one for Xmas."

Smoothly the woman reached over with a broad sweep of her arm to slap the boy quiet.

"Thanks, Mom, that really straightened me out," he lied, for his head seemed rendered crooked, "with her awful hair and all."

The father offered only a look of revulsion to the boy as he and the dog guided Melody into the house.

The Hopso was sweet and prancing. Melody wanted to kick its butt.

"You stay here awhile," Bishup instructed her, and left with his dog, locking the door behind.

Looking through the front window, Melody saw the farmer rip the onion ring away and fling the necklace to his doorstep. Then he entered the trok with his family, the father taking the controls. And with a semi-muffled roar, they left, revolting son and all.

Glancing about inside, Melody saw that the house was virtually empty, some books and old pillows lying about, bad furniture here and there, not a sound. She intended to examine the rest of the building, wondering why she had been left alone in this bizarre manner. About ten seconds of search Melody would allow before attacking the openings, just enough time for the family to be down the road a piece. But upon entering the hallway a moment later, Melody noticed an odd smell. Then she discovered that she was not alone, but had a killer for company. And she could feel the other presence, the building's contents, for Bishup had left his home full of flames.

# CHAPTER 6:
## *Cool as a Witch's Vulva*

With a shriek, Melody flung herself around and ran
back into the main room. To the windows, beat on the
plastick, kick the unbreakable panes, Melody nearly
wild, but moving toward freedom, not panic. To the
door, the clear fumes of a chemical fire to her back,
and now heat. Somehow Bishup had reversed the lock
panel; so a key would be needed from inside. Franti-
cally, Melody looked about as though flinging her
vision. One more window to try, running toward it,
closed as the first, glued closed, so it seemed. She
thought of going into another room, but the flames
were coming from every entrance. No matter. Melody
would be on fire in seconds; and for an endless second
she went blank, ignorant, nothing to do, helpless,
hopeless. An endless second of defeat before looking
about again and again, ready to plan, trying
to . . . And the door opened.

"That idiot rock farmer can't do anything right,"
Jid sneered as he reached inside to grab Melody by the
arm and yank her out. "I'm taking you home to burn
you properly."

With his free hand, the farmer reached for the

discarded onion ring which he stuffed into his pocket. Then he pushed Melody toward a small, open kar, the semi-seared girl unable to gain her breath or her bearings. Behind them the plastick sizzled. Ahead, Melody saw that they were not alone. A youth about her age was in the kar, a large male pointing an ore fork toward her, obviously unfamiliar with this device used as a weapon, his grip and aim uncertain.

Shoving her between the shoulders, Jid pushed Melody into the back of the low kar next to the boy, who moved to the vehicle's edge as he brandished his ore fork, looking wide-eyed at Melody's sprawling, unclad legs as she settled in an ungainly lump and tried to breathe.

"Dad, if that's a witch, I want one for—" and the farmer knocked him cold.

For an endless moment, Melody thought only of that terrible smack of fist against face, a sound so ugly it hurt. But then improper contact became immediate, the farmer with his hands on her. Before they were established in their journey on the dirt road, Jid reached back to grab Melody's nearer arm to pull her into superior view, the kar swerving a bit, but okay. Then he grabbed her closer calf and planned on holding it, as though to tie her down with his grip; but recovered Melody had felt enough of him.

"You know you're getting warts wherever you touch me," she averred with a nasty tone, and gave him her best cackle.

Astonished, Jid looked down to his hands as though hair grew between his fingers. He found nothing, but did not touch her again.

Minutes later, the three were at a farmstead similar to Bishup's, though somewhat neater. Jid had been driving with difficulty, in that he needed to guide the kar with one hand on the steering bar, one on an ore fork to guard the witchghost. The boy did not come to until Jid had driven behind his karbarn to a thick metal post planted in the ground, its base surrounded by a stack of short tree limbs, small branches. There the farmer and his son guided Melody with very little speaking from any party, dragged Melody and tied her with rubber hoses to the post.

Jid did not touch the witch, of course, but prodded her with the handle end of his fork, Melody avoiding sharp contact after the first few bruises. The son, however, was so brave and strong as to drag the slight girl about, his hands all over her arms and elbows. He had no idea what his father meant when saying, "Them warts will serve you right."

Then Melody was at the post and being secured. As they proceeded, Jid spoke further to his son as though instructing him.

"Burn your own house down just to kill a witch —that's crazy. Everybody knows you got to have real oke and a iron post and rubber tie-downs to kill one proper."

This was all happening too quickly for Melody, never with a decent chance for recuperation. First the machine's eating, then in the dirt, a few breaths and here come the ore forks. Then the dragging and burning, Melody still uncertain of her locale, stuck in an unknown world. Then prodded everywhere, lashed down, and now burned again.

She hated them. They were really going to burn her. No longer did she want to escape from these people —she wanted to punish them. Escape, after all, seemed impossible. But punishment was easy.

"You fool," she crooned calmly to Jid in her deepest voice. "A metal post is no good. If you use a *metal* post to burn a witch you will find it in your woman's womb."

The man was shocked motionless, his jaw dropped open again. But after his shock came fury, Jid shrieking so hard he shot spittle.

"Gahddamn! you curse my *wife*, you witch!" and he reached for the nearest branch, the nearest club.

Cool as a witch's vulva, Melody told him, "Strike me and toads will grow in your mouth while you're sleeping. Can you do nothing right, mortal?"

Another pause for shock from the man; then quick, nervous moves as he dropped the branch and told his son:

"Get back, get back, she's going up right now," and he reached into his pant, bringing out a fag torch. With a flip of his thumb, he formed a small flame which he applied to tiny branches inches from Melody's feet.

She wanted to curse him genuinely, with a religion that she believed. She wanted to scream, "Why the rush? Where's due process or expert opinion?" But of course these were fanatics, and fanatics listen poorly. Too late for talk regardless, because beneath her was a fire. Then Melody felt a berserk tightening in all her muscles, an unchecked urge to leap from this heat. She wanted to spit or pee or bleed on the flames. But the flames were minor. The tiny branches crackled brightly, then were gone, but the larger branches would not ignite. Agitated, the farmer tried again with his pocket torch, until his son finally explained.

"They're too green to burn, Dad."

The father reached out and hit him again, that smack against skin which now seemed insignificant, the boy with only a welt; but what is even a broken jaw compared to incineration?

Jid stood back, thought a moment, then looked over to his son as though struck with brilliance.

"We'll try some raw idea on it."

Rubbing the side of his face, the boy replied, "But won't that put it out or make it cold or something?"

Jid shrugged. "I don't know, but we're gonna try it."

"But how do we get it here?"

"Go ask your mom."

After the boy left, Jid searched through his pocket for scraps of paper which he proceeded to light fruitlessly. Finally Melody had to speak. She was still alive; things had slowed. Those tiny fires were driving her mad. She was still alive.

"Can't we talk about this?" she asked in no witch's tone.

"What?" Jid shot back. "So you can say talking to a witch puts a curse all over your azz?"

"No, no, I'm not a witch, really. I'm just lost and scared; and since you're trying to hurt me, I've been talking mean. I haven't been trying to hurt you, after all."

With a discomforting anger, Jid then snapped, "You've been cursing me and tormenting with your body all day."

"I can't curse you if I'm not a witch," Melody pleaded.

Then the farmer concluded decisively as he thrust a branch with smoking leaves toward her, his voice absolutely final, absolutely unkind.

"You're a fokking witch and I'm gonna burn you tid and bone!"

For a long moment, the cruelty of Jid's voice seemed worse than the damage he was attempting, as though Melody's hurt feelings could be worse than charred flesh. Then she literally had to think beyond painful impressions, for here came a man running from the woods, a man Melody knew. The other farmer, Bishup. He held a sort of rubber club at the ready as he moved without sound toward the burning post. Violence was with him like motion, but Melody knew to remain soundless because Jid's being clubbed would aid her. And so he was. Bishup ran to his previous friend and whacked him to the uppermost part of his skull with a blow so dull one might doubt its success, except that Jid dropped into a crooked heap, nose inches from his latest attempts at conflagration.

As Bishup stomped the meager fire out—nearly ripping Jid's ear loose in the process—he looked up to Melody, then ran around to work on her bonds. And when he spoke, he spoke with exasperation.

"You couldn't even get out of the house yourself?"

With no pause, Melody retorted, "The doors and windows were locked. How was I supposed to get out?" as though it had all been planned to her knowledge, as though this conversation were expected.

"Not in the cookroom one wasn't," Bishup grumbled.

"By the time I got there it was ablaze!" Melody sputtered. "I couldn't even *look* there."

"Be quiet!" he whispered fiercely, but had no further reply as the last rubber rope fell away. But Melody knew he was thinking, thinking something on the order of: Did it spread that quickly? Didn't I really leave her any time?

With a sure step, Melody leapt from the post and woodpile, certain to stay away from now-moaning Jid. And she was ready to jump and run farther, with certainty or with desperation, but she did not know where to run. Bishup told her.

"Go by the road edge in the woods. They'll be looking for you to hide in the hills; so head toward the city. Now run!"

But she couldn't. As though that initial leap had taken all her energy, Melody's continued movement was an unsteady slowness fit for childish fear, not a deathly predicament. Her legs would not function together, and her ankles seemed about to collapse. Still, she moved, in the direction Bishup had indicated. All the thoughts of nakedness and unnatural shock, of unjust hatred and fire attacked her again just as she was set free, and Melody was slow to recuperate. Too slow for Bishup, who after too many seconds of watching her plod away ran to Melody and grasped her by the waist, lifting the incompetent girl and carrying her like a sack to the edge of the cleared area about the house. There he dropped her—hard, on her feet—and ordered her unkindly again.

"Move, girl—or stay here and burn."

She moved. Better now, Melody with a look behind to her benefactor, finding enough energy to tell him, "Thank you," as she turned and finally ran.

Yards, yards, and Melody was moving as though normal, thinking clearly once more, thinking, "Girl, be frightened when you're home in bed again. In these woods, run like a bunnit rabbi or burn like a, a . . . witch."

A glance behind: Bishup out of sight, wobbly Jid now on his hands and knees. Melody then placed her concentration solely ahead, and soon gained a glimpse of the road. She heard no one coming behind, and tried to run quietly through the dry undergrowth; but then she was not running at all, for ahead on the roadside was a large commercial trok and men about it.

She tiptoed while slowing those final steps, looking around bushes and past trees toward the road. Adults there wearing hard caps. And the trok: the same color as the pipes, the same Iron Knot. But above it, another new world, another shock for Melody; for she was reading her name. The trok said MEL, no question, and Melody thought that somehow she was looking at herself, and froze. But then she looked closer, and read more than the big letters. She read the small ones, too: Marzian Energy Limited. Melody sighed wonderfully, for this was the greatest relief she had received on this world, this obnoxious universe.

A repair crew. They were working on the pipeline. To get past them, Melody would have to cross the road, since before her was a bold, bald hillock that would reveal her presence if she climbed it just as surely as though she stepped onto the open roadway.

No panic, think carefully, she told herself. As crazy as these people are, those workers will probably snatch me on sight. But there's no place to hide around here, and I believe Bishup when he said it's best to head down the road. So where do I go?

She decided to return. They expect me to run, she thought, so they won't be looking for me right in their backyard. There were some hollows by the bigger trees and some dense bushes—I'll hide there until nightfall, and *then* take the road.

Her plan seemed sensible, Melody intending to concentrate on her hiding, finding a fine, barely penetrable bush so near the farmstead it seemed like another shed. But once there, Melody had to concentrate on the scene beyond, had to see exactly who was tied to the post this time.

It was Bishup. He struggled with his rubber bonds to no avail as Jid bent to work on the fire. Melody could hear the latter's loud words as she watched.

"You can *kill* a man hitting him upside his head! At least I knocked you in the kidneys."

She had done it. Melody knew that if Bishup had not needed to help her run, he would never have been caught himself. The closest thing to a friend on this world, and she was burning him.

Jid worked on his tiny branches. Additional, futile seconds later, he stood, leaving his torch.

"Well, I'm wasting my fire here. What we're gonna do is throw some raw idea on it. That ought to work for a traitor, a man cursed by a witch so much he goes to clubbing his best friend and releasing her heinous evil on the world."

With the term "raw idea," Bishup began struggling further: a pause to hear Jid's speaking, then great, useless grimacing and pulling against his bonds. Standing back, Jid watched him a moment, then looked to his right; for there came his son carrying a common bucket covered with a strange fabric that seemed a bright, self-illuminating metal woven like cloth.

He carried the bucket as though its contents were

precious, the father calling out, "Careful, careful. Watch the insulator—it's slipping. Keep that shid in or it'll be all over us."

And through the crack where the fabric covered imperfectly, Melody could see the contents leaking, a light rolling out she had seen before, a non-gaseous refraction which seemed negative yellow.

Melody was glad she did not have to flee now, because this she wanted to see. Together yet apart, the three males functioned to make the scene she viewed, the son cautiously carrying, Bishup with a strenuous struggle, Jid forming another feeble fire. But his latest was aided by the bucket, Jid taking the container from his son to quickly pull the odd cover off and fling the raw idea onto the burning sticks from paces away. Melody still could not discern the contents' state, for her impressions were only negative: not a gas nor liquid nor projection. Its effects, however, were clear; for as the neg-yellow wafted through the air onto the woodpile, instantly the small fire erupted into a total, blinding inferno that roared to drown out the world, all reds and yellows and burning blue gases which filled everyone's senses so that nothing else was experienced but this ultimate bonfire—a fire gone as soon as it came. A false inferno come and gone as quick as an explosion. But regardless of its instantaneity and apparent scope, the only area affected was the burning pile, not the surrounding ground. Left behind was the silvery metal pole, as though untouched; and below, the finest, thinnest layer of black soot, no steam, no smoke. No farmer.

The three observers were taken by the experience, the event, Melody and the remaining males watching, all dumbfounded, for that following moment. And

Melody was horrified, for with all the threats and incompetent attempts on her life, finally here was death, human destruction come so quickly, so absolutely, that she was sickened.

Before Melody could think, before she could react further, Jid began hollering, Melody with the initial, partial impression that he was yelping joyfully at his success; for did this not fit his character? But, no, before Jid landed from his second yelling stomp, Melody saw another movement and understood, saw a man crawl out from beneath the house with difficulty, Bishup pulling himself onto the lawn yards from the fire, Bishup without a singe.

Melody was either overjoyed or amazed, and did not care which. She was about to cry in relief; but instead of fully emoting, Melody again had to fully observe; for the three people were forming another scene to view; but now only one was moving, and two were foolishly speaking.

"What happened, Dad? Why didn't it work?" the boy asked, looking anxiously between Bishup and Jid, the former nearing the latter with strong, angry strides.

"You never know what idea it's gonna work on," Jid tried to explain, looking at the completed fire, thinking so hard of this he could pay Bishup only zero heed.

"If you don't run the stuff through one of them scientist's adapters, you don't know what it'll do," Jid concluded.

Thoughtful Jid realized Bishup needed some attention just as the latter began clubbing him with both fists, powerful, certain blows against the side of Jid's face.

"You could kill a man hitting him there!" Jid gasped, inadequately covering his violated head with both folded arms until Bishup rendered him as quiet as himself, but much less conscious.

The son was not moving. Twitching a bit, the father reached for the blood on his face, but was unable to gain it. Erect and proud, Bishup walked away, toward home. Melody did not wonder about the fire there. Melody was getting the heill out.

Too many thumps for her, too many smacks of fist and club against human flesh for Melody to be comfortable, regardless of justified retribution or deserved salvation. She was thinking about neg-yellow on this Marz and hers, of Chas' and Nan's conversation, thinking of where anyone she knew could be. But Melody had some raw idea as to where she could be: she could be away from these horrid farmers. She could be down the road, and that's where she was heading.

This latest beating seemed a type of resolution, as though the initial portion of her bizarre journey were through, and Melody could continue. No, she did not know where she was or why, but at least she had a goal: to remove herself from an area whose raw ideas were concluded, whose bad concepts were complete.

Perhaps her ideas were too raw, for although this notion of leavance seemed reasonable, Melody was not manifesting her thoughts properly, because she was being followed. Before reaching that decisive site of bare hill and populated roadway, Melody heard a crashing in the undergrowth behind her. Still running, she glanced over her shoulder to see children: Bishup's three, and Jid's big one. The two larger, though youths, were adult-sized and dangerous. Melody began running totally, and there was no more looking back.

Upon reaching the hillock, she decided her course at once: there would be no hiding. Melody was going to attack the workers. Without pause, her long shirt flying, she ran directly to the trok body, past wondering men who stared at her but did not react with action, with violence. Pushing and pulling and twisting the handle until the door slid open, Melody jumped inside. Then the men reacted, the nearest worker dropping his blackprints to shout at the intruder and rush to the trok's door.

She had locked it. Before the man could reach her, Melody as well had slid and latched the driver's window. Quickly to the fore and aft windows, Melody seeing that the last side window was stationary. The man was pounding on the door now, yelling at her to get out. Being educated, he hollered more fluently than the farmers, but Melody's heart was beating just as ungrammatically as before.

Hearing him yell but studying the front panel: a guide bar for steering, but no key port. Instead, a multi-button lock, and Melody did not know the proper sequence. All these pieces were common, but never before had she seen the specific arrangement in a vehicle. Nevertheless, she knew enough to bend beneath the panel, looking for strip contacts. She found wires. Thinking of the types of motive power available for such troks—from steam to aqueous to no-cycle—Melody began pulling connectors away, checking their sources, then trying combinations. First she got sparks, which made her gasp, and then she got ignition.

After shoving the six proper wires together, Melody

returned to the seat, the steering bar. Looking to the floor—and hearing two men beat and yell now—she saw a foot throttle, but no trans selector. Off with what seemed a finger brake, and down with her foot. Unfortunately she pressed the wrong side, and the trok leapt backward, nearly running over a worker who looked exactly like old Randy. Melody ignored this impression, not because it was so preposterous, but due to a stronger sight which needed response; for she had backed directly against the pipe's loose joint which ruptured, a stream of neg-yellow slowly lolling out, covering the trok's lower rear as the nearby men jumped away, screaming now in a different manner. Ahead she saw a worker hurriedly begin wrenching a huge, linear valve. Looking through the go-back screen, Melody saw the blue flow cease. She also saw that all three rear wheels were now perfectly square.

Leaving these raw ideas was still her best plan. Pressing the go-board properly this time, Melody was pleased that the trok moved forward, but she was severely shaken by the rear tires' horrendous imbalance. And since these were the steering wheels, Melody proceeded down the road, then off, directly against the pipe again, another rupture, the neg-yellow rolling out around the trok's front as the same man ran down the line to the next juncture. Melody passed him before he reached the valve. She read his lips as he looked at her hair and shouted, "A bleeding witch!" But Melody could only think, I don't want to bleed . . .

The latest non-blue flow had taken effect on the trok, Melody finding her travel easier now, because the square rear wheels were no longer on the roadway —nor were the front. Melody was flying.

No vibration now, Melody laughing in exquisite relief as she steered the trok. The wheels seemed a foot or so above the dirt road, but truly Melody was moving through the air, an effortless traversal, nothing ahead but the scenery of her new planet, and behind, nothing she cared to recall.

# CHAPTER 7:
## _Hemorrhaging Brunch_

Before the crew was out of sight, their confiscated vehicle dropped to the road's surface again, Melody having to fight the bar to control a weaving that threatened to overturn the trok. After next gaining control of her thumping heart, she continued in a now-standard vehicle, guessing that the power of the negative yellow was temporary, perhaps dependent upon the exposure's duration.

She presumed communication. Nothing so archaic as stretched wires were seen, but certainly if the farmers wanted to tell their neighbors, some way was possible. Melody thus thought herself into depression, for of course someone must be waiting for her ahead. And the repair crew had not come from plastick sheds, but a more permanent society. Perhaps the city Bishup had mentioned as being her best goal, this idea still feasible to Melody as she traveled the narrow road up and down gentle hills, around sweeping curves, past dirt intersections, until the surface turned a deep, consistent brown with pink markings: pavement—civilization ahead!

Soon there was traffic: a disheveled auto, a three-wheeled cyke, more troks, more of everything. After blasthorn blares and swervings, Melody learned which side of the road was proper. She took gusto in handling the bulky trok well, leaning on the stiff steering bar, firmly applying the other controls, putting her weight behind it, which of course was a good ninety-eight pounds again.

Largely in command of her vehicular destiny, Melody became part of the traffic around her, passing scattered buildings, people standing about, walking, driving, Melody presuming the outskirts of a town, all the people and their products familiar in style. She passed a commonstore, and of course the signs were in Inglich. The people were dressed in clothes that were not unusual. The only consistent abnormality was the pale blue MEL line, fat pipes along each road, near every edifice, Melody assuming that smaller pipes led underground to the buildings. And she thought that if they didn't need repairs so often, even the fat pipes could have been buried, thus precluding trok thieves from damaging them further. But apart from the pipeline, Melody saw nothing that would not have fit a thousand similar Erth locales. But this was not Erth.

Before she could again become amazed at the confusing facts of her position—why? where? how? —Melody saw something different, something not of her Marz or her Erth. To her right, the east, the scenery of hills and woodland opened. Down a shallow valley was a grand establishment of some nature: buildings small and large, vehicles, machines, rows of unplaceable constructs, all within high fences, several acres. Nothing odd in this periphery, but the center of the compound was filled with a huge, conically roofed building of UR blue that seemed as cold as, as . . . raw idea, perhaps, an impression caused by the faintest neg-yellow tinge about the edifice which had nothing to do with the paint job, not a flow like the ruptured pipe, but an impression of this material, this force. And, of course, emanating from the building's lower levels was a layered web of pale lines which only in the distance were small, for when near they were not lines, but pipes, large pipes which paralleled each road.

Melody continued so long she was beginning to wonder where she was going, when her trok would run out of steam. Then, on a long straight, she saw her goal: buildings, many, tall—the skyline of a city. Traffic patterns were becoming more complex, Melody needing to pay close attention to avoid the minor wrecks available all around. But on a quiet straightaway she saw a group of people waving to her—*waiting* for her, so it seemed—four people looking in her direction, gesturing and smiling as soon as her trok neared. They wanted her to stop, and she thought of it, for these people seemed familiar. In a flash, she recalled the pipeline worker who resembled old Randy—identical, in fact—but these people were identical to no one she knew. To see them clearly, Melody slowed, denoting every face. Familiar, yes, but she did not recognize them: a thin blackman, a middle-aged woman; an older, quite pale, quite bearded man; and a strikingly beautiful young fem. Melody knew many Neegores, oldies, and beardoes, though few stunning folk of any gender. Something about these four, however, was special. Melody knew she was failing here, knew she should have recognized them. But she did not, and thought of trickery, that the farmers or Em Ee El workers had communicated ahead and a trap was set with semi-familiar individuals as bait. They appeared friendly, expectant, but their deciding trait was hair color: every one of them hair brown. No way was she stopping for a pack of witches. Melody drove by, looking to them but not staring, calling out, "No riders!" as she passed.

Kilos later, Melody found herself thinking again, for there were fewer potential accidents to avoid. Although proceeding well in general, there was no action to keep her mind sharp; so Melody was stuck with feeling, literally feeling now; for she did not know where to go, what to do, or why she had to rethink an entire planet. And she thought that, yes, she should have stopped for those people, should have taken the chance; for now she had a knot in her belly so painful she had to hold her side; for above all else in the world—any world—Melody did not want to be alone. A mile later she was not, for there was another pack to stop her, but these people were not asking, but forcing.

The same group was ahead of her again, standing on the edgewalk exactly as before. They looked toward Melody's trok in the same manner, waved and smiled identically. Their actions and relative positions were so similar that the scene seemed a refilming of the previous, true event. This was so weird an occurrence that Melody considered it proper for this new, bizarre Marz. Besides, these were the only people she had seen on the planet who were friendly, not flame-boyant. This time, Melody was stopping.

Firmly she thumbed the brake button, all the while looking toward the group on the roadside. Just before coming to a stop, however, she discerned a further oddity about these people; for around them—at their edges—was a hint of blueness which Melody had seen before.

She kicked the go-board, but too late, the trok too slow to escape these people who changed instantly into tall men with firm expressions and colorful uniforms, UR blue. Men who moved as quickly as they had changed, one throwing a metal blanket over the hood—just like the flexible lid on Jid's bucket —and the motorvator stopped dead. The other three approached the trok's doors with small items in their hands; and regardless of interior latches, they opened. An unfamiliar young adult—a little too pale, a little too friendly—looked up to Melody and spoke.

"Hello, would you please come with us?"

"No, I won't," she replied coolly. "Who are you?"

"We're the local constables of Marzian Energy. As you might not know—being a stranger—all this city and the outer farms are owned by the company; so you're on private lands. Name, please," he requested.

"Melody Preece. What am I, trespassing?" she tried.

"Well, you know you're lost, don't you?" he added like a helpful uncle. "I know you don't have any place better to go than with us. If you do, I promise to get you some clothing," he said with no lecherous tone, though he nodded toward all that exposed leg.

"Do I have a choice?" Melody asked. "You going to force me?"

"No, you don't have a choice," the constable stated with no rancor, "and of course we can take you with no force at all, no discomfort. And it doesn't matter if you cooperate; because, you see, I've used my allotment of words for this case."

Melody was going to say something else, but as soon as her mouth opened, the man reached out with the swiftest of fluid moves, touching her with something she barely saw and did not feel, for Melody went blank, completely, as though dead.

She awoke in a comfortable chair centered in a room so vast it seemed boundless. Melody had clear recollection of being taken, of losing consciousness utterly, immediately. And now she awoke as cleanly, with no grogginess, Melody not needing to blink or shake her head, normal breathing, just come to in this wonderful brocade chair from an antique culture and era she was unfamiliar with. Cleanly awake in a dimly lit room whose ceiling was so high she could not discern its texture, walls so distant the floor faded into darkness before they were seen. But the temperature was pleasant, and weren't the faintest strains of fine music to be heard? Beneath her feet, the carpet was so thick her shoes sank past the surface.

Shoes?

Yes, fabric shoes that fit so well they were almost unnoticed. The dress was also her size, a deep green gown of a clinging fabric cut modestly, long sleeves, classically semi-formal. Reaching a hand within the apparel, between her legs, Melody felt a sort of undergarment, one piece from crotch to bosom. Comfy. And she was clean, hair soft, no dirt beneath her nails, no sand between her toes. Melody then had the ridiculous thought that if someone(s) had been this close to her, had they also been intimate? She wondered whether she had been sexually violated, but how do you tell? After being half eaten by the thresher and partially burned twice, she was sore all over, regardless of unconscious mistreatment.

Then the room became brighter, but only in two areas: about Melody's chair, and about his—the man facing her from so far away she could not distinguish his face. Average-aged and overdressed, he sat in a high-back chair like Melody's, a small table to one side. Oh, yes, there was also a table at Melody's elbow, she noticed. And when the man became visible, he spoke, Melody screwing up her eyes in confusion; for his voice sounded like a whisper two feet away, not a hundred. She saw no sound source in mid-air before her, only a man so far away she could scarcely see his mouth move.

"Would you care for something to drink?" he offered pleasantly with a formal tone. "Perhaps something casual to eat. Or a meal not so casual, what with the difficulties our more unfriendly folk have caused you."

With the man's first words, Melody found another disparity, a problem with identity that was by now typical on this Marz. That voice: she knew it, but could not place a name or face with the sound, perhaps due to the precise, overeducated enunciation. And since she could not solve the voice's source, she dealt with its content.

"Yes, a bit of a snack would be welcome," Melody answered politely. "I haven't eaten since, oh, the last few times I was burned."

With a convincingly sincere tone, the man replied, "I can hardly convey the sorrow and anger I felt at my own sharecroppers for their foolish attempts to harm you. Truly these people are being spoken with so that we might educate them as to the immorality of their groundless fears. Had we found you earlier, you would have been treated as you deserve."

"And how is that?" Melody returned. "What sort of treatment do I deserve?"

"You deserve the treatment of a special and unique person," he answered pridefully.

"You mean witches aren't always burned?"

Seriously the man then maintained, "To the best of our rather thorough knowledge, no appearee has ever been harmed by the local farmers. Lately, however, fears have been breeding for no good cause, their results a terrible rumor that proper response for appearees is burning. Such ritual executions are supposed to solve the problem of, er, ghosts."

"But what *is* the problem? What did I do by just appearing? And there were others? How many? Where'd they come from? Where are they now?"

The man remained so calm that he did not have to request that Melody ask fewer questions more slowly with less gasping—for she *was* excited—calming her with his own unagitated answering.

"Over a two-year period there have been four appearances, plus yourself, each person having come from a different Marz. We spoke with all of these people who are now free. As for the problem, the appearances have caused none for the farmers, except fear, and that is a very real concern. Certainly the greatest difficulty is for you and your kind. You have lost your true worlds, and we would like to return you. Also, something, somewhere, is very wrong to have engendered these appearances, a problem we must resolve; because—frankly—certain of the more sophisticated city folk are becoming concerned as to their own physical positions being in jeopardy. But unlike the common farmers, our urban citizens understand the cause to be technological, not magical."

Before Melody could reply, a voice called out from the darkness behind her host, this sound tonally honest in that it seemed a hundred feet away in a reverberant room.

"So do we!" the voice shouted. "We believe in technology, not magic—we've had enough of your magic, Chairhume. And as for jeopardy—"

The man interrupted, throwing himself around to snap, "You will wait for this interview!" Remarkably enough, *his* voice was now yards and yards removed.

"You interrupted the meeting because of her," the second voice barked, agitated now.

"She is more important than your treachery—now you will wait! I am still the Prime Chair."

No more voice from behind, the man turning to Melody again, his speech no longer loud, no longer a hundred feet away—only two.

"You would forgive the Board's overexuberance," he intoned sweetly, Melody becoming aurally dizzy from the change of speaking distances. "These are more people whose positions are in jeopardy."

"Oh," Melody responded, "are they going to vanish as I did?"

"No, no, Mizz Preece," the Prime Chair explained. "I was referring to another type of transferal. None of our people has left Marz in this manner; your type only appear here."

"What is my type?" Melody asked the faraway man with the usually nearby voice. "What does my hair color have to do with the appearings?"

"The characteristic is not mere coincidence, because all appearees have your hair color, but certainly the trait is not causal in itself. We can only partially explain the reason for your having appeared. Suffice to say that the cause is your sensitivity, as though with music or art, a sensitivity you people have to the conceptual matrix that is the ether which has led you to what is a tremendous source of pure idea: our Marz, our controlled conceptual power."

And the Board shouted out from the distance, "Partially controlled, else her type would not still be coming!"

This time the Chairhume ignored the voice, but Melody was listening. She wanted to know more about her type, their current status, for example, Melody recalling how she had been tricked into stopping her trok: those people, all those hair-brown people.

"What about the other appearees, Mr. Chairhuman?" Melody asked. "Do they bunch together in public?"

"And how intelligent you are to have deduced that the vision we, er, 'lured' you with was that of the other appearees. We thought you might recognize them by their hair brownity."

Something was wrong here, at least incomplete. Melody had seen the group first, and then the imitation. But was the first sighting unreal as well? And if not, where could she find these semi-familiar folk? But before Melody could delve further into these ideas, another man entered the room, entered the speaker's light sphere: an older man in deep green and white—servant's attire of the ancient Third Reik. Certainly this was not the Board, because the Chairhume spoke without anger toward him.

"Master Jipson," he began, his tone more formal than even the proper voice used with Melody, "you will be so gracious as to have your food preparers concoct a repast suitable for our guest, in accord with her condition and desires as you may now ascertain."

Jipson then turned to Melody; and as though on a conveyor belt, was whisked to her in seconds with no effort displayed, no movement of his legs. And then he was by her side. Looking carefully, Melody recognized nothing about him.

"What do you want?" he asked curtly.

Melody was proud because this drastic contrast in speaking was unsurprising to her. With no bashfulness she told him, "A little white whine on the racks, some organic fruit with carbos for ergs. Tiny fat, medium protein, about ten, eleven ounce total plus half again in liquids."

"Bier and salad," Jipson determined.

Then the other orders came, a rush of voices emanating from behind the Prime Chair.

"Large piece-of."

"Berger, no holding."

"Double hand samwitch."

The Chairhume then whirled around and shouted in his distant voice, "Eat idea!" and the Board went quiet. Their orders were not taken, Jipson already conveyed out of sight.

"We might next introduce ourselves," the Chairhuman continued calmly, the change to a too-near voice still disorienting. "I am the Prime Chair and Excessive President of Operations of Marzian Energy Limited, an organization whose acroname I am sure you find amusing."

"Yeah, bleeding hilarious," Melody mumbled.

"We are a subsidiary of Krautzi Inkorporated," the Chairhume added, "and on this planet, the only employer. We have no public government here, only the korporate. And who might you be?"

"I'm not sure who I might be," Melody returned. "I used to be a stu'ent working with the miners of Marz on the middling force ore crop, but now I guess I'm some kind of witch."

"No, of course not at all," the Chair laughingly replied. "Regardless of how affecting the opinions of the worst people of a state may be, the worst is seldom the generality, the majority. The official position toward you is that you are worthy of our time, our concern."

"Am I under arrest or something?" Melody next asked. "Is this detention official?"

"This is brunch, not detention," the Prime Hume told her, "and yes it is official, since I am the representative of this planet's controlling concern. But if you will be so good as to speak freely with me awhile, I assure you that as soon as is reasonable you will be released. I also assure you that alone, you will never see your home again."

This was suitably impressive to Melody, who was again struck with a pang of loneliness. Of course she wanted nothing more than to return home, regardless of how fascinating this Marz might be. And though she did not trust the Chairhume, what choice did she have but to cooperate? But more important, she had to learn of her position: a little knowledge is never enough for the mentally greedy.

"Mr. Chairhume, where am I?" she asked blithely.

"Why, you are on Marz, Mizz Preece."

"But it's not the Marz I left."

"One of the main goals in bringing you here is to ascertain exactly where you came from and how.

Suffice to say, in preliminary explanation, that to the best of our initial studies' revelations, you and the other appearees are from separate Marzes existing simultaneously and in parallel with this one. Theory describes these planets as having been manifested on different layers, shells, or frequencies of the ether, the matrix from which all ideas naturally turn real. Thus, although the basic natures of the various Marzes are equal, important ideas of and on each planet have been actualized diversely."

"But why am I on the wrong Marz?" Melody demanded, a concrete girl dissatisfied with theory.

"Unfortunately it seems to be our fault. Evidently our usage and dependence upon processed conceptual power is adversely influencing certain exceptional people: you and the other appearees. It seems that the area in which you appeared is the one geographic form all the affected Marzes share; yet only on our Marz is there a significant growth of the ore crop. On all other Marzes, this area is barren. Discussions with previous appearees have shown us that when a sensitive person is exposed to Skopein Plain for a sufficient duration, he 'bleeds through' at this shared point of Manifestic similarity to the Marz which draws him conceptually. The great ideational force on our Marz draws you people here as though you belonged."

"I don't belong," Melody asserted. "I want out."

"Of course you should be home, but we cannot return you until we learn more of the general causes for appearees and your specific case."

"What about prevention?" Melody asked, still seeking knowledge to help her, not depress her. "What are you doing to prevent further appearances or hemorrhaging or whatever?"

With this, the Board behind its Chairhuman turned especially lively.

"Yes! What is being done to prevent the bleeders, and what is being done to prevent more occurrences such as Ideatown?"

This commentary was from the Board's first voice, but others followed again. No brunch orders this time.

"The Primary Chair is conducting an interview, Mister Second Gleeson. No time now for your perhaps fine ideas on AM influence."

Glieson?

"Influence!" that first voice returned, a voice which now seemed familiar to Melody. "Influence is when you say, 'pretty please.' Manifestic energy seeping through the generators' walls and causing bleeders to appear is not 'influence.' Unchecked conceptual power driving people pschyotic is not 'influence'—it is damaging and dangerous."

More oddness here, Melody noting that as the Board leapt into this discussion the darkness about them began receding. Seated people in dim light getting brighter as voices rose. Soon they would be fully visible.

The Primary Chair wanted to join or end the conversation behind him, but could not get a word in folded flat.

"Pschyotic is too strong a term, Mister Second."

"No it ain't," the piece-of desirer inserted.

"Yeah it is," said the samwitch, "but crazy-azz-bonkers is better."

"Bleeding mind blown," the berger noted, the light around the Board pulsing now.

"Plain insane," said someone.

"You're all an azzole," another seethed.

With the following, most extravagant addition, the Board appeared in bright light a few paces behind its Prime Chair and to one side. Only one person, one name she knew, Melody seeing a dozen men in pastel oversuits crammed around a tiny table, their knees certainly touching below. And above, lots of gestures and twitching, even from those not speaking. "Speaking," however, was not the proper term for the next sound from a Board member. Crazy-azz-bonkers was better.

"Pschyo! pschyo! pschyo is the notion, the realized notion, for people gone rear end over head bone!"

All this from a frothing elder whose comments turned to blather as Jipson reappeared to take Frother's seat and convey it away with one finger. As soon as these two reached darkness, Blather's voice was no longer heard, as though abruptly cut by the light's end.

Of course Mr. Prime was responsible, Melody noting that he was seated quietly, though the Board's noise grew, the Chairhume facing Melody and gesticulating, pointing for that man to be taken away. But the Prime continued pointing even after Frother was gone. Oh, yes: again came Jipson, now lightly pushing the table and all its members into the darkness, the sound of their heated speaking ceasing with their disappearance. The light behind the Chairhume then ended, and he lowered his hand to his lap. Satisfied was his face. Crazed Board Runs Mad Marz, was Melody's headline. Apart from this phrase, she was unable to form a clear response: fear, humor, perhaps plain insane. Sick of seeing the Chairhume's pleasure in his own power, Melody decided to end it.

"Trouble with energy, eh, Chair?"

"Nothing uncommon, Mizz Preece. As a person of your obvious education well knows, the various powerful sources of energy available to run a planet are not without their dangers."

"What about salar?" Melody offered.

"Oh, Melody, you must be bright enough to know the sun is not bright enough on Marz to allow solar energy to be viable."

"What about something clean like, er, fusion?"

"There is too great a danger that someone will be tempted to make weaponry. Unions, perhaps."

"Well," Melody tried, "I've heard you can make conceptual weapons."

"Yes, Melody, but as you might guess, we would not likely have many concept bombs on Marz. What would we use them against, witches?"

The Chair laughed foppishly after his minor humor, Melody returning a smile that resembled a sneer.

"Besides," he contended, "no other source of power would allow us to grow the ore plants at will."

"And what do you do with the ore crop?" Melody asked, aware in her sly perception of the forthcoming reply.

"Why, it is the raw material allowing us to produce AM power on our great planet."

Melody nearly swooned, rolling her eyes and moaning. This was her characteristic response to questionable positions. After the Chairhuman's explanation, Melody slid her eyes left and right, the corners of her mouth tightening as her throat groaned. Normally she might attempt to subdue this sort of reaction, but at a hundred paces, Melody felt she didn't have to. Besides, the physical action was so tangible a response that it consistently helped her make a verbal—an intellectual—reply. Most important, being abnormal was normal for this Marz. On her planet—her Erth —many people found the self-justifying aspects of harvesting the ore crop unsatisfactory—what did this populace think? But Melody wasn't asking. She was too busy salivating, for Jipson had returned with eats.

He slid next to the Chairhume with a floating kart, and Melody could see steam, the vapors of warm victuals. And as though only a yard away, she could smell, smell preparations, not merely food: dishes, a meal, cuisine: quality foodstuffs prepared with the experienced care of a fine shef. Hungry Melody was made anxious, however, by the routine the Prime Chair had to undertake just to gain a glass of whine. With his hand held out, Mr. Prime pronounced:

"And now to take this liquid as brought from our fine eatmakers by this finer delivery elder, received with gratitude and appetite, I am to thank you each one for the good work and hereby swear to enjoy as well as consume."

The Chairhume had been fluent in his speaking before, but this speech seemed rote, a form discourse wherein he simply filled in blanks. Jipson then glided rapidly to Melody with his kart. As before, the journey was too brief for the distance covered. Although uncertain of the protocol she was to follow, Melody was thinking of simply grabbing a handful of food and stuffing it in, claiming to be a witch and thus with excusable manners. But Jipson spoke first, and Melody did not have to be polite or witchy.

Perfectly erect Jipson looked over Melody's head as he pronounced, "Enjoy your grub."

"Thanks mucha," she said.

Melody dug in. Mushrooms with wide sauce and some kind of pale animal flesh she did not resist. A species of asparagrass, oh so tender. Smooth whine that went down like spit. Melody hoped she wasn't secretly being drugged by this Marz' lying government, but mainly she didn't care. Starvation, et cetera.

She tried not to be the wild animal, using the wooden mouthsticks provided instead of fingers. During their repast, she and the Chairhume chatted lightly, briefly, about vantage years for Marzian berries, saturation-heat ovens, processed ideas as fertilizer, and so on. Although aware the solid metal kart which held her meal seemed supported only by air, Melody was not prepared to examine this aspect of Marzian technology. Perhaps later, after dessert.

There was no dessert. The Chair made no offer, but Melody was belly-bloated regardless. She was not feeling contented, however, but fat and mean. With all that food, she was likely over a hundred pounds, and that made her special. Looking across to the Prime Chair, she saw him dabbing his mouth with a corner of his outfit. Same MEL blue as the uniforms of the constables who took her, but too blousy, too loose a cut. It looked more proper for her than any man. Melody did not mention this, instead turning her bad instincts into businesslike procedure.

"Well, Mr. Chair, real good eats—and thanks. Now what? Let's get me home, please."

"Mizz Preece," he intoned slowly, lowering his glass, "to learn how to return you to your proper place, we must first learn more about you."

"What can I tell you?" Melody replied.

"Your speech and self-knowledge are unacceptably limited within the realms of data we seek. For you to 'tell' us, we would like to begin by your submitting to a complete and complex physical examination."

"You're not going to burn me, are you?" Melody wondered.

"Of course not, Melody. You won't feel a thing."

That sounded bad. Complete removal from life's sensations is not exactly life, is it?

"Can I pee first?"

"Of course, dear."

That sounded bad. Not even the young and innocent, if thoughtful, appreciate patronizing. Melody may have been young, but was innocent mainly by circumstance.

"Shall we?" the Chairhume proposed, and stood.

Melody was becoming perturbed. All this food within her was turning to energy, the concept of power turned real by eating. She was dissatisfied, however, because it seemed she was being herded again. Like the farmers, but not with forks—with words, ideas. Considering her own experiences with AM—from the experimental station on her Marz to the leak-modified trok—the Chair's claims about concept power were believable. Intellectually Melody had few doubts but that she actually was sensitive to the force of ideas which had attracted her to this Marz. But emotionally, it all seemed nonsense: simultaneous worlds, naked people bleeding from planet to planet because they're sensitive, like psikik healers. Melody was perturbed because she knew too little about this new science to formulate a plan to help herself get home. And she was upset because in this fascinating, unquestionably real universe in which she found herself, Melody was a witch. She did not like being a witch. Melody was angry.

Cooperation with Marzian Energy and its Prime Chair was the only sensible idea to her. In order to gain a superior position—one nearer home—she would not only cooperate with the First Chairhume, but reasonably seek his aid. Melody, however, had begun to twitch in her seat even before the Prime's last phrase. Herein she was not adverse to cooperation, but examination. Dr. Searle had been bad enough—what could the Board's mediks be like? Where would cooperation lead her? But, too late, it seemed, for the Chairhume was conveying himself toward her—directly toward her—as though gliding. And when he neared, Melody knew exactly where she was being led. Her course was disaster.

It was not his clothing which upset her, Melody discerning the fabric as chiffon, unpleasant on this man, an adult she had seen before. It was not his face that chilled Melody literally stiff; not his face, but his other identity, his true identity in Melody's universe, on her Erth. For that's the world where last she saw him, and a poorer world it was because of Josef Hagen.

# CHAPTER 8:
## Pus Yellow Surgery

She was mellow now; but is that the term for energy gone quick as blood from a body slit? The man was before her now, his expression pleasant, but this meant nothing to Melody. Although she knew that on this Marz, Hagen did not know her, and that even on her Erth he was not evil; nevertheless, no one she had ever known so affected her toward fear as did Josef Hagen, his memory, a million miles away, but now right next to her. And Melody was stiff in her mind but limp in the body, feeling not terrified, but terrible.

She showed scant reaction: no smile, but no horrified eyes, Melody appearing calm, but feeling an illness that negated life as certainly as burning. After Hagen requested kindly for her to follow, she rose with no shown emotion, though she was sick; Melody moving firmly, though she was decrepit, emotionally deceased. Melody followed, but she was going to run. Her striking impression was that she no longer was on another Marz, but an afterworld, an afterlife where she was the same, but Hagen had been reincarnated whereby he could finally gain vengeance on her, a world where with impunity he could break her back.

This Hagen was different. Melody could see the experience of a world leader in his eyes, see the intensity of responsibility and conflict. With single syllables she responded, saying, "Fine" and "Yes" to the Chairhume's descriptions of superior doktors and concept scientists to ascertain her condition, to help her, return her as soon as possible. But Melody was thinking of more than Hagen now, she was thinking of those other appearees, those four people waiting for her, four people alone, without aid or interference or association with the Chair and his company, Hagen in charge of another concern wherein Melody was disruptive. Those four people on the street, not the false image used by Hagen's constables, now seemed the proper representatives of this Marz for Melody. And she believed in them, believed that first sight to be as real as the second was false. She could have asked Hagen, "Where are my people? I want to see them first, before any 'examination,'" but she was saying nothing. I should be with witches, she thought, not bureaucrats wanting to knock me out. She recalled that the four people had seemed familiar; but were they partially known because she barely knew them in her other life, or because Melody was "sensitive" to them as she was to AM? Or had Hagen examined them so thoroughly they were no longer the same? After all, they had yet to be returned—how soon would as soon as possible be?

"Fine" and "Yes" as they moved, not walking, feet stationary on the smoothest moving floor a girl of Erth could know, moving in a huge room —unchanged, but now cold and uncomfortable —toward a dim wall, and there a door which opened without order to a conventionally bright hallway of average dimensions where they stopped and began walking. No other people, only handsome, slick slabs of minerals on the walls, woven coverings on the floor, potentially warm, but not inviting.

She was going to knock him out. Over the years, working Melody had learned enough to physically disable a non-physical person; but she had never hurt anyone with this training, and she could not presume Hagen's reactions to be as insubstantial as his chiffon. Despite the softness of his attire, Hagen gave no impression of weakness. Perhaps Melody could have stuffed him back into the huge room, perhaps not. At least he didn't have an ore fork, didn't have his kin about . . .

She was not looking to him now, and they were not talking. Suddenly, Melody knew. She stopped abruptly, turning to Hagen, looking to his nose, not his eyes, not looking into Hagen's eyes. Melody turned to him and cheerfully announced:

"I'm anxious to get on with it. Let's run, okay? That will be fun," and she was off with no pause or lack of energy.

"Wait, Melody, don't run!" Hagen called out loudly, not running himself, no anger in his voice, perhaps disappointment. Perhaps not.

Melody knew how to run on any Marz, a .6 g field requiring a special, low-moving technique to keep one's feet on the ground: bounding was slower than running. Melody was concentrating on her form, shortened strides and a low knee action providing her with a speed no athlete on Erth could match. But Melody was also looking ahead and to both sides for people to come out from the several doors she passed, people to trip or grab her, perhaps those thugs with their devices which could anesthetize a motorvehicle or a person. And soon she did see people ahead: a woman coming toward her, two men moving away, Melody noting surprise in them, but they made no move against her.

Hagen was no presence behind, Melody continuing alone, not looking back, not yet. Coming to an angled juncture in the hallway, she proceeded down the broader corridor. Melody was looking for a way out, but far ahead no exit could be seen. More people she passed, their attitude one of work before the runner startled them. And Melody felt herself dreamlike, moving amongst people yet apart because of her running, running forever while they stood still, Melody untouchable because of perversion, not superiority, the perversion of being alone.

A glance behind revealed no one following, and Melody slowed, began walking. Around her the people seemed unconcerned with a fugitive, Melody seeming to fit once achieving their pace. The style of her apparel—formal business—prevailed, no one with any special markings, nothing that looked like a constable. Having attained their rate, Melody next sought their attitude, trying to look as though she had somewhere to go. "Nice shoes," a woman smiled to her, Melody with a grin as she continued.

She began looking past doors. Opening the first, she heard much agitated speaking which ended as soon as she glanced inside. A half dozen heads turned to her and stared, six people becoming silent and displeased. "Oops, wrong planet," she muttered, and moved away.

Yards farther, Melody looked back to see a man from that room look into the hall and stare firmly at the intruder. Melody continued, the man finally slamming the door behind. By then she was in a less exotic area of the building, floor and wall coverings no longer special, the doors average sliders instead of the semi-magic, self-opener of Hagen's huge chamber.

No longer did Melody see the point in opening blank doors. None were marked, but she knew only trouble was to be found by so proceeding. What she sought was a hole marked "Exit." She wanted a level map or listing to guide her. What Melody found was a window, one which nearly filled a short wall around a curving corner. She stopped, looking outside from a height stories above ground level. Far in the distance were the mountains of this Marz—any Marz —Unverit's handsome peak. Nearer, the greenery of forests and fields of ore plants. Nearer still, roads, buildings below her, vehicles, people moving. And to one side an incredible flowering of tiny, pale pipes which led to a huge, cone-topped edifice which seemed only yards away, but the vehicles below described the distance to be a kilo. Melody looked out to see the road on which before she had traveled, at that time looking from her trok to view this very compound. Apart from relative position, another discrepancy was time: Melody viewed a mid-morning scene; yet she had traveled the road an hour or so later. Hagen had thus kept her overnight—where had she slept?

Regardless of potential abuse, Melody now had her bearings. Got to go down, she thought, then head for the road, and somehow find those people—my people. Melody had just begun looking for doors on the window side of the corridor when she heard a whisper from around the next bend. The voice was not the first heard in the hallway, but only these words caught Melody's attention—because they were about her.

"—girl wandering about supposed to be detained . . ." Then, excited buzzing, another voice continuing, ". . . to get her in . . . all of us!"

Abruptly Melody turned to the nearest door and entered. Dim inside with many people, but no one looked to her. In their rows of seats on a sloping floor, they were looking away, looking through a huge window to a brightly lit chamber below where people with covered hands and faces stood, people with pale yellow uniforms moving about a covered table wide enough for only one body.

An operating theater. On this world, the color for medicine was pale yellow—pus yellow. With no pause, Melody walked deeper into the room, turning left to an empty seat, the only attention paid her an "Excuse me" and "Oh, I am sorry" when she brushed a knee and nudged a foot. No one followed from the hall, Melody settling in a position where she did not stand out from the crowd; yet a clear view of the hall door was available. One of the physicians was speaking, pointing to an impressive, translucent machine situated next to the operating table, his voice heard as though he spoke from the audience's center. Melody listened.

"—today is a procedure commonly used for exploratory surgery in these and other cases. Only precise control of conceptual power allows the patient to survive, considering the pervasive rearrangement of internals and the accompanying shock. The idea which is enhanced by the aura of idea force is that all these pieces, once rejoined to each other, should form a living whole. Since the surgery is so rapid with the ideational mechanics of the concept surgeon, we will demonstrate beforehand with the exact process on a corpse."

Not a machine or an idea, but a person's hand next rolled up the fabric cover. Only then did Melody realize that a body was below the cover which was not form fitting, but flat like a box lid, not touching flesh. Melody did not want to see this, for autopsies made her sick; perhaps because she was first made to view surgery at the age of eleven, too young to accept people being cut, intentionally or not. The corpse's being a thin, young woman made the scene no better or worse. As the physicians moved and adjusted the machine—this "concept surgeon"—accompanied by technical explanations she only partially understood, Melody tried to avert her gaze, to keep watch on that door, the other two doors in the theater. But then a non-blue glow caught her eye, and Melody had to look.

A negative-yellow emanation covered the corpse as the physicians stood back, their hands on the large machine supplying the color. Gracefully flexible extensions like arms reached down to the body. Melody could not tell they ended in cutting devices until the several arms touched the thorax and skull and abdomen at once, moving with such speed she could barely follow their paths. But she could see the lines of blood all over the skin. She could see skin and flesh pulled back, ribs plucked out, then organs, each organ in that body exposed, touched by the machine entirely over every wet surface. She could see the skull split in half precisely, right between the eyes, left and right halves flattened to the table as the brain was entered by smaller extensions, as though fingers, cortex and cerebellum and all the wonderful parts pulled precisely asunder by this wonderful machine.

All this in seconds, a kinetic display around and within the body too rapid for Melody to follow. Over in seconds, and then reversed: all the organs again tucked inside, the skull pressed back together, the ribs situated normally and re-covered with skin, all the blood replaced, none on the surface, only the faintest scars left, innumerable scars like the pipes outside: fine, pale lines visible now that the blue non-light returned to the machine as though an organ itself, an effervescent tongue sucked back into the animal after lapping the victim first dead, then alive.

The speaking medik stepped forward again, but Melody found difficulty in listening. She heard his last words, though, for these were pertinent, Melody no longer looking toward the door for vigilantes, stunned Melody without concentration.

"—to now be performed on the patient herself . . ."

She no longer looked at the door. She was looking at the physician. She was looking at him because through his transparent mask she could see him looking at her. As were all the other mediks, looking up into the audience. Directly at Melody. And this was no illusion: there was no mistaking the individual whom they viewed; for around her, every person in the audience turned, staring at Melody, only at Melody, as the physician concluded.

". . . just as soon as we bring the young lady down."

# CHAPTER 9:
## *Squandered Statues*

She was flying, suspended a thousand feet in the air above a city's buildings. A bland view to her, though floating facedown a kilo up should have been exciting. But Melody was not enthralled, looking down at the view only because she was facing this way. But then she slowly blinked and focused to see that she was not floating over a huge structure: Melody was flat on her back beneath a machine she had seen before, in some terrible dream. And then, with the first movement of a person to her side, Melody understood. She was on the operating table beneath the concept surgeon. She was nude and numb, unable to move her limbs, her body. She could move her head somewhat, but nothing below the neck. Even looking was lethargic for her, but she could think, she could feel.

A man in a pus-colored surgeon's gown bent over her, but this was no doktor: it was Hagen. He looked down with a convincing smile, a concerned expression Melody could not bring herself to believe. His words, not his face, told her everything, Hagen not speaking to the audience, but to Melody alone.

"I especially dislike the way you seemed so sweet

before you ran. That was cruel of you to falsify your friendship just to catch me off guard, then take advantage of my warmth. I will always remember that sweet smile of yours just before you hurt me. But nothing has changed. I did not lie before, and will not now, for I never lie. You will soon undergo the examination I described, the procedure you just witnessed. We will learn much by this, and if possible, we will help you."

Subtly his expression changed as he spoke. With his final words, Hagen's smile would have convinced no one of the bearer's claim, his kindness.

"I will not harm you, as promised, even though I ought to *break your back*."

He stood away as busy physicians reached to the machine, pressing its parts, making adjustments just for Melody. With a greater effort she could have seen more of their movements, but the sight of the machine above her was so pervasive she could not look away, though she did not want to see this thing, not ever again in her life, especially now that it was about to work on her. About to cut her. About to pick her to pieces. Of course, it would only last seconds, Melody thinking that if she could just fill her mind with *anything*, it would all be over.

Of course she could concentrate on nothing but the activity around her. So silent, all these surgeons —human and machine—making no sound as they prepared. But what was all the gasping, then? Why did Melody hear shuffling feet as the human physicians began scurrying around the room? And there were other sounds, strange hissings, vibrations which shook the table, though the machine above seemed unaffected. And then came shouts, unclear words from upset mediks who were surprised and frightened, the entire room confused.

With difficulty, Melody strained to look toward the wall behind the concept surgeon. There she saw people entering the room, but through no door. The thick, grainy substance of the wall turned to powder as people moved through forcefully, people she had seen before: the group, the four appearees on the street, none hair brown now, but black and blonde and auburn. And a strange combination they were, working in unison. The pale man's eyes were glazed as he stood near the oldish woman who was all alertness. This man whispered in her ear, looking nowhere as though blind, his mouth loose as though he were in a trance. The alert woman, however, looked everywhere as she called out loudly and gestured.

"Him! That entrance! The wall's end—aim the refractor!"

Straining to look where this woman pointed, Melody saw that her words were instructions, instructions followed by the remaining two people: the thin blackman, the voluptuous fem. The former carried on his person—somehow strapped to his shoulders and back, around his hips—complicated devices or a single, segmented device Melody could not distinguish, but it was the same material as the machine above her; it was the same nature. The woman held an object that seemed a profound baking dish: strapped to her forearms, its interior was mirrored with no glass, no substance known to Melody. These two impressive instruments were connected via a thin pipe just like those on every roadside, a thin pipe that looked rigid but flexed as the younger woman turned, aiming the refractor.

Unless the larger device were made of a unique new matter, the carrier's burden was great; but he showed no strain as he turned with the younger woman who pointed the refractor high and low in accord with the shouted instructions from behind. Then came a buzz Melody felt through the floor, through the table, and everything in the room shook, Melody thinking that the machine above her would topple, so stiff, but now it shimmied as though hot rubber. And from the refractor, a neg-yellow flow coming quick as fine ideas to wash first Hagen, then the talking physician, a closed door, a wall with equipment.

"Cut it!"

The non-blue wash ended after the woman's order, and everyone in the room went still. All the un-touched physicians were standing away, fearful of this power. They did not want to move, but the directly affected men could not move. Rigid as the unchanged walls, the medik and Hagen seemed welded solid, lips twitching, eyes blinking, but now more statues than men.

"Save it," the speaking woman called loudly to her companions, then removed the pale man's hands from her shoulders, and touched his neck with a small tube, Melody recognizing a quick-fill chemamp. A moment after the ampule dropped to the floor, the man blinked, shook his head, then turned largely normal, looking about until he spotted Melody. He walked rapidly to her table, bending to do something which Melody could not see, only feeling thereafter a shaking. After glancing at this activity, the older woman walked swiftly to Hagen, looking up to him from inches away.

"She won't be the last one we save, Mister Chair,"

the woman announced with an energetic tone, her voice all success. "We're saving the entire planet. And now you'll have one of us to confront who's completely human."

Quickly she turned and stepped to Melody's table. A glance to the patient as she reached down for this and that somewhere below. Then she straightened, and the table smoothly rose several inches. She and the paler man began pushing it, for the operating table now floated in the air, like Melody in that previous pseudo dream. Then the woman shouted.

"It won't last—let's go, bleeders!" and the pair pushed Melody toward the dusty hole in the wall, the man and woman with the equipment following.

They had spun the table around, Melody then able to see the room's interior: above, behind glass, scores of people staring and jumping and silently shouting. But her last view before leaving the room was of Hagen, frozen, expressionless Hagen looking nowhere, straining to speak. And though no sound was heard, Melody read his lips, that final phrase.

". . . Your back," he said. Your back.

Once into the hole, the five proceeded in the dark for several seconds, then a change, a turn, and they dropped, going from dark to light as though falling down a shaft in the building, Melody presuming an elevator of sorts, perhaps pneumatic like the table, but the sensation of movement was slight. Soon they stopped, more turning and shuffling, Melody seeing a ceiling and flashes of the four people moving beside her, quick words of guidance. Then the ceiling changed, becoming coarse, not the finished interior surface seen before, this one with pipes and wiring and other mechanical channels. And the air was different: not so cool, now drafty, more humidity perhaps, Melody sure they were on ground level, dim light, a long path here. And finally other people were seen: those uniforms, the constables on the street, these like statues, many of them passed; and soon, bright light, outside into the Marzian air.

All along, Melody had heard the occasional firm whisper about this way and that, move faster; and, yes, the four people surrounding her were straining to run as they guided her table, the two machine-laden individuals in the lead. But now a more significant cry, the pale man looking back, then quickly to the woman to snap:

"They're coming to!"

"Too late to hit them again," she replied. "Move!"

Half in and half out of the light was a large trok with massive rear body. The vehicle pointed toward many others, this area of the compound congested with troks, loading stalls, and opaque fences. Beyond, doors closed on full bods as several vehicles began leaving, Melody hearing their precise whining, unexcited voices of drivers and other personnel. At the nearest trok now, Melody realized they had moved through an opened fence panel which cryptically led to this area. Then the table clicked beneath her, and she and her support were inside the vehicle along with three of the group, the older woman closing the hissing door from outside, and then they were under way, Melody noting their rate: insistent, but not desperate.

They were breathing hard now. Melody was still in that odd, pre-surgery state which insulated her from all the excitement about her, any desperation of her own. But she could see. The people sitting on the trok's floor were like statues themselves now, very still, but motionless from fatigue, from a mental stress anesthetic Melody had missed. She could sense their state, however, and by now had sensed their identities, Melody presuming, hoping for safety as they drove, beside her a tall woman Melody had seen on her Marz as a handsome Sueedish man. And the dazed-first, normal-later man: Dr. Searle with a beard and a squandered expression Melody presumed to be permanent here. So skinny yet stronger than ever was Chas Chaeung, kneeling with his burden still against him as he looked to Melody and spoke.

"Let's go, Mel," he whispered from exhaustion; while ahead, an older Nan Flamini drove.

# CHAPTER 10:
## *An Aftermath of Admonition*

"You say I am to do it? With the chems in me, that is a problem. The hand is twitching, you know."

This voice she recognized: Dr. Searle's, though somewhat slurred now. The next voice, however, was a surprise.

"You could at least cover her up. It's not nice to leave her with no clothes on and everything."

Melody did not have to stretch around painfully to determine who was speaking. The voice was feminine, so certainly the young woman spoke; but the sound was that of a child, not at all fitting that mature face and figure. Dr. Searle then replied.

"On my Marz, I took this girl's appendixes out, you know. I've seen her tummy before."

"I'm not talking about her tummy, Doktor," the girl/woman returned with some youthful agitation. "You are nasty."

"I am a doktor is what I am, Mizz Pushka," Searle replied as firmly as possible considering his affected condition. "But for now, I am not much of a good one. The chems which keep me from hearing all of their communiqués make me unsteady, you can see.

So you, the big lady with the little voice, you can give it to her."

"Me! I hate shots," she whined.

"You don't do it, I look at her chest," the doktor threatened.

"Oh, you grown-ups can be real llamas!" Pushka fumed with her upset-child's voice. Then, with a bit of a young huff, she moved near Melody's bed, standing on her knees. With a shaking hand, the doktor reached across nude Melody, who saw the corner of an inject-ampule between his fingers. She was not thrilled with shots herself, and was glad those unsteady digits would not be administering the dreg, which Melody presumed to be beneficial for her recovering from Hagen's stiffness. Pushka, however, ignored Searle, reaching instead to the bed's end where the cover was rolled tight. After fussing and fiddling with the simple mechanism, Pushka finally released the fabric so it snapped loudly across the bed, covering Melody from hock to hairline. "Oh!" Pushka pronounced in surprise, then managed with less difficulty to uncover Melody's face.

Apparently the patient did not care, unable to form an expression, her blinking languid; and this was fine with Melody, because her changed companions should have been stunning. She thought of Hagen's "examinations," looked for scars, but found none on the bleeders. Nothing else about them was normal. The doktor looked hurt, Melody liking him more in this weakness than she had on her own Marz. And the Sueede, here the most profound human view, more handsome as a woman than a man, all these voluptuous forms evident even beneath conservative clothing, Melody wondering why she hadn't received more of these attributes. And that voice, Melody looking now to an elegant, dramatic face, strong eyes, baby talk from the lips of a woman. Nan so old—nothing terrible here, for advancing years prove advanced life—but she was due more late youth before achieving the beginnings of old age. And Chas: how did his bulk go without taking his strength? for carrying such equipment was nothing thin people do. He had removed the gear now, but placing it on the floor shifted the trok's balance, so great was the mass. All of this was odd to Melody but it should have been irrevocably weird. But then Pushka took the ampule, whined, "I hate this again," and popped it precisely into Melody's bicep, reaching beneath the cover, looking into the patient's eyes to tell her, "I'm glad it was you who came," smiling so sweetly, the baby, that Melody wanted to smile in return, but not yet, coming around, but not at once.

From the half-segregated front segment of the vehicle, Nan called back, "Let's get the clothes back on. We don't have to show off anymore," and around Melody the bleeders began covering their average attire with terrible clothes pulled from bags: jackets and shawls of the nastiest, acid hues, awful cuts but fine stitching, indescribable coverings, pointy pockets for Chas and a pointy hat for Searle. Soon the bleeders looked like a group from a planet Melody wanted to know nothing about.

"When do we leave it?" a slow voice asked from behind, the unmistakable voice of a huge man now in some ways reduced.

"She'll be able to walk before we have to rid the trok," Nan answered, her voice as old as her appearance. "I hope she can walk. We'll have difficulty carrying both Melody and the doktor."

Pushka returned to her place after patting Melody's head once, leaning against the trok wall for a bit of comfort. The doktor had taken a similar pose, Chas sitting erect, breathing deeply.

They drove. Only one window back here, and that covered but for a slit. Seems they were hiding. Several times Pushka craned to look through the opening, mentioning once, ". . . No one following," to Chas.

Melody's view here was more relaxed. Through the window she saw the blue Marzian sky, again having the purple tint of morning. Flashes of buildings and tall troks interrupted her view. Around her, minor conversation Melody did not follow. Her arm did not hurt from the injection; so Pushka must have poked it in correctly. And here again was Pushka, bending over to peer at the patient, to check her condition, but Melody could form no response. By now, Melody had determined that Pushka was One Sweet Girl. But their position seemed one due heroics rather than sweetness. And regardless of how courageously Pushka had performed in the operating theater, Melody would have preferred her as the male of her Marz. She could have used a conventional hero, a man to bat her blue eyes at and perhaps more, much more. She was no baby, after all. Dr. Searle, on any Marz, was just not correct; and Chas was Nan's. Ever since that scene in the cubicle, she could have him. Melody was thinking of a guy to squeeze her hard and do some serious saving; yes, that would do. But no such creature was available. To Melody it seemed she was stuck with just another friend. But, fee-cees, with those hips, they couldn't even wear the same clothes . . .

They drove. Melody felt . . . fuzzy for a length of time whose duration she was unable to judge. But soon she found herself stretching both legs. Then, fabric flopped on her midsection. Reaching one arm out from the cover, Melody prodded the cloth. Apparel. A type of loose pant with waist-cinch, like the Sub Amerigans wore, but this was a putrid, impure orange. A floppy shirt with serrated sleeves of a clashing fuchsia, nearly as bad as Pushka's.

Feeling more mobile, Melody lifted her neck and shoulders to look about the trok's interior. To her left, she saw Dr. Searle looking nowhere. To the right and behind, Pushka was staring intently at the opposite wall. And Chas . . . Melody looked closely to him; and, yes, this was her Chas, skinny but still the same solid expression. And he was staring at her. Melody gave him a tremendous, somewhat embarrassed smile. Of course, Chas did not change his expression, but his response was perfect.

"Good smile," he said loudly. "Healthy-girl smile; I like it."

Quickly Pushka turned to her. One look and she had the same silly smile as Melody. "How do you feel?" she asked like a thoughtful niece.

"Good," Melody croaked, and cleared her throat. "Getting dressed now; all boys turn around."

"I don't have to, the doktor," Searle pronounced with a tired voice, but Pushka excitedly corrected him.

"You better turn around or I'll put something on your face!"

Searle complied in a manner, raising a lax forearm before his eyes, while Chas decisively turned away, as though performing an important deed. Sternly

Pushka watched both men for peeking as Melody crawled from beneath the troublesome cover, and dressed. Thick, pulp paper shoes on the floor for her.

"They didn't even get you any undies," the girl-voiced Pushka observed, perturbed again. "I cannot comprehend."

From the front of the trok, Nan called back, "How are you, Melody?"

"I'm fine, er, Nan. Haysus, this is weird."

"No cussing," Chas admonished from his reversed position. "Bad for nice girl."

"Okay, everybody back to normal looking," Melody allowed as she pulled at the obtrusive collar about her neck, and shaped her hair with ruffles of both hands.

"I might have been peeking," the doktor intoned with half-closed eyes.

"You better not have!" Pushka fumed, looking about the trok for something to throw at him.

"Calm down, Pushka; he's just teasing," Nan told her, and Pushka settled, sulking. Then, from the front compartment, a creature came flying, thrown by Nan.

It was a wig. Red. Bright red.

"That's yours, Mel."

"Red?" she sputtered, stupified. "A clown red wig?"

"It's all we had left," Nan explained. "Besides, you'll fit right in where we're going."

"Then I don't want to go there," Melody mumbled, and turned the wig about, trying to align it, and donned the thing, stuffing her hair-brown waves beneath the red, the ugly red.

Just as Melody looked up, Pushka guffawed. A baby

guffaw. "Backward," Chas explained.

"You, help," Melody insisted, pointing to Pushka.

They leaned forward together, Melody bending as Pushka plucked the wig away, then pressed it firmly over Melody's skull.

"Let's see," Pushka ventured as she and Melody straightened. "Looks bad," she said brightly, and giggled. "You want to see in a mirher or something?"

"No thanks," Melody grumbled. "Just make sure it's on right, because I hold a grudge."

Smart Pushka giggled again, knowing better than to believe Melody's stern expression.

The patient looked around. Searle seemed removed, Chas impassive, Pushka pleased. Not much to be seen through the rear window's slit, but Melody was curious, and needed to catch up. No, she was not energetic considering that the chems of Hagen and the bleeders pulled her in conflicting directions; but she could manage some listening, some thinking. The commando scene most recently transpired she could interpret. The pack of bleeders—or sensitives or appearees or witches—had broken into the MEL complex using harnessed-idea devices, freezing the bad guys, commandeering a vehicle, leaving in an area of normally high traffic. Real good thinking, she granted them. Real good ideas. Melody, however, needed more.

She was going to speak with her companions, but the situation was so odd here—these people were so odd here—that Melody was uncomfortable with the prospect even before opening her mouth. Nevertheless, on any Marz, regardless of their manner, these people were still her friends.

"Very well," she proclaimed to the bleeders, "I'm ready for stories now. Who wants to convey at me the whole scenery?"

"Oh! I do, I do! Please, Nan," Pushka implored, jumping excitedly, breasts bouncing in disaccord with that voice, the nature of that excitement. Melody would not soon be accustomed to this sound and that stature, Pushka's adult face. "Please, Nan, I want to tell her everything."

"Go ahead, Pushka; you'll do fine," Nan replied agreeably, no pique in her voice.

"Okay, Melody, this is it," Pushka began, rubbing her hands together. "Well, we're all the same. We're sensitives who bled through our Marzes to this one because on this one none of us exists and MEL has all this concept power leaking out everywhere which makes some of the workers mad—called 'Antis,' though I call them 'Ants'—who want to riot and they're on our side but not many because everyone gets paid so much they just take the money."

Already Pushka was panting.

"Easy, Pushka," Nan suggested.

"Okay, okay," Pushka agreed, breathing slowly. "Well, we all bled through because we were on Skopein Plain too long, though I was on a hill but didn't fall, just showed up on flatland, and you must have done the same thing and we all saw ghost plants and then turned into ghost people. And we all came through naked, but that didn't bother me because I was a big old man and brave and everything, but I would be embarrassed now, and I bet it was *really* bad for you, Melody, because you're little and sweet, wasn't it?"

"Well," Melody replied in a rush, "being nude

wasn't so bad because I landed right in a thresher which tried to eat me, and I thought I was—" and she stopped abruptly. "Wait a minute, wait a minute," she pronounced carefully, "I'm starting to talk like you."

Chas nodded, Nan laughed, and excited Pushka continued.

"Oh, we heard that, we heard that. Since Dok is connected to MEL communications, he learns everything, which is too much because it all comes at once when he's not chemmed away, but you were the only one. The rest of us just popped into the ore crop here and there and wandered around. You were the only one to get threshed and the only one ore-forked and the only one nearly burned twice, and I'm sorry." Pushka was now nearly in tears. "I wish we had found you sooner because it must have been terrible, all those sick, nasty farmers trying to hurt you, but you're nice and everything and didn't deserve that."

Pushka had slowed now, looking so sad.

"Yeah, but I'm tough," Melody claimed with a non-serious, non-believable expression of power. "Go ahead, Pushka, tell me more."

"Well . . . ," she began, still upset, having trouble with her new start. Melody aided.

"We all bled through at about the same place. At the same time for you gals, or what?"

"No, no," Pushka continued, her pace regained. "Nan was first, then Chas, then Doktor, then me, then you, but only you got burned and stuff. Nan's been here well over a year and Chas about a year and Dok less and me months and months and you just got here."

Although at a normal rate again, Pushka seemed to

have lost her story. Melody aided further.

"So you wandered around and . . ."

"And we all got taken by MEL and they didn't know what we were or where we came from, and the Board and Mr. Hagen were pretty nice to us until the Ants got themselves going and started being very mean because of Ideatown especially—which is where we live now—which is the worst place for weird things because of power leaks; so MEL needed to figure out what the whole problem was and there were all these ghosts being seen and witch rumors —and that was us few and a lot of ore crop—so they had to figure us out because we were the most, er . . . , er . . ."

"We appearees were the most obvious and significant aspect of the entire concept power problem caused by Em Ee El's misuse of this new energy form," Nan explained.

"Yes, that's what I meant, thanks," Pushka told her, and continued with Melody. "So they had to figure us and began making all these tests, and . . . ," but Pushka had paused again, becoming upset once more. "Oh, this is the hard part. I'll have to go through this real quick. They studied us by checking our insides like they were going to do to you, but more than once, and each time they drowned us with the concept power until our, our . . ."

"Basic natures."

"Basic natures, thankyouNan, were changed. And they worked with a different idea on each of us and it all got turned around and we came out a little more different each time. They adjusted the machine so it messed with Nan's age—so she got old—and Chas' size—so he got skinny—and Dok's er, er . . ."

"Capacity for lingual and non-verbal communications."

"Yes, that, and he ended up being able to hear in his brain everything they say with factingrates and stuff or over the tellherfones or anything. And with me they messed with my sex, because I used to be this big guy, but it seems funny to think of being a man, because this feels okay to me—do you think it's okay?" she asked sheepishly.

"I don't know you that well," Melody began cautiously, "but I like you tremendous already."

"Oh, thank you," Pushka sighed with an almost pitiful relief.

"So they changed you all and what happened?" Melody asked.

"Well, they changed us, all right, trying to learn how we came here and trying to get that power for themselves so they could do it or something like it, but when they changed us they changed too much. They made me a lot younger up here," she noted, tapping her forehead, "and Dok started hearing everything they said, though they didn't expect that. He was just supposed to be able to tell *them* everything *he* knew, but—girl—did Dok fool them. And Chas got even stronger, even with his skinniness, and Nan got smarter because she can figure all the stuff Dok is saying. But we all wanted to get out by then, so Dok listened and Nan figured out where and when to go and Chas busted us out before Mr. Hagen and them really knew what the two guys could do because they and Nan knew all along to hide what they could of that, although Dok was still getting better or worse or whatever even after we got out. So we got out and hid in Ideatown which is where we're going roundabout to hide the trok first, because we met the Ants and they arranged it, and they call it that because it's downhill from the ether flow and all the extra concept power puddles there and changes things because—"

"An ether eddy where Actal Manifestic current stagnates," Nan explained.

"Yeah, that's it," Pushka said, "and we hide there because we're hard to find there because people are funny and some machines don't always work so well and even the bad guys don't like to go there and we've been there ever since trying to figure out what to do and we were gonna take over something in MEL until we learned of you through Dok so we knew that's what we wanted. We wanted you. We wanted you before you got changed. And we got you."

With those last, short sentences, Pushka turned alternately fearful and sad and finally satisfied.

"Wow," Melody replied, on the verge of dumbfoundedness. "How am I supposed to thank you all?" and her lost look to her friends was genuine.

"It was nothing," Pushka beamed.

"Worth it," Chas mentioned. "All of us are worth anything."

"But, but," Melody began, looking from Pushka to Chas to Nan's back, past semi-conscious Searle, "what were you going to do in Em Ee El before you learned I was there?"

"The surgeon," Chas said, "we were taking the concept surgeon."

"Mel," Nan stated seriously, needing to be loud because of her separation, "they were not going to be so nice with you. We were treated rather mildly considering Hagen's potential, the potential for change via AM. But after we escaped, the Prime Chair decided the next witch was expendable. Melody, with you it would have been all or nothing."

"We didn't want you with six legs," Pushka whispered fearfully.

"Or no body at all," Chas added. "But they didn't get you. We did. We almost got you first. On the street, but you drove past. Then Hagen copied us, but we got away. If you had stopped, we'd have you and the cee surgeon now."

"She couldn't tell it was us," defensive Pushka explained.

"I almost stopped," guilty Melody mumbled.

"You stopped for Hagen instead," Chas said.

"I thought they were you," guilty Melody mumbled.

"She didn't know it was them," defensive Pushka explained.

"God bless your universe regardless," Melody whispered. "But if you had gotten the surgeon, could you have changed yourselves back?"

"Likely, yes," Nan replied, "because the device is unlimited. MEL's medikal force makes good use of the instrument with normal persons, but an AM sensitive allows vastly more potential for experiment and change. But the only sensitives are us. Had they retained your, er, services, they might have destroyed you. Or—and I won't lie—they might have gained ultimate control of AM power without damaging you and thereby solved every problem."

And Melody sighed, "They could have returned you."

"Had the best occurred, yes. They could have returned us and ended the bad influence permeating Marz as exemplified by Ideatown. But they needed a sensitive and we weren't letting them perform their conceptual vivisection on us anymore—or on you."

"But what do you—what do *we* do now?" Melody asked.

"Next we go for the surgeon again," Nan told her. "But it will be more difficult this time, because we'll be expected."

"We could have had it," Chas stated flatly, looking directly toward Melody.

"I'd rather have Melody," Pushka maintained.

"But we *do* have Melody," Nan insisted, "so we've succeeded. And soon we'll have the cee surgeon for our own."

"And then?" Melody asked. "What can we do with it that they couldn't? Aren't we going to have to experiment on ourselves?"

Her answer was silence. Finally, Nan spoke.

"Mel, we would never ask you to volunteer. There are four of us who've already gone through it."

"But I owe you—I owe the group."

"No, Melody," Nan contended, "because we've received from you exactly what we wanted. We got you alive, well, and normal. Who could want more?"

"I don't like that machine," Pushka declared, "but it's not that bad. It wouldn't be if we were doing it to each other."

"We have to try," Nan added.

"This is no one's world," Chas said, and Pushka concluded:

"I want to go home . . ."

"Well," Melody sighed, "when do we go get our surgeon?"

"After some planning," Nan told her. "But, frankly, Mel, you'll have to stay behind. You're too inexperienced here. You're too normal to help us."

After one tick of her brain for reaction, Melody became red, and was no longer calm, no longer sighing. When she spoke again, she was virtually twitching, trembling with intensity.

"Well, maybe it's for the worst that they didn't change me," she blurted angrily, "because I think that normal me is meaner than any of you here. And I don't think all of you put together can stop me from going when we get the machine."

And then she was silent, throwing her arms tightly against her chest, a blow so hard she thumped. And the aftermath she left was one of admonition, Nan breaking the silence after this moment had passed.

"The same old Melody," she stated firmly, "on any Marz."

"Some things," Chas offered, "should not be changed."

"Some things," the doktor snored, "just won't burn."

# CHAPTER 11:
## *Poke Your Holes With Racket Roll*

Dr. Searle was turning into a teletalk machine. Through the front window, glimpses of dense architecture could be seen beyond, Melody told this was Ideatown. And then, as the nulling chems in his system became diluted by Nan's additional dreg, the doktor began prattling mathematics. With one eye half closed and the other wide open, Searle started mumbling numbers, chemical and mathematical symbols, formulae with factors Melody could only guess at. As soon as he began, Pushka moved quickly over to press with her fingers into Searle's collar. Melody then noticed the throat recorder which Pushka activated.

"We have to record everything down so Nan and the rest can go over it later," Pushka told Melody gravely, then returned to her place.

"What's he saying?" Melody asked no one in particular.

"Tapped into MEL's communications," Chas answered. "Could be saying anything. Valuable data to be sorted by Nan and the Antis' factingrate."

Melody tried to listen, but interspersed with the math symbols, Searle was conveying business and

personal fone calls: ". . . meet you the month . . . ,"
". . . where's . . . at supplies?" ". . . outer finances
are fringing, even . . . ," "Gahd! I love you forever,
girlhood!" Some phrases with detailed names and
sources, others anonymous, then almost constant lists
of inventories mixed with the rest, followed by musi-
cal signals Searle hummed beautifully, then secretive-
sounding reports of miners' and employees' activities
("apprehended Ideatown, removed . . . returned after
holding . . . min fine payable in . . ."). But soon all
these phrases and facts were coming in increasingly
irregular snatches, short and long, the total so complex that it became beyond Melody's ability to sort,
turning into an abstract flow that was entrancing in its
complexity, a nearly soothing buzz.

"Poor Dr. Searle," Melody whispered to Pushka
and Chas as though not wanting to disturb his buzzing. "How often does he do that?"

"Constant," Chas said.

"He goes until he's so tired that he falls asleep,"
Pushka reported, "then he does it less. He's only
really quiet when Nan nulls him, but that stuff is
dangerous." Then she looked to Searle with her sad,
adult eyes, and agreed with Melody. "Poor Doktor."

Before Melody could decide whether to concentrate
on Searle's words or try to ignore him, Nan spoke an
order as she guided the trok.

"Stay down, everyone. We're here."

Pushka and Chas slid to either side, leaning so they
would not be seen through the front window. Melody
flopped flat on her bed. A moment later she saw
through the slit in back a city, streaks of tall buildings
that were immediately unusual: acid colors, too many
angles, nasty curves. Soon, noises, whooping and
screaming intermixed with loud, semi-human speak-

ing. Although the trok was still moving, Melody saw bodies flying past the slit, slaps and thumps against the body panels accompanied by odd shouts without content, all these voices adult. Surprising to Melody, Nan had not closed her window, but opened it wide so she could poke out with her still too long, too rude fingernails as she growled like an animal, this last a stunning act for an intellectual, more intimidating to Melody than the initial ambience of Ideatown. Melody was thinking of the slums of Singherpoor, but—as the name suggested—that was an unwealthy place with desperate people. Those voices outside, however, sounded a little crazy to Melody.

The street had turned rough, the driving erratic. After several turns, Nan had yet to come to a complete stop, the hornblares and tread squalls about their vehicle perhaps not Nan's fault. Twice she sharply called out through the window, "Stay there, father; I'm not stopping!" and leaned on the go-bar, Melody imagining recalcitrant pedestrians scurrying. After minutes of this, Nan slowed, turned abruptly, and the world became dark.

They were inside some structure. As soon as the darkness surrounded them, Pushka and Chas began moving, preparing to leave. Then Nan's door slid open, the trok having stopped, and a dim light snapped on outside the vehicle. Pushka and Chas were unloading their equipment, Nan having opened the vehicle's larger, rearside door.

Melody was fully alert, and ready to move. The conflicting chems within her caused some wooziness now that her heart was pumping at plus-norm, but she could function.

"What do I do?" she whispered to Nan, who stood

outside as Pushka left, followed by Chas moving past the bed with all these machines which seemed to grow now that a mere man had to handle them.

"Try to get the doktor out," Nan answered.

He was conscious, but not with them, not surprising with all those data in his head, all those calls and queries slipping from his mouth, words clear but too many for Melody to follow. "Let's go, Dok," she told him, and nudged a shoulder.

"Don't be gentle," Nan described with a partial smile. "Grab hold and pull or he won't notice."

With a semi-ferocious glare, Melody looked to Searle's face and ordered in her roughest, deepest tone, "Let's go, fast-talking man," and yanked his shoulders with both hands. His eyes focused beyond infinity, Searle complied, moving stiffly, slowly, Melody continuing to guide until they stood on the floor outside the trok.

A packhouse, some sort of storage, with huge, round paper canisters or rolls Melody could not identify. Attaching the refractor again, Pushka stood back and cringed like a child as Chas shook the floor by placing his burden inside one of the hollow, evidently false containers, arranging the plas and metal items with no gentility. Nan then joined Chas at the devices' controls. After some talk and finger pressing, the machine hummed, Pushka's segment glowing the faintest negative yellow. Already Nan had returned to the trok, reaching within the driver's compartment, coming out with a handful of noses and cheekbones.

"What?" Melody uttered, mostly to herself. Her answer was Nan's continued action as she handed everyone a new nose and cheeks, even a chin for herself. Melody got a whole mouth. Dr. Searle also got glue, Nan tacking the fake pieces against his real face, bare skin against beard. Then she herded the group closely together.

"Hold them against your face," she told Melody, "and look into the refractor."

"Smile!" Pushka told them as she aimed the device at her friends.

A dollop of non-blue rolled out at the speed of thought, and Melody felt her face change. Holding the obviously plas facial pieces against her skin, Melody saw the negative color, then felt the false articles expand or move against her or . . . something. And then the light ended and Melody dropped her hands, but the pieces remained. She looked to Nan and Chas and Searle. They looked different. They seemed to be different people. All the phony pieces had become part of their faces, not false additions. As Chas moved to turn the refractor against Pushka, Nan explained.

"Via concept power, this instrument has expressed the idea that these false faces be real. The gear is rather crude compared to the concept surgeon, but more immediately versatile—and temporary. The effect is real, but it won't last." She then spoke to everyone, "So let's go, gals."

Now Pushka was also different. None of them were recognizable as their former selves, and some of the effects were bold. Pushka's fake nose looked masculine, so her new face was that of a man with just *darling* lips, Pushka resembling not her original male face, but a third cousin, perhaps, with a strong Lateeno bloodline—and a wonderful chest. Since Chas' false cheekbones were white, his new face was moolotto, lips thinner to match his rather

Cockassion, phony nose. As for Searle and Nan, both were somewhat older now, the clean-shaven doktor's hair white and frizzy, Nan heavier in the face. No one here was recognizable as herself. Melody had no idea how she appeared, and was not asking.

"Gal, you look awful," Pushka spat as though gagging on the words, and turned away from Melody.

The lately ugly newcomer had no reply, Pushka along with Chas proceeding to the trok to don long part-coats from the vehicle, Pushka blousing hers around the torso so her unchanged figure would not be evident. Then the girl/woman moved to the doktor's side, grasping Searle by the shirt as though a large rag. "I'll take him," she announced cheerfully, her old voice and new face absolutely ridiculous together.

Nan and Chas had by then surrounded Searle, looking between the gabby doktor and Pushka. "I'd say he can walk, yes, Pushka?" Nan remarked.

"I am very sure he'll be real good for a while, Nan," Pushka claimed with certainty. Nan then turned to Chas.

"You can go ahead and not worry about returning here."

A half nod and Chas was gone, moving past to enter the trok. As Chas started the motorvator, Nan spoke to Melody.

"We're walking home. We couldn't get the trok any closer without being suspicious. Pushka handles Searle best; so you and I will move together. Chas is going to vacate the trok outside the Town, then come on his own. It's too dangerous walking all together."

Chas reversed the trok toward the blank wall which split, and there was Ideatown. Out of sight with him in a second. Then Pushka, with an assured look that fit her stature more than her voice, turned right with her charge in hand, leaving without pause.

Nan followed with Melody. "Stay right next to me," she stated. This would be only the first of her suggestions for travel in the area.

Aurally and kinetically this section of Ideatown was relatively quiescent—compared to those they had passed through—with few people immediately evident. But it was a riot to Melody, who had to force her jaw not to drop, force herself not to hang on to Nan like an infant. And like a mother, fast-walking Nan was giving instructions as she firmly took Melody's hand and pulled the younger fem alongside.

"Move quickly, talk to *no one* regardless of what they say, and try not to react to what occurs or what you see. Watch me, follow me, pay attention to me. Do not release my hand."

Okay, but still Melody had to look. And first was the architecture, multi-story buildings with irregular, angular additions sticking out over the street, threatening to fall, the buildings held together with struts of lumber and coarse, cast metal. And right before her: walls jutting from nowhere onto the roadwalk, she and Nan already having to dodge about these anomalous, seemingly useless pieces. The organic material smeared and slopped on the edgewalk was no help to unfamiliar Melody's navigation, but there was no stench, just a thick, distinctive odor comprised of these biological stuffs and perhaps fragrances from distant sources; and, yes, yards ahead some acrid chem came flying through a doorway.

"The architectural 'style' developed only recently," Nan described, noting Melody's stares toward the buildings. "Before the conceptual influence took hold, the city was relatively normal."

The colors could kill. The favorite hues of the area were a deep reddish maroon and acid yellow which beat together like bad notes, applied as paints and slick panels and textured fabrics which deteriorated in the elements. The favorite sheen here was gloss. As they rapidly proceeded, Nan had further explication for her guest.

"The place is a company town like those formed in Ameriga during the Gold Rash days. The few farmers who've been on Marz long enough to establish flatland locations are family-oriented, but the miners working multi-shifts in the crop smelters are solo. Ideatown provides services for them: entertainment, cuisine, gender. The only people who live here work here. If the miners lived in Ideatown, they wouldn't be able to function at their jobs. Living here is illegal for them."

"But *you* live here; how does that affect you?"

"Being sensitives makes us insensitive in certain respects. Athletes are not only stronger, they can take more physical abuse than the average woman. Raw ideas don't affect us, only coalesced concepts, ideational power purified, by the concept surgeon, for example. But not all normal people are affected by the constant exposure here. Those unchanged knew enough to leave. The residents remaining are essentially 'pschyotic,' as they say. The only normal people still living in Ideatown are insensitve Antis, a few aides for emergencies."

This was clearly a back street they traveled, the buildings having big doors for deliveries, small windows, smaller signs to denote the businesses in a language no one spoke, not with that spelling. Melody kept looking up, hoping those nasty-colored outcroppings would not drop on her; and she wondered how people functioned in such narrow, often angular rooms. As for the people, they all seemed ahead, Melody seeing a corner, a wider street, folk beyond in increasing numbers. And though Melody thought she was prepared for the more active area where Nan led her, upon turning that corner, shocked Melody wanted to run back.

People were shouting in her head. At once Melody recognized tawdry come-ons to buy this and that —"Our eats feed your belly better!" and "Poke your holes . . . our beauties!"—but the words did not match any speaker, the nearest people in doorways inviting passersby only with gestures, as words entered Melody's head. And she recalled Hagen and his chamber, the discrepancy between his voice and his position.

"Perceptual projection," Nan explained. "Crude compared to Searle's mental receptions, but still different from the MEL norm." She then added with confidence, "You'll get used to it."

Perhaps, but not easily. And this was not Melody's only problem: the entire experience was a chore, the two women being barraged though Nan remained composed. All the mental screaming and people with loud clothes begging with their semi-sane eyes for one to enter their premises, aided by blade-sharp storefronts requiring pedestrians to walk onto the street and the paper and food droppings and broken pieces of a city that were scattered there, smashed and smeared by the kars which zoomed and skidded everywhere, including the roadwalks, avoid them by staying close to the pointy buildings, protruding ledges head-high as though for decapitation, kurbs like craters; and, yes, there was crashing, Melody gasping at the sound of rented plastick but little damage with this material, a great deal of bounding away, the din from this and the perceptual entice-ments, the drivers laughing here and serious there, people dressed okay and others intentionally in tat-ters, as though disguised themselves. And Melody could discern the difference now: there were miners here, the normal folk, some as shocked as Melody, some not so unfamiliar, composed in these surrounds. And the other persons with tatters, those laughing in wrecks where the miners were serious, those with eyes seemingly inches deep in their skulls and mouths permanently garbled; whereas the miners just looked like people, and not a woman, no one deadly hurt, no children present; but, yes, there's one crying; but, no, just another resident luring miners to buy some get-up chems, but luring peers just as hard. And the colors which stung her eyes and the projected shouts inside her head and now all this sub-music, this racket roll, and the frightening people close enough to smell, often bumping her, poking with fingers for her to pay attention, spastic fingers, clogging bodily smells, ber-serk bumping, all of which she had to avoid though the experience washed over her like sewage, and the pointy buildings spearing her and the unspeakable stuffs on the edgewalk she at once could not bear to look at, just step over, and when you missed, thank God you couldn't hear the squishing over the din of mad traffic and look away from him and him who looked at you too hard, their smell, oh, just follow Nan, and try your best, girl, to stay remotely sane, but don't look or listen or smell on purpose, keep away from everything, and for Haysus' sake *touch nothing*.

In the entire multi-level area, only one bit of peace was found by Melody, but certainly her calm discovery was even less desirable than the raucous ambience.

A pale blue kar with part of her name and a 2D, steel cable. No one bothered this vehicle which sat in a pool of calm, neither resident nor miner coming near, avoiding the driver equally. He was walking toward his kar, dressed as the constables who had stopped Melody's trok, this man with extra accouterments on his person which Melody could not quite discern: wristcuffs, it seemed, no weapon, a bag at his beltline as though for trash.

"Bad guy," Melody told Nan, who conveyed the proper terminalogy.

"He is a MEL Officer of Detachment, Investigation, and Enforcement Services," she explained with an unpleasant smile. "The residents call them 'oddies.'"

Melody determined the acroname, then wanted to kill, telling Nan, "I hope whoever came up with that name dies long and terrible."

"Hagen," Nan snickered, Melody deciding her response was appropriate.

The two women continued with no concern for or from the oddie, not with the endless folk about them, Melody soon forgetting this officer, overcome once more with ideas gone bad around her. After several endless blocks of Ideatown's bombardment and a pair of turns, Nan led her to a block whose style was similar but less intense. But apart from reduced jostling, this place was worse; for with the sparse people, Melody and Nan were noticed more than before, when they were part of the crowd. A very young man soon showed Melody something new. Many of the upper-story porticoes were shy a wall or portions of a wall, and there were no barricades or rails to prevent one's rapid, vertical exit. The very young man with huge, green moustache and bald, pinkish head pointed to Nan and Melody from a second story, er, pyramid across the street, wiggled in excitement, then leaned deeper within to manipulate a panel with his palms. In the women's ears thus came a deal.

"Grow up and we use you always! Both of you together would make something for a mining man!"

This advertisement, as the rest, had a tremendous range, closer to flashing lights than shouting, Nan and Melody hearing his voice when they were stores removed. Then the voice was joined in Melody's brain by her own, uncomfortable thought.

"Nan, how can you let Pushka come out here by herself—especially when she has to worry over Searle?"

"There's a lot of talk here, but no action unless you pay for it," Nan described. "These people aren't nonsane, just odd, and remarkably straightforward as businesshumes. They don't cheat, steal, or hurt each other on purpose. As for Pushka, she can handle plenty. Besides, she's just not Ideatown's style."

After a few more minutes of torrid walking, Nan nodded to a building with a broad opening as though a typical store display, but here with a yellow and green picket fence instead of glass. From this site came more gender enticements that Melody was beginning to ignore. But she understood Nan's reference; for behind the fence were two seated women, both the fattest things Melody had ever seen, huge softies each with a man on her lap clothed in postage stamps on his nipples and about the genital area. There was some foolish laughing and quaking of flesh going on, some genuine exertion, but Melody was looking no closer. And she was not thinking of that other Nan on that other Chas, for there was no comparison.

"I'm throwing up," Melody threatened.

"They're just having fun," Nan claimed as she squeezed Melody's hand and pulled her along.

"Well, after seeing all this, it will be fun for me to throw up."

"Try not to, Mel," Nan told her. "Someone would like it and want you to do it again."

They could still hear the voice inducing them personally to get together and please a miner. But then his speaking ended abruptly, the man calling out, "Catch me!" with no humor. Turning quickly, Melody saw him falling to the roadwalk—he had slipped from the building's unprotected edge.

She gasped and jerked Nan still. It was over in seconds. Not even in a sub-Erth field is falling thirty feet inconsequential; but with his shout, several people had rushed directly beneath the man, holding their arms up, waving their hands. And, yes, they caught him, the whole handful of folk slapped down with some brief but loud grunting upon contact.

Now Nan was jerking back, pulling Melody along again. "I told you not to react so," she told her companion firmly. "It happens constantly, they don't get hurt much, and they wouldn't want us helping them even if they were hurt."

Melody was now breathing as though she had fallen

herself. But Nan was still guiding her, and they continued, a few more blocks, more turns, until they came to their incongruous home base.

This section of town was quieter, the buildings lower, some flat and expansive. Montei Unverit was just visible in the distance, smaller than when seen from the Powerhouse's more easterly position. And between the garish buildings, across from the partial view of Unverit, was a precise white construct, odd in its clean lines, its plain coloration, its centuries-old style of peaked roof and steeple; for their home was a church, a lovely country church.

"Oh, this is perfect," Melody whispered as though not wanting to frighten her pleasure, to shock it away.

"No one bothers us here," Nan informed her. "There are few Xians in Ideatown."

Then Nan looked sharply to Melody, stared at her face a moment, and began running, pulling the girl along.

"We better hurry, Mel. You're changing back and we're out in the open."

Yes, Melody felt her face trembling, could see that Nan's disguise was beginning to look like a disguise instead of a genuine face.

They were moving quickly—but then Nan was stopped by a vision, pulling Melody aside as she nodded down the block with an unpleasant exhalation. Nan gestured so that Melody would look, look at the oddie.

"He's seen us," Nan told her, "keep walking."

Quickly then, Nan glanced down to Melody's figure. "Damn," she growled, "you walk like a fem."

"Aren't I supposed to?"

"Not with that face—it's a man's. The refractor did

that. Pushka was worse top to bottom, but at least we had the sense to cover her."

Gripping Nan's hand, but ready to flee, Melody asked, "Will he stop us?"

"Only if we're suspicious. Then we're through—the oddies have every bleeder's headscan, including yours."

Nan was thinking, the oddie a half block away, walking directly toward them. Nan was thinking, dividing and devising the variables.

"Not much gender manipulation in Ideatown, but some. Not many slim women, but nothing is unheard-of here."

With only her eyes, Nan was looking left and right, to the church, to the oddie, to Melody; and finally she decided.

"We've only seconds left," she declared with a rare, excited tone. "Either we run away and appear guilty, or run toward him while we can, and appear as normal as possible. Listen, Mel: close one eye, and insert a finger in your nostril."

This seemed ridiculous, but Nan was so uncharacteristically anxious that regardless of bad hygiene and mediocre embarrassment, Melody complied without hesitation. Seemingly satisfied with Melody's pose, Nan grabbed her by the shirt with a final order.

"Let's go! Ignore me and look right through his forehead—and try not to wiggle."

"What's this wiggling krap?" Melody scowled to herself. "I'm a lady."

Then Nan was running, pulling Melody along. After several hard strides, Melody realized she was holding her nose on, for Nan had seen that it was going first. Holding her nose on just as she had held her breather when on that other Marz, the real one, she had turned into a ghost, a witch, a bleeder.

They were running directly at the oddie. Without revealing his thoughts or intentions, the officer continued to watch them. A dozen meters away, Melody stared at his forehead while Nan began shouting in a voice due professional examination.

"Move, oddie, that's our spot!" and she waved her free hand wildly, happily, the second still grasping Melody, who kept her one eye closed, one boring through that forehead, finger wearing out her nostril.

The oddie looked, but now he saw nothing, trying to look away, not wanting to associate with happy residents, his part smile as false as Melody's nose. The same smile the constable had used when taking her from the trok. Company policy, she presumed.

And then they were past. Nan and Melody looked to one another once away from the oddie. Almost simultaneously their faces fell to the edgewalk. They stopped to pick up the pieces, then continued via a back route to the church's side door. And then they were home.

# CHAPTER 12:
## The Spitty Image of Turmoil

Pushka and her charge, the supra-glib doktor, had already arrived, their faces normal. Chas was not expected until later. Meeting her new friend at the door, Pushka asked Melody:

"How do you like our town?" Her voice was bright but with a touch of evil, baby evil.

Melody could only shake her head, roll her eyes, and moan. "Not even any *cladaks*," she finally managed to say.

"Oh, yes there are," Pushka piped forth, "you just didn't see them. But there are *uber cladaks* on the west side."

"*Uber cladaks!*" Melody whined in amazement. "How *vulgo!*"

"Double vulgo!" Pushka cried.

As Pushka and Melody enjoyed their gallish laughter, Nan briefly checked Searle's recorder, then continued into the church, the main sanctuary, stepping from the hallway where she and Melody had entered. The church was compact, a highish but not high ceiling, a dozen rows of pews split by a path for walking, a carpet, well-oiled wood from floors to ceiling to choir loft, a warm and natural usage of materials in antithesis to the remainder of Ideatown; and Melody was comfortable at once. But not for long.

There were more people in the sanctuary, Melody recognizing an old-time Beible family at first sight: the tall, straight-backed father with dark, archaic suit, vertically hung tie, no hair on his face. The missus with long, full dress, hair in a bundt, small spectacles. And the eldest son: adult but still in the household, heir to the pulpit, this new generation larger than the old—as always—but otherwise the spitty image of his father. The three stood passively as Nan entered the sanctuary, Melody close behind. She was not recognized, for no Melody existed on this Marz, but she knew them. Not the boy, but she knew the Sueedish woman who had been friendly to her. She knew her own dorm director.

Pushka guided Melody and Searle behind Nan. Pastor Telak looked to these three, then growled to Nan:

"Where the heill have you been?"

"And where the shidload is the surgeon?" the mother scowled. Then the son moaned and covered his face.

"Oooh, they sucked up again," and he turned away in pain. Preacher and Missus still faced the bleeders in disgust.

Calm Nan glanced to Searle, asking Telak, "Have you pushed his facts into the data integrator?"

The wife answered, "We're collating what he heard now, Flamini. You don't have to worry about that; we always take care of that. And you don't have to change that subject."

Anxious to be speaking again, the preacher began exactly as his wife finished, as though they shared a throat.

"Where's the surgeon, Flamini? Our people at the packhouse said you still had the refractor—you were supposed to *bring* the surgeon even if you had to *leave* the refractor. And who is *that*?" and he pointed to Melody.

In all her innocence, Melody looked everywhere around the room; but, no, there were no other strangers present.

"We didn't get the surgeon," Nan described as she faced her persecutors. "We learned about Melody, so we changed our approach."

The preaching family went rigid with the term "Melody," all three looking for a goon, finally realizing in their intelligence that the word was this non-goon girl's name and not her occupation. Pastor Telak was fully recovered as he continued his confrontation.

"Look, Nan, we can't get Hagen to put controls on AM usage by petitioning the Board or asking them nicely. Only Gleeson makes sense there, and he's only number two. Hagen won't listen—he doesn't have to. None of us have any rights on Marz: we're nothing but employees. If we don't like it, we can go home, and that's Irth. But we're staying and we're making changes—and we can only do it with power. We can only change Em Ee El by using their own power against them. Now, just exactly what are we going to do with *her*—with another of you bleeders?"

Calm Nan showed neither weakness nor hesitation as she stepped nearer the preacher and replied, as she informed him.

"Firstly, I am not letting Hagen turn another friend of mine into a freak. And secondly, I am not letting

MEL experiment on a sensitive so they can learn more of AM and thus become even more dangerous. They were experimenting with Searle to learn how to read minds. How will you Antis hide when Hagen knows your thoughts?"

Unimpressed, the son whined as though in pain, "Sucked up again. Let them go on their own and they suck up complete."

Pastor Telak then countered, "Let me tell you, Flamini—we didn't get that refractor so you could waste it. We had a hundred twenty people each with a little part in getting that, a hundred twenty people risking their careers before you even got here, and what do you do with it? You bring someone else here to feed."

"I don't eat much . . .," Melody said, strictly to herself.

"This is the only appearee who's normal," Nan insisted to everyone. "Her potential is unlimited. With the refractor, we'll get the cee surgeon as soon as possible, and then with Melody we'll learn what Em Ee El cannot—because they don't have a sensitive. The worst thing we could have done was leave her for Hagen."

The missus, religiously shocked, then confronted Nan with, "You brought that girl here so you could experiment on it? One of your own kind?"

Having been bandied about in name often enough, Melody then piped forth, "No one is 'experimenting' on me," she told the three Telaks. "We are going to study my condition. It's my choice."

"Just what are you going to do, girl, with all your choosing?" Preacher Telak demanded, "steal the concept surgeon by yourself?"

"What I am not going to do is wait around for

profundities from your mouth," unhappy Melody retorted. "Why don't you go pray or something." She was additionally displeased at not knowing someone she knew, unhappy at Niklas' different behavior.

The Telaks wanted to say more, but they were rendered silent by a force from the hallway: Chas had returned. As he entered the sanctuary, Chas virtually ripped off his part-coat, revealing an unimpressive body. Even his face was thin on this Marz, but those eyes were still Chas'; and regardless of bulk, his manner was expansive. Chas stepped near and filled the room.

With no violence, he strode to the preacher and pulled at his collar, coming away with a small colored patch, pulling hard enough to upset the man's balance, to frighten him, for Telak had expected more. The pastor shuffled his feet to keep from falling as Chas spoke.

"Got the wrong color here," he said, glancing at the patch which he then dropped to the floor. "Stay longer and you'll be like the rest."

As though emphasizing that Chas was not being destructive, Mrs. Telak reached beneath her own collar, coming away with a patch which she examined.

"That's right," she confirmed with a cheerfulness as false as the cheeks in the bleeders' pockets. "We came back too soon—our exposure to that seepage hasn't worn off yet." Turning to her son, the woman then added, "Let's go, man and boy. That would be bad for us to turn into a resident."

Pastor Telak had now regained all his poise, turning to Nan with a semi-pleasant look, barely affected by Chas inches away and staring.

"Tomorrow morning, Nan, we're going to move the

refractor out of the Town."

Immediately Nan was displeased, demanding of Telak in a louder tone, "How can we get the refractor if it's not nearby?"

"You'll still make the best use of the instrument, Nan; so we'll always let you know where it is. Don't worry; I don't lie."

"Neither does Hagen," Melody muttered.

Telak then smiled as he turned to leave, an expression whose sincerity Melody could not judge. The three walked to the front of the building, gathered their things, and left the witches alone.

"Don't forget to lock up," Telak called out lightly as he stood by the door. "You don't want to attract any MELODIES," and he smiled to the latest bleeder. Then he and his family were gone.

The sensitives mulled about momentarily. Nan checked Searle's recorder needlessly. Chas said, "Eat," nothing more. Now that all were respiring normally again, Pushka danced over to Melody —quite a lightweight prance for such a solid body —the girl/woman offering to display their home.

"Let's go, Pushka," Melody told her, "it's getting too adult around here."

As Pushka took Melody's arm and guided her away, Melody asked, "Do you have any Telaks on your Marz?"

"Yes, but just Mr. Telack and his brother Klaws there. Ingot is only on my Urth, they're not married, and none of them speak Englich. How about your Telacks?"

After Melody explained her versions, Pushka offered that each bleeder had a different variety of relations and situations with the various people they

knew, though all knew the same persons. Melody told
Pushka about her handsome Sueede and how they
were connected, then asked about herself on Pushka's
Marz.

"I'm the same sort of guy as on your Marz, and you
are this real important ore plant advisor who comes
around once in a while. I don't know where you live or
anything, but I like you because you're funny, but I
have a galfriend so there's none of that, though I think
you're sort-acute. And you have real blond hair that's
real light and real pretty, because all of us are hair
brown only on our own Marzes. That's why the me on
your Marz didn't bleed through and why the you on
my Marz didn't either—only the brownies bleed
through," Pushka mentioned. "And this," she said,
touching her hair, "is dye so we can hide better and
I'll get some for you, too—what color do you want?"

Blond, Melody decided. A real pretty and real light
blond. Pushka ran for the hairosol, and in minutes
Melody was a goldhead. Pushka loved it. Melody was
sure she looked better hair brown. This was a terrible
shock to her. She'd stick with the clown wig.

Again Pushka had to run ahead, for one aspect of
the interior could not wait, the girl/woman returning
with her most personal, prideful part: a doll Chas had
found on the streets of Ideatown. A typical pseudo-
flesh baby, but with no legs. Chas had partially
explained that such dolls were used by a type of
unmentioned service in the Town, the legs always
removed because they got in the way. From that story
on, the doll made Melody sick.

On with the tour. Towering Pushka took Melody's
arm, guiding her through the building. Chas was
taking care of Searle, and Nan was taking care of the

household: locking the doors, for with the Telaks gone, the church was supposed to be closed, empty, the oddies aware that the preaching family were not residents of Ideatown. Block the windows at night so the bleeders' lights would be unseen. Worry about the angry Antis tomorrow.

No worrying was Melody's attitude. In the church now with only her friends, Ideatown unnoticeable outside, all but the future was serene, and Melody needed to be without concern for a time. As Pushka took her upsteps and down, Melody was at ease with her guide, so relieved at the overall tranquillity—at being away from the turmoil of burning and running and surgery and preachers—that she could scarcely pay attention in her mental exhaustion, trying to be courteous and smile as Pushka showed her the cookroom and drainroom and sleepsect and more. And though Melody was pleased with the company and with the tour; nevertheless she was too spent for full appreciation.

Soon, Melody was in a daze. Pushka was babbling on, and really didn't need much in reply; so Melody remained quiet. Chas cooked dinner and everyone ate something that was good, but Melody was losing her grip on this day. Nan was self-contained; moody, perhaps, but not unpleasant. Poor Dok was not really amongst them, but neither was Melody.

Darkness came, became established. Someone made the windows opaque. Melody glanced at the tiny hollow lines running from the coldbox and cooker to wall connectors. She imagined the negative yellow flowing there. She imagined being absolutely alone in the universe, but was too tired and too satisfied with her improved companionship to seek sympathy. Unclear Melody could not discern her condition. So much was terrible: transported to a different universe as though directly to heill, there to be burned crudely and butchered with sophistication. Yet so much had improved: safe now with friends who offered hope. Sympathy? Her last decision of the day was that she deserved none, not compared to her friends, the other bleeders who had truly bled, who had never been threatened but genuinely cut, and often. Bleeders who had suffered by being present for months, for months, but Melody's time was an eternity as she lay on her personal bed, other people in this room but not close. And she was warm and would sleep deeply, completely comfortable except for the world about her, the void that was this universe, Melody in the midst of the densest town whose only idea was emptiness.

# CHAPTER 13:
## *Gross Bodily Collateral*

"Damn, I think he *is* a liar."

This was the revelation coming to Nan late in the morning as she read Searle's most recently collated receptions. Standing before the pantry closet where the data integrator was hidden, Nan suddenly looked up from the long printon she held, spoke her profundity, and turned to Melody, blinking. Melody was doing dishes from breakfast which their shefs, Chas and Pushka, had prepared for the group. Pushka was still helping Searle eat, who needed great quantities of any sort of foodstuff, such was the energy requirement of his overfunctioning brain. Nan had nulled him a bit through sleep, enough so Searle could rest, not using sufficient dregs to harm him.

"Who's a liar?" wet-handed Melody asked in reply.

"Not the doktor, is it, Nan?" a hopeful Pushka ventured as she steadied Searle's eatstick; for with his semi-nonconscious receptors in full bloom, the doktor's physical abilities were impaired, as though he were retarded.

"No, not the doktor, Pushka. I think Telak is a liar. It just struck me that perhaps he and the other Antis are as disgusted as they seemed yesterday. Heill, Telak lies to Em Ee El constantly; maybe he's about to start lying to us."

"About what, for example?" Melody asked as she stacked the crocks.

"About moving the refractor but still having it available for our usage. I can see that the Ants might need to store it elsewhere, but I can't be sure any other place is superior. There are hundreds of Antis with a very aware underground, but they still have a hierarch, and Telak is as important as any of their leaders. Perhaps he'll decide to move the gear where only the Antis can get at it, and try to use it themselves. What a waste."

"When do they come here, Nan?" Melody wondered, having finished the pats and pens.

"Just often enough to handle church duties, to keep their cover intact. But today they're moving the refractor, and we're keeping the doors locked."

Then Searle was standing unsteadily. Pushka knew the problem, the change. Searle stood and Pushka called out to Chas, who was doing laundry in the next room.

"Chas, Dok has to use the jane!"

Looking into the dineroom as Searle stumbled about aimlessly, Chas held out an ugly shirt covered with tiny white speckles.

"Lint everywhere from sinus papers in the poke. Trouble when I find who does this, the one with the running nose." Then he took Searle's shoulders, the two men disappearing.

The three fems returned to their work: Nan examining, Melody drying eatery, Pushka cleaning Searle's mess. A moment later, as suddenly as her previous declaration, Nan looked up from the closet shelf to state sharply:

"I'm going over there."

Just as quickly as she spoke did she move, Nan donning eyeglasses and false teeth as she told Melody and Pushka, "Everybody stay here. I'm just going to check on the Telaks."

Before leaving, Nan finished her face, applying artificial pinkles and heavy eyebrows, a saggy hat; then on with the pointy overclothes, the sideways pockets, the chafing collar. And Nan was a man, her manner of gross bodily movement to be hidden by apparel. No refractor was available to make her disguise real, but this one would not wear away. Besides, Nan looked so terrible that she was appropriate for Ideatown.

Nan moved too quickly for Melody to think of questions before she was out the back door and gone. So Melody went looking for Chas.

He was collecting the garbage. Searle was in a corner, lips twitching.

"Chas," she asked her multi-Marz friend, "Nan went to the packhouse to check on Telak while the refractor is moved. She thinks he might be lying about still letting us have the gear. Do you think she's all right alone?"

"Did she say to go with her?"

"No, she said everybody was to stay here."

"Then we stay here, and she's all right. I've never outthought a Nan yet. You neither; quit trying."

Melody just smiled and sidled away. Not being in on the thinking was so foreign to her as to seem perverse. Besides, it was her fault the Antis were perturbed at the bleeders: had Nan and company not rescued her, things would still be normal. Not Melody, but everyone else, relatively. In a vain attempt to outthink Nan, Melody thus decided that her older friend really did need help, and who was a better volunteer than the troublemaker herself?

Melody then realized this type of decision exemplified a problem she had recognized that morning. Not just a problem, but a character flaw; for Melody's gloom of the previous evening had been replaced as soon as she awoke with a fulfilling, invigorating optimism. Melody just could not stand thoughts of being on this Marz forever; so she felt—without due cause —that things would certainly work out for the best if only she continued to try to help herself and her friends, if only she did not fail to make a proper effort. But now, as she selected a shirt from the bleeders' wardrobe—an item she thought of as puce-puke because of the colorful, everwet patterns—Melody realized that she was virtually looking for trouble, in her semi-brilliance discovering that with her, optimism was not an attribute, but an illness.

Sick Melody was going as a man: beard, wig, dark goggles. A terrible thincoat to cloak shemale movements. Looking in the mirher, she saw scant resemblance to any sort of man; but in this town, okay.

She snuck out the same door as Nan. As soon as she inhaled that first exterior breath, as soon as she felt that side of the universe known as outside, Melody was taken by an acute feeling of oddness, but not misgiving; of alienness, but not fear. All the previous day's experiences of Ideatown returned to her, the strong impressions which this day seemed less dangerous; Melody, perhaps inappropriately, feeling that this town would not hurt her unless she tried, unless she was more foolhardy than usual. With the fulfilling impression of a rich voyage ahead, an optimistic journey, Melody scratched her phony hair and stepped into the alley.

This place stunk. Trash from the last several decades was stored here, Melody seeing frightening, mutated rats which turned out to be foot-long Marzian moles. This sight stunned her so much she stopped short to stare, but then Melody noticed a man and woman playing in a trash heap—no, playing with the moles, but *eating* from the heap—and she began walking at once, immediately rethinking her ridiculous optimism, the insane notion that this town would not consume her one minute just to spit her pieces out the next.

Although cursed with optimism, Melody was blessed with an exceptional memory for directions. She knew that with little effort—even in Ideatown —she would be able to find the packhouse with the refractor. Then she would sneak around, not be seen by Nan, yet manage to view the Antis' movements without being molested by residents or captured by MELODIES.

Not an illness—a malignant disease.

Only the first block was Melody going the back way. She was passing too many people in the garbage heaps for this path to be acceptable. Selecting a broad thoroughfare which seemed intrinsically safer than that claustrophobic alley, Melody headed for the main straight whereby she and Nan had gained the church the day before. Here were troks backing, kars careening; and in the distance, a plastick crush and screeching, the squealing of treads on roadway, loud voices as she continued, many, crazy voices everywhere ahead, in her head and in the air.

She just kept moving, not looking mean, but self-contained; for she was trying her hardest to feel apart from this town, to be unaffected, pay attention only to avoid involvement or injury, and always keep moving. And she was successful, dodging the acute and arbitrary architecture which threatened to stab her, carefully but quickly stepping over discarded food and broken kurbs, staying clear of the autos which nudged the edgewalk, not listening to the racket roll, the head projections, ignoring the shouts and laughter, the people moving by, some so near—too near —some occasionally nudging her. All of them smelling too sweet or too sour, and here was the difference. On Erth, in the intercities, people pretended to ignore you while brushing close to steal what you carried, to crash into you because it was fun. But in Ideatown, people brushed against each other because when you walk that crooked, you got to be running into something. The difference was that the people shouting were not shouting in anger. The people screaming were not screaming in pain. The people who wanted things were not going to steal them. The sellers and panderers may have been asking for too much, but they were taking nothing.

An ease on Melody's burden of getting through these sensations was their number and intensity. There was so much and it was so bright and loud that no one could pay attention to everything; so the parts merged into a thick, undifferentiated background as Melody proceeded.

Lot of miners on leave that morning. They stood out with their practical clothes—no getting dressed fancy for this occasion—their awed or intimidated expressions. By now, Melody felt like a regular, and was about to gawk at the concept virgins about her. Pretty weird there being near zip women mining ore crop on this Marz. The men, though, must have been spending their monies, for in they went past this door and that. With all these temptations, who could resist? Melody could, especially the bar pledging: "Pain of all types—we promise! Ohyesohyes with our burning the skin and boiling the insides and cut brains and smashing everything flat—but all mental with no damage at all atallatallll!" No temptation from: "Expert tickling in all the galaxy! Every portion even those you thought dead: our girls tickle your toenails—yes—our gal-oes tickle your marrow!" The laughter emitted from this emporium was less than inspirational to Melody. Didn't sound like torture, but didn't sound like fun. On she went.

Melody saw another well-colored oddie, but he wasn't interested in seeing anyone. Especially not the resident who found interest in this officer, a man standing by a punctured window, leaflets to distribute in one hand, a skinny pipe with valve in the other. After a time of typical Ideatown begging, the resident spotted the MEL constable, then opened the valve on himself, a non-blue wash changing his tune.

"Excuse me, sir, but I would like to give you a copy of our brochure. No obligation, but perhaps you would be interested in our poisoning services . . ."

With no further thrills, high-momentum Melody found the packhouse, and continued to the loading site, a narrow alley now filled with a huge flatbed trok upon which several residents were loading some of the paper canisters with a hydraulic lowlifter. One of the residents standing about pointing, looking knowledgeable, was Niklas Telak. His brother was driving the lifter, his wife the trok.

Not being near enough for an acceptable view, Melody carefully selected the best doorway to hide in. No, not that, some residents playing a game there, hiding from the boss instead of working. Yes, this one: deep and dark, a dim alcove with busted doors, obscure plasglass windows, Melody sneaking around a kar, a trash heap, some type of rolling, exterior shelf, and inside the niche.

To be grabbed at once by a resident, a terrible hand thrown across her face—stifling Melody's screams —the other arm wrapped about her chest to snatch her back into the alcove, Melody off balance, held upright only by her heinous captor, an overpowering semi-human who whispered unkindly in her ear:

"What the heill are you doing here?"

Melody went still, the hand on her face moved, and she could speak. "Nan?" was all she said.

"Is there any universe you're not dangerous in?" Nan scowled with more exasperation than anger.

"Maybe heaven," Melody replied thoughtfully.

"If you were there, it wouldn't be heaven," Nan returned. "What are you doing here?" she repeated, her exasperation, on second effort, implying anger.

"Shhh, Nan, let's watch," Melody tried, and nodded toward the flatback.

Nan said nothing further, but moved ahead of Melody, into position for best viewing, one hand against the dangerous girl's sternum so that she would remain behind.

For several minutes they watched without incident, without word. Then a gnarled resident passed two meters away, saw the women, and stopped to stare with either uncertainty or enlightenment.

"Keep moving or I call the taxhume on you," Nan growled, and the man was away like a dropped rock.

After another minute, Melody whispered to Nan, "That's the one with the refractor."

"How do you know?" she returned, staring at the huge container.

"Because it's falling apart."

And so it was. The false walls were not sturdy enough to be hauled about on a lowlift, the contents jostled, a corner of concept-proof plastick splitting through a seam.

The Ants panicked. Niklas looked everywhere, trying to see who was about to discover this disaster, as he ran to the lowlift, arms flailing impotently, eyes so open, as though he could gather the unraveling container with his vision.

Klaws stopped the lift at knee height, jumped from his seat, joining his brother on the platform. Ingot, looking through the trok's backviewer, was completely silent as she pointed sharply behind. The other two residents revealed their falseness by competently aiding Niklas and Klaws. These four men managed to shove the refractor's components back within the too soft container, battening them down with articulated props so that the equipment could no longer tumble side to side. Then Niklas stumbled down too hard to ground level, sinking to his knees, rising with a limp to disappear within the packhouse, returning in seconds with a hand-wide roll of strip adhesive. Recovered enough from his fall to clamber back onto the loader's platform, Niklas with Klaws began wrapping the container, the preacher again looking for observers. Melody and Nan were not noticed, but the oddie was. Telak's gaze went rigid, eyes aimed at the alley's far end where an odd stood staring, obviously watching the Antis' loading operation.

Too far away for Melody to be sure, but wasn't he familiar? No panic from the Ants. The oddie remained still; so the Telaks continued with their task. Following Niklas' guidance—his newly assumed, nocontent shouting—the Telaks tried to act crazy, but weren't even fooling each other. With less noise, Niklas then joined his wife in the trok's front compartment, while Klaws sprawled on the back, between containers. Unfortunately they would have to drive past the waiting oddie. Ingot was still at the guide bar, showing good control of the vehicle and even better control of her nerves as she steered the bulky flatback past the stationary, staring officer. No problem until Ingot overextended her resident imitation by accelerating too rapidly at the alley's end, screeching around the corner to smash into the oddie's parked vehicle.

Now he was moving. Although he had not watched the trok once past him, with the sound of the giant thud, the odd whirled about, saw, and ran the few yards to the accident site. And though his brief running had been frantic, after those several wild steps, the officer stopped calmly, looked for a moment, and proceeded with his investigation and enforcement services.

Boldly Melody ran out for a superior view, Nan having to follow to a position inferior in its concealment, the women poorly hidden, but who was watching them? Not the oddie, a man recognized now that Melody was closer, a man last seen on another Marz telling her that following rules wasn't all that difficult: the bunk balloon's food server.

He pointed to Ingot, and gestured for her to leave the vehicle and stand beside him. Ingot was stiff, weak, but she complied. When the driver was within arms' reach, the odd began moving.

He stuck a metal pad on her forehead, then touched one finger to his ear. Melody had seen this on Erth: the officer was reading Ingot's headscan, checking his kar or base factingrate. No record of this brain, for the oddie retrieved his instrument, then returned to the matter at hand.

"Negligent destruction of Marzian Energy Limited property," he stated as though making a public declaration. "Adjudicated and applied by the constable. Your fine eight or twelve hundred. The amount disclosed when retrieving your collateral."

As he spoke, the oddie reached into his bag, coming out with a tag with attachment band, the kind used to mark museum pieces or legal evidence. With his other hand, he removed the bracelet-like device from his waistband. All done fluidly and quickly, Melody thinking the odd was going to secure Ingot's wrists and take her away. And he did reach out with the bracelet thing, snapping it around Ingot's left wrist. Melody did not understand the oddie's action, and Nan telling her, "Don't look!" and trying to pull her away was no help. But Melody refused to be moved, looking over Nan's shoulder as the older woman turned to stare at Melody's face as though desperate to study the coming expression, looked at her reaction to the sight of the oddie clicking the bracelet onto Ingot's wrist, and coming away with her hand.

Melody and Ingot were equal here, for both went inhumanly rigid, but made no sound, each face a display of unparalleled shock. The difference was that

Melody knew enough to be quiet regardless of the horror she saw; whereas Ingot was incapable of sound, because the horror was hers.

A swift click of the device and Ingot's hand dropped into the odd's waiting palm, a move so facile that Melody inferred practice. No blood, not a drop, a cut clean and cured instantly. He then pulled the hand to his waist and applied the tag, tearing off the bottom segment, reaching out to place the piece in Ingot's collar; for she could not reach it, could not grasp. The hand he let fall into his bag.

"The address is on your receipt," the officer described. "You have six days to pay your fine, or we bury your collateral." Then he turned to Niklas and Klaws, who were slumped as though sacks.

"Someone get this trok away from me, or I'm taking it for myself."

Now Nan turned around, having seen enough of Melody's face, turned around to see Niklas lead his wife into the vehicle, making tiny sounds to her that Melody was glad she could not hear. And then the three Antis were in the trok and gone, Niklas driving like a normal man, but no one doubted his identity.

As the oddie examined his kar, Nan imitated Niklas; for Melody was still the same as Ingot and needed to be led away herself. Nan tried to aid with an explanation, but on any Marz, Melody knew that understanding is not necessarily acceptance.

"They can reattach it surgically if she pays the fine. It will be as good as new."

Melody began moving on her own, but now she was like Niklas, a normal person devastated and incapable of hiding the destruction, emotional destruction. Nan tried to explain, that the occurrence was common, no pain felt, no physiological shock induced, nothing to recover from later but a large expense. But the emotion, the emotion ... And though Melody listened and believed, Nan told her nothing, the stricken girl only aware that on any world of persons, understanding is not agreement, and enlightenment is trivial compared to terror.

# CHAPTER 14:
## *A More Adamant Axiom*

To Nan's surprise, the still-loaded trok was parked behind the church when she and Melody arrived. Ingot was in front, the middle seat, erect and not blatantly affected by her ordeal. Utter blankness, however, can hide emotional subtleties just as surely as death. Nan and Melody only glanced to her, seeing her full face through her minor disguise, but Ingot gave no reaction as she stared back without expression. The two sensitives had no response, wanting to enter the building quickly and not be seen by oddies or residents. And, no, truly they did not want to see or be seen by damaged Ingot, not beyond the minimum.

Niklas and Klaws were inside with the bleeders. Everyone stood in the sanctuary, between pews or near the podium. They were not close, but all were connected. Chas seemed normal, but Pushka's face revealed that the story had been told. Klaws was all gloom; only Niklas would speak. And Niklas seemed unable to gain his breath, his voice odd even in this company, for his chest and throat were constricted as he strained for control.

Everyone turned to the hallway as Nan and Melody

entered. When Niklas spoke, he looked only to Nan. He did not ask how or whether she knew of Ingot, accepting this knowledge as though universal law, like gravity; for in this universe, what axiom was more adamant?

"We are still taking the refractor as planned," he began, a labored sound which hurt Melody to experience. "I think we can continue without being stopped, now that we've been punished in advance. As soon as the refractor is delivered, I'm collecting the funds from whatever monies we have to retrieve the rest of my wife. And I tell you, Nan, that you will never see us here again. You will have to find us outside the Town. We were only here because your people could best hide in the church. But however we get together, if we get together, you bleeders will have to come to us; because never again will we come to you."

Then he turned with his brother and left, driving away with his family. And the bleeders were left alone, alone in Ideatown.

No one moved. The sensitives did not look to one another. Pushka was trying to smile. Chas was not. Finally Pushka said she had to check on Dok, and ran off, Melody inferring relief in the girl/woman, relief in being away from the dour trio that remained.

Nan began moving about, shaking her head, breathing these grand, painful sighs. Nervous Nan with her arms akimbo then looked to passive Melody, looked her up and down sharply. "Take that stuff off; you don't need it," she snapped; her words, perhaps, intended to aid more than order; but Nan was incapable then of being pleasant. Nan did not remove her own disguise, however, because she needed hers.

"I'm going out," she stated, already walking toward

the hallway, the side door. "I'm going to call some other Antis and see what we can expect. I have to check. I have to check on something."

Nan had her momentum up as she reached the room's end, but then she whirled around, stopping to point sternly at Melody.

"Don't you follow me this time, girl. Don't you follow," and she was gone.

Melody was going nowhere. She spent valuable time not thinking of anything, looking at the carpet, a corner of the pews where Chas consistently let dust collect, each base, the same corner, spotless rug elsewhere. After Melody reinforced this profound discovery with repetitive observation, Pushka returned. These three bleeders then collected like dust in the choir loft, assembled like a trio, looking out at the congregation of zero to sing the appropriate song: sing nothing.

"Tough without the Antis," Chas said. "We get supplies through them. Communications."

"But the Telacks," Pushka added, "are no fun."

"I see," Melody nodded sagely.

Chas soon left. The girls, too. They moved around here and there, trying to have fun. But wherever they went, Chas was cleaning something: scrubbing surfaces, shining wood, collecting the dust he had seen that Melody had seen. Watching him wipe one too many scrupulously clean tables, Melody decided that Chas was driving her mad.

"What are you, Chas, the bleeding janitor?"

"Keeps me from going nuts," he said, and continued with his chores.

Nan returned after noon. Unhappy Nan who had asked other Antis of the Telaks, and waited for an answer. Gone to pay for the wife's hand. Too expensive for us, this cost. Their implication claimed the bleeders to be at fault. And what of the refractor? Where is it? Can't tell you, they replied. Can't trust this fone system. Maybe later.

Nan came home to lay down the law.

"Perhaps Telak will be more cooperative once Ingot is back to normal. But one way or other, we're going ahead with our plans. We are getting the surgeon, and then we are getting out of here."

"Of course," Chas said, not looking up as he polished the spotless podium.

This pep talk was so inspiring that the bleeders' next bout of moping about the church found them in better spirits than their Nanless rambling of that morning. Melody even found the initiative to play unstructured games with Pushka and her discomforting doll. And in an impoverished way, Melody's health was superior to her condition upon rising, for now she suffered less from that illness of optimism.

Before long, however, all the sensitives became enthralled; for as Pushka wiped Searle's mouth for the seventh time that day, the poor babbler became agitated, gasping loudly not for air, but for words. Nan recognized the problem.

"He's heard something important," she announced, and ran to a drawer where she rummaged for seconds, returning to the doktor's side with a chemamp she injected into struggling Searle's neck.

"He's trying to tell us, but just can't do it. Sometimes he can, sometimes he cannot," Nan described.

"Is that the stuff that nulls him?" Melody asked as Nan stood away from her patient.

"No, actually it intensifies the workings of certain

mind regions dealing with success-intent. Dok wants to speak on his own, and this chem helps him fulfill that desire."

"Why don't you use it more often?"

"Because it causes vomiting and high blood pressure. The way Dok needs to eat, he can't be vomiting, and his metabolic rates are too high even before this."

With his initial excitement, Searle had partially stood, trying to straighten, remaining half bent at the table. After Nan's injection, vigilant Pushka leaned forcefully on Searle's shoulders with soothing young words and all her adult weight until the doktor was seated again. And then he was also speaking.

After a few faltering attempts, Searle regained a clear voice, his agitation inverted, Dok speaking more slowly than usual, his words precise and loud. Nan termed this manner one of "accumulated significance." He was collating his own data.

"Telak goes to traffic court, pays fine with marked barter, wages for those suspected of being Anti, large amassment implying it was collected by some group, Telaks' background checked vis-à-vis Antis, previous record of suspicion now confirmed enough, Niklas and Ingot taken to Hagen, told to describe the Antis' org or Ingot will lose more pieces to be returned as ground bief. The Telaks fight well but realize imminent defeat; so arrange a bargain: fix the wife, let us run, and we'll tell you of the bleeders. Yes, Hagen says, yes. The bleeders live in Ideatown, Telaks managing to avoid details, no mention of the church, no association with preaching, because they are known only as farmers."

Searle then collapsed, Nan examining him. "Only asleep," she described, and told Pushka to have Chas carry the doktor to his bed. Thereafter, Nan began thinking. And Melody, always prepared for plotting brazen moves, helped her cogitate, asking:

"What do we do and how much time do we have to do it?"

"This is a big town, so we have opportunity to react properly. With over a hundred thousand residents and relatively few MELODIES, we're in no immediate danger. Still, reducing the plus-million population of the area to one locale is significant for MEL. Our biggest mistake would be to rush out and get caught on the outskirts. We have time to plan; so we should use it."

But Searle disagreed. From an exhausted sleep due to chemistry and exertion, Chas and Pushka still at his side, the doktor sat upright in bed as though thrust from a nightmare, sat up and shouted so that even Melody and Nan downsteps could clearly hear.

"Here comes the bomb!"

And then a whistling screeched their sky.

# CHAPTER 15:
## *Rash Aspect of Era*

They all looked up, then as suddenly down; but there was no place to hide, and no time. Nan and Melody met each other's eyes, sharing an instant look of resignation, as the whistling reached its orgasm of intensity, and the bomb exploded.

A direct hit on the church, they knew this at once, because the blast was in their midst, the noise ungodly in its volume, a sound to bypass the ear and crush hearing, this sense just as useless as sight because the erupting gases burned vision blind with a tactile light that seared the bleeders' minds, as overwhelming as the blasting concussion felt through the skin and bone and into every heart, smashing every lung, the experience so complete that Melody's final thought was not that they alone were dead, but surely all of Marz would be seared and burned and melted.

And then the blast was over. The smoke did not clear because there was no smoke. The dust did not settle because there was no dust. Only human senses settled and cleared, the sensitives astounded because they were still alive. And then, when they were able to see and hear and think again, the witches blinked to see that the world still existed, that the church still stood, that nowhere about them was there any damage. The damage was outside.

Downsteps, Nan and Melody were limp and looked disheveled, though not a cell was misplaced. Breathing roughly, erratically, rubbing their eyes and holding their ears, the women did nothing but recover. And then, a movement from behind, a shaken Chas and Pushka entering the sanctuary. All okay with them and Searle. And better with Nan, who began to think, and then to understand.

"Of course," she proclaimed, holding her head as though it were falling, "it's a *concept* bomb. What we experienced was the *idea* of a bomb, but there was no real blast or flash—the explosion was only an idea expressed by the device."

"Nan," Melody wheezed with evident dissatisfaction, "Hagen didn't go to the trouble of sending an airkraft just so he could scare us."

"But Melody," Pushka whined, "nothing happened to us, did it?"

"Something happened," Melody claimed, "but not to us, not directly to us," and she stepped toward the front doors.

Looking closely all about the interior as Melody moved away, Nan submitted, "Mel, I don't think the church has changed."

Opening one of the double doors a crack and peering through, Melody whispered to her friends as though something had exploded within and taken her breath.

"Maybe not—but everything else has!" and she pulled the door open wider so that all the sensitives could see.

Four heads peered through the doorway, looking out at a road, a dirt road. The edgewalk before the church was no longer seamless and artificial, but greyish-tan lumber, weathered and ill-fitting. Between dirt road and wooden walkway were skeletal post and lintel affairs. Down the street they saw not kars parked, but wagons, wagons pulled by horses—Erth horses—real horses which pawed the ground and whinnied, more horses tied to the wooden post constraints. And the buildings: none higher than two stories, and none made of plas or metal. Everything was wooden now, frame buildings with clapboard siding, the formerly plastick church also changed to this material. And the colors: limited to greys and white and tans, for these colors were only paint. Certainly the windows were glass, not plas, with painted signs in brighter colors than the walls reading, "Plover's General Store," instead of a perceptual barrage transmitting, "Hot eatstuffs for *you*!" More signs in antique, gilded lettering denoting, "Main Street Saloon" and "Elegant Ladies." And there were water troughs for the horses and weeds and grasses sprouting through the walkways' cracks. And, yes, there were people, people wearing greenjeans and flathats—horseboys! Horseboys as though from an Amerigan Eastern, the difference being that these boys looked around and saw nothing, blinked as though lost, and then understood, walking on with a horseboy's swagger seen in a thousand film-flams, some passing through swinging doors as though done a thousand times, one mounting a horse as though he owned it, one boy going on with his loading of that there wagon, grabbing sacks as though he knew all along persactly what he was up to. And of course, they all did. After that pause, they went on with their lives, and not a one behaved like a resident.

Pushka was absorbing every sight, the smell of horse droppings, the feel of dust raised by animal traffic wafting through the door. But the two other fems moved back inside, Nan astounded, Melody delighted.

"Nan, all it did was change the nature of things," Melody offered.

"Yes, yes," Nan said weakly, and Melody continued, active now in her thinking—unlike shaken Nan —and active in her speaking as well.

"Now Ideatown is just like a company town of a hundred years ago. Still the same basic idea, but the aspect of era was changed drastically."

"But why did the bomb do this?" Pushka asked, more curious than fearful as she continued to stare outside.

"It couldn't have worked the way they wanted it to," Nan stated, more settled now. "What could be the purpose of this?"

"I bet they never tested it on such a scale," Melody determined. "They just hoped it would do something else, but what did they expect? What did they want?"

A somber voice behind them said, "Us."

Nan agreed. Looking around to Chas for a moment, then over to Melody, she told them, "There's no question but that they wanted us sensitives. Since they affected everyone *except* us, obviously the bomb was a failure."

"Certainly they didn't want to change everyone in Ideatown," Melody ventured, Nan replying:

"No, they didn't. The Town may be weird, but it's useful to miners; so it's valuable to MEL."

"Then the bomb must have worked backward," Melody proposed. "I bet that Em Ee El wanted to affect only us, and expected everyone else to stay the same."

"Ideas worked on us before," Chas said, his unspecified reference to the bleeders' changes: his size, Pushka's gender, Searle's brain. Too-old Nan had an interpretation.

"The manner or nature of conceptual power as expressed by the concept surgeon altered us, but the Powerhouse's uncoalesced seepage does not."

"Because they're different, er, intellects, sort of," Melody ventured.

"Good assessment," Nan remarked. "There are different types of conceptual power just as there are different types of ideas, of intellects."

"And Em Ee El got the wrong one," Melody added.

"Perhaps," Nan submitted. "One thing we've known all along is that MEL's scientists need and want to learn more about concept power. They worked on us to learn more of AM's potential, to gain more understanding. Obviously with concept bombs they lack full control. Perhaps this was not only an assault, but an experiment."

"Will it last?" Melody asked. Then she compared the idea change of her trok when escaping the farmers to the bleeders' conceptual surgery: one temporary, the other permanent. Which would Ideatown be?

"I would guess temporary," Nan replied, "but for a different reason. It would take too much energy to hold the Town like this for long. Again: the point is that MEL wanted to change *us* permanently—not Ideatown, not the residents—and once you're killed, that lasts forever. If they could have increased our conceptual alterations enough, we might have become barely human, or dead."

After a group pause, Pushka whispered slyly, "Why didn't the church change?"

"Already old-fashioned," Chas said. "It fit this style."

"The outside is wood now," Melody mentioned. "I guess it changed enough to fit even better."

Finally the awed child/woman closed the door, moving inside to face her friends.

"What do we do now, Nan?" she whispered as though hiding her voice from the changes.

Having been lately peering through a front window, past the opaque curtain, Melody turned to the other sensitives to offer, "Why, I know exactly what to do. We take a stroll, partner."

"Now, Melody, calm down," Nan warned. "You're becoming overinterested again. Our clothes stayed the same, and we don't have any disguises to allow us to blend in. I'm certain MEL still has constables of some nature out there, and to be safe we have to assume they're looking for us."

"Maybe we're still wanted, but we'd be hard to get now, I bet," Melody presumed. "And I know the oddies are still out there because I just saw one," and she pointed down the street.

Everyone looked as Pushka slid the door open again. Down the block, headed their way, was a horseboy like any other, except this one wore a gon on his hip and a badje on his chest. His only business was looking around.

"No communiqué devices, and nothing to catch us with but that old gon," Melody reported.

Nan was astounded.

"*Melody*," she moaned, "that firehand is probably real, just as those horses are real. And if that gon functions, it shoots heavy-metal projectiles which kill people."

After an overdone expression of disbelief—as though pained to be dealing with a dimhead —Melody looked to Nan and scowled:

"Come *on*, Nan. How could a lousy antique gon stop us sophisticates—we're *conceptual* and everything."

"By blowing holes in our guts," Chas said.

"Those aren't real oddies anymore," Melody retorted, "they are *peace* officers. They wouldn't shoot us on first sight."

"No," the experienced Pushka described, "they holler out, 'Hold it, renegade!' and then they shoot us on sight."

The conversation continued in this manner until certain persons were prepared to throttle Melody. But then they all went silent, because Melody heard a sound.

"Listen!" she whispered harshly, and peered outside, peered upward. "I can hear this one coming."

They all could after Melody's observation. Since Ideatown was now a quiet burg, the plane was audible, a plane flying low blocks away, going past. But not far enough.

A glance to the airkraft, and the sensitives returned inside. Nan spoke.

"It may be the same plane. It's likely observing the results of the bombing. And probably a ground crew will be sent thereafter for closer observation."

But Melody was all apprehension as she stared only at Nan and disagreed.

"I don't think so," she said, speaking quietly but quickly, all these ideas. "They were rash dropping that bomb—too hasty, no planning. As soon as Telak told Hagen we were here, he dropped the bomb—he didn't even take time to get his own people out. And I have a feeling that Hagen is still rash. I have a feeling he'll—"

And a shrieking whistled throughout their sky.

They looked up, then down to one another. Then they could no longer see. The blast engulfed them totally, all their senses obliterated: a sound beyond noise beyond hearing which exploded their perceptions, their vision burned to blindness with a light so hot as to be tactile; and the feeling, the compression of normal air so dense against them that their blood and brains and bones were crushed thin as skin, the totality of the explosion's effects so perceptually, mentally destructive that the sensitives knew they experienced not war, but death.

And the blast was gone. As before, there was no settling of debris, of destruction, for none was evident within the church. And the people: they were still there, still alive. The difference was that although Melody's friends were still around her, in reality she was alone.

# CHAPTER 16:
## *Spreading South Marzgut*

The first thing she noticed was that Nan's hair was a new color, the concept behind this change obvious; for the color was grey, completely grey, because Nan was old. Her face was shriveled, shoulders stooped, Nan more frail than before, looking about with rheumy eyes that saw little, turning slowly left and right with the stiff moves of a person who's seen a century.

Pushka was certainly not shriveled, no more beautiful than before, but surely no less. And unlike Nan, who seemed confused, Pushka was babbling happily with words Melody could not understand, because children of this age—regardless of their figures—have not yet learned to speak. Nor walk, for the blast cleared and Pushka was sitting on the floor, playing with her breasts as though newfound toys, happy as she looked up because her friends were near.

Pushka was closest to Melody, Nan two steps removed; but yards away was Chas, having collapsed on an unchanged pew. This one looked ill, Melody running toward him. Even before nearing she noticed how his nature had been altered: normally massive, later thin but strong, now emaciated, bones showing in his arms, cheeks sunken as though he were starving. Chas looked upward, straight to the ceiling, as Melody bent over him.

"Chas, Chas, are you all right?"

He was breathing strangely: weak inhalations, strong, voluminous exhalations, blinking normally and barely able to speak.

"Weak," he said, voice so soft, but not meant to be a whisper. "Feel okay, just can't move . . . nothing." Literally too weak to move, Chas nonetheless concluded by telling Melody, "Okay. I'm . . . okay."

Generous Chas perhaps overstated his condition; but still, did he not seem adequate? He wasn't bleeding or choking. Whatever aid he ultimately required, Melody could not provide. All she could do was squeeze his bony shoulder and try not to gasp, try not to jerk her hand away, because no one likes to touch a skeleton. Just stay near her friend and agree: "Okay, Chas," she told him. "Okay."

Nan sat, almost creaking as she lowered herself to the pew near Chas, looking at her sometimes loveher to croak in an ancient voice, "Don't I know you, son?"

She didn't know much, Nan looking about quizzically, recognizing nothing in the church, though nothing had changed. No help for them, Melody thought, then realized what she should be doing: Dr. Searle was upsteps alone.

There were two restrooms in the church, one for the preacher's family, one with a row of four beds for indigents. The fem bleeders used the latter, Chas and Dok the pastor's. (Nan and Chas did not sleep together on this Marz; it just wasn't the same.) Entering the boys' restroom, Melody found Searle on the larger, broader bed. At once she knew something was wrong, because he seemed unchanged. Moving nearer, she could hear quiet words coming more slowly than before—was this the only difference?

As Melody stood beside him, looking down, the doktor turned to her, eyes focused nowhere as usual, though they seemed to glow. Were his irises lighter now? Unable to discern any blatant physical change, Melody asked:

"Are you all right, Doktor?"

He pointed to his mouth, a normal signal which Melody recognized, one given Pushka often.

"Are you hungry?"

He nodded.

"Any other problems?"

Unfortunately Melody received another gesture she understood. Dok pointed to his waist, pointed lower.

"You have to go to the drainroom, don't you?"

Nod.

"Oh, good," Melody muttered, "that is so good."

She helped him stand. He was heavy. Searle could walk on his own, but slowly, erratically, Melody with an arm firmly around him regardless. With Dok's mouth so near, Melody could distinguish those new sounds, Searle making noises as though imitating machines. And his slower words seemed to be both parts of a conversation. Melody could not study this, however, at the drainroom now, taking Searle inside while thinking: Treat him like a child; you had to help babies in the nursery years ago, remember?

In a coup of problem attacking, Melody unfastened Dok's pant and without pause pulled it to his knees. She didn't remember seeing anything like this in the nursery: the broad expanse of pale skin split by a cleft with hair; and when she turned him around with soothing words, certainly nothing here had she direct knowledge of, not on this level, and Melody wanted none for the future: no husband, loveher, family, not ever, a firm decision on Melody's part as she thought: I hate this, I hate this. But she said nothing unkind, only, "Sit down, Dok," not wanting to embarrass the man; for she knew that most of his mind still functioned perfectly.

His internal cleansing systems worked equally well; for as he sat, Dok released volumes of noisily rushing solid material, a bit of gaseous product, and a stream of urine to fill the drainpot, Melody then reaching not the end of her ordeal, but the climax, the worst part of all.

She had to wipe him.

Although not through with her coup, Melody hesitated. She looked down. Most upsetting were not the man's draping gender portions, but his thighs spread on the seat like water animals out of their habitat. Melody was out of hers. Still, time had come for another decisive move, Melody reaching for the kraphersheet roll, firmly telling Dok to stand. Just as he cleared the seat, she reached beneath him with a handful of sheets so that her skin would not meet his skin, his materials; and she moaned, unavoidably, sensing warmth and wetness.

Drop it in, hit the box's drain, jerk up the doktor's pant, and guide him back to his room after washing her hands twice. Melody was trying to be pleasant, and was pleased to be leaving, but there he was pointing to his mouth again, and Melody became depressed.

"I'll fix something, then come back and get you," Melody told him as quickly as possible, voice flat, and left the room, no more pleasantries, wanting to get away.

Incredible, incredible: Melody realized she had to go downsteps and take care of the rest of them. And even more incredible: she would have to take care of them all constantly. Nan, although senile, was probably the most self-reliant; for Pushka was a baby, and Chas could not move a bone. How was she supposed to rear all these former semi-normals and figure how to end this crazy concept situation simultaneously?

"You okay, Chas?"

"Yes."

"I bet you're uncomfortable on that hard pew."

"Okay."

She did not believe him. Standing by his side, Melody looked down to stiff Chas, looked at those clothes so loose on his body that he seemed covered with rags. He must have weighed seventy-five pounds *Erth*. Most bizarre of all was her next realization, that Chas now weighed less than she. And Melody knew what to do.

"I'm taking you upsteps, Chas."

"Okay . . . here," he said, speaking slowly because each word was an effort, each syllable work. "Don't . . . bother."

She reached beneath him and lifted. Chas weighed nothing, not fifty pounds Marz, clothes like a sheet. At the vet's one year, Melody had carried heavier dogs. But this was no dog—this was her friend.

"Oh, God, you poor sweetheart," she whispered, nearly choking. Realizing such sentiment would embarrass Chas, Melody swallowed that pitying tone and

told him plainly, "No problem, Chas." Then she
turned to carry him away. But Nan had to argue.

"Just a moment, young lady—where are you going
with that man? Bring him back and take care of your
baby. Can't you hear her crying?"

Yes, she could hear. Evidently Pushka had been
frightened by the sight of Melody's carrying this stick
figure in rags.

Deal with her later. Move quickly to the hall, up the
steps, place Chas next to Searle on the bed, kiss him
on the forehead, Dok sounding worse, pointing to his
mouth with both hands at the first sight of Melody as
received words kept rolling from him, another promise to feed him—but nicer now, since she'd kissed
poor Chas in poor Dok's vicinity—run for Pushka's
horrible doll, downsteps to the baby-woman, hug and
soothe her till the pitiful, pitiful tears stopped and the
grown-up face smiled sweetly, doll in hand, run past
crab Nan demanding Melody's identity, her own
location, the cause for her situation and nature thereof, into the cookroom to dig everywhere, find enough
crusts to last Searle a meal but none for the rest of
them, none for further meals.

Run upsteps. Chas okay. Guide Dok to the
dineroom. As Melody guessed, guiding him
downsteps was easier than moving Nan anywhere
who griped each step as she was led into the dineroom
until Melody finally convinced her that she needed to
quit worrying so much about herself and help her
friend. You must remember Dr. Searle, don't you?

"I . . . think so," Nan replied as she looked to the
seated physician. "I ought to remember my own
friends."

"Good, because this is one of them."

"But I don't remember . . . you," she told Melody, pointing an old finger at her with that final word.

"That's all right, because you're not feeding me."

Onto the table with a cup of water and the crusts, nothing else to drink, to eat. Instructions on how to feed him—small bites—Nan replying with annoyance that she knew how to *feed* someone: she wasn't a baby. The baby was out there crying—can't you hear her?

Yes, yes, Melody could hear her. Run back to Pushka, who was old enough to say, "Lonely, lonely . . . ," Melody having to carry her into the foodroom and set her on the floor next to Nan, a frightening job because Pushka was a hundred thirty pounds Erth if she was an ounce, eighty Marz, and Melody had to grunt to lift her, moan to carry Pushka, and grunt and moan and strain to lower her to the floor without breaking her own back or smashing Pushka, but the baby was satisfied to look up to Melody and coo, "Mama, mama . . ."

This was enough to make Melody ill, worse than carrying her. Silently she staggered away to be alone from them all, flopping out of sight on a pew, but she could still hear Nan griping at Dok not to eat so fast—You're choking; what are you, a baby? *That's* the baby; you can tell because she just wet the floor.

No moving, not a bone, Melody just like Chas. Why me? she thought, and had a rational answer which offered no comfort, Melody aware she had not been altered by the bomb because she had never undergone conceptual surgery as had the other sensitives. And perhaps Nan had been correct when telling the Antis about Melody's being uniquely valuable. But what of Searle? Melody was certain that he had also changed, but in accord with the rest, in accord with his initial conceptual modifications. And since Dok's changes had been re language/communication centers, surely the latest alteration was in his head, where Melody couldn't see it, not on his body where she had to clean it up.

Practical, practical, got to do pragmatic stuff before I theorize, Melody thought. No time for rest. Got to clean the damn baby's fat azz, then get food else Dok will expire in hours. If his head is more active deep inside, he'll need even more eats than before, Melody guessed. And how do I get grosheries? I don't even know what kind of monies they use on this Marz. Then Melody realized she did not know what Marz this was, what with the latest bombing.

Drag herself to the door. Look out. Same horsetown. People moving about on this quiet end, slow wagons, clomping horses. The general store, old man Plover's, that's where she needed to go—with no monies. What about barter? What did she have to trade? Melody wondered what she could get for the downsteps factingrate: a pound of biens and a cup of flowr? But Melody decided she would worry about that after she made it to the store, but this might not be easy, for Melody did not fit in this burg. No clothes which looked right. No placket shirts, no buttuns or snapps. No tight leg pants of natural fiber, only ugly red plastick. But so what? she decided. What'll they do—shoot me for looking strange?

Probably, for as she opened the door to move out, a kar passed by, an Em Ee El auto with an oddie inside.

Melody stood still in the doorway. No use jumping. Too late, but the odd had not seen her, Melody thinking: What in the universe is that contemporary vehicle doing here? But, of course, the world had not changed, just this area, just Ideatown; and Hagen was sending troops to check his success.

Thinking, thinking . . . Good time to run, because he's gone. Quickly outside, look both ways, wagons about but the single kar out of sight, run across the dust which for an instant horrified Melody, not because of the danger, but because she recalled her own Marz, that empty Marz and her empty life, but a full and rich, wonderful world only forty million miles away. But here, removed by infinity, by forever. And the dusty street reminded her of another road, one down which she had been led to a burning.

Melody ran, ran as though fleeing the area she traversed, as though fleeing her recollections. Enough thinking, enough feeling, all empty everywhere within except for her procedure spot, that place always filled with going on. Run to the opposite walkway, left to the intersection, down the street with Plover's, past the Marzian Assay Office and the miners with shiny rock samples. On the hard boards, to the door she couldn't open until learning the round thing had to be turned, not pulled—a flash of stealing that trok—and inside.

People there giving her funny looks right away as Melody stepped in, though she was dressed for parts outside Ideatown. But not this far outside. She was wearing a tight pant, but needed a full dress like this woman telling her man to quit staring, ain't polite; and they moved to another row of shelves piled with new-old goods, like an antique display. Bold Melody walked past a man studying a rake who dropped it upon spying her, but not a blink from Melody because this was expected, not a pause as she walked to the low counter, nicked wood stained with scratches and oils, walked to an older couple behind it who stared at her real hard.

Melody did not know this man from any world, but the woman was called Nuri on her Marz. With difficulty, Melody stopped herself from grabbing metal she did not carry, as the presumed Mrs. Plover spoke.

"Ooo-eee, girl, you must be one of them foreigners," and Melody agreed.

"Yes, I'm from . . . South Amarziga."

The wifey then added with a homey smile, "And what can we do for a little foreign girl today?"

"My friend is starving," Melody told them both earnestly. "I need something for him to eat."

"Why sure," Nuri purred pleasantly. "We've always got victuals for a hungry hair-brown alien—as long as she's got money."

"I have no monies," Melody admitted.

"Then you better find a friend who already ate," Nuri announced, she and Hubby laughing mildly, looking to each other with down-home idiocy.

Melody was glancing to the kash register, sacks on the floor and on shelves, wondering how to go about stealing something, thinking of coming back at night, but Searle would be starved by then. She was ready to come forth with more of her artistic words when a tall horseboy with chips and spars sauntered to the counter. Setting down the box he was buying, the horseboy looked to Melody, looked all the way down her and all the way back up. Even with a flathat and no face hair, this man was known, Melody recognizing Seitz, the human pinch artist.

"I might be able to get you some money there, little

lady," he offered with a horse drawl, and paid the Plovers for his purchase.

"And what would I owe you?" Melody asked, having heard similar lines from him before, in another outfit, on another world. But she knew that subtle changes had occurred Marz to Marz, knew by Seitz' eventual reply.

"What do you got?" he asked, Melody responding with an even tone, looking him right in the eye.

"Nothing but gratitude."

After a pause, still looking the little foreigner up and down, Seitz decided. "I'll take it," and he flipped Melody a tarnished coin, taking his box, out the door.

She was going to stop him and say, "Thank you; isn't your name Seitz?" How gracious this would have been, but how foolish to look deeply enough to find the Seitz she knew. Melody took her money, and let him leave.

Confidently she turned to the owners and dropped the coin on the counter. As it rattled around and settled, Melody ordered.

"I want some basic food, real nutrients. Something I don't have to cook."

"Don't have to cook?" Nuri pronounced incredulously. "You people from South Marzgut eat raw beens or something?"

Deciding she needed to get at this era, Melody changed her verbal tack.

"Fruit," she tried. "What do you folk have in the way of fruit?" speaking with a fake horseboy tone, trying to look as though she'd be a-sauntering at any moment.

"Well, we got your peeches and your abbles," the

man said, vocal now that kash was on the line.

"Well, mister," Melody sauntered, "gimme what you can outen that, and leave me a little change so I can come back and spend it in this here fine establishment tomorrowday."

Melody hoped she sounded as stupid as these two quasi-humans; but they weren't impressed, Nuri looking on with remnants of her laughter, a potential chuckle as she studied Melody's clothes, the hub filling a medium basket from big bins, handing Melody a smaller, duller coin and her purchase, the foreigner out the door, and good day.

Look left and right. No oddies. Run across the street, down an adjacent alley, *then* backtrack to the church so no one could place her there and come a-looking.

Into the church, back door, to the dineroom. Ignore Nan with her questions and complaints about leaving the wet baby, care for Pushka after placing the basket before Nan the granny and telling her to feed the one sticking both hands toward his mouth. Step to baby.

"Wet, wet . . .," Pushka cried softly, looking up to Melody, sprawled on the floor clasping dolly.

"Yes, wet, wet but not lonely," Melody offered as she knelt beside Pushka to hold her and pat those poor, sobbing shoulders, soothing words as she pressed her flat on her back, pulled her pant off, sop up the puddle with cookroom rags. Run upsteps for a clean pant, down to calmer Pushka—who cares about undies—ignore Nan wondering what kind of mother Melody could be to stuff a rag against her baby's crotch, pull on the pant, sit her up in a corner away from the damp spot, this one better to work on than

Searle, girls being neater here, all of a piece, no loose parts for entanglement, hair less coarse than Dok on Pushka's bottom or in Melody's imagination, drag her to a corner away from the damp spot, and:

"Will you please just feed the doktor and be quiet for a moment!" then pat the baby, preclude her crying from the shout before running upsteps to Chas after washing her hands twice.

"Okay, okay," but Melody wondered.

Walk downsteps, not such a hurry, Searle still eating, don't listen to Nan, the baby playing with her detestable doll and a peech pit, not trying to eat the latter, just skid it across the floor, ignore Nan, Dok adequate sitting upright for a while, feed everyone later fresh fruit, Melody stranded in a hopeless state just as she was becoming used to the last, semirational domestic situation; but with a new Marz every minute, what's a girl to do?

To the pastor's study, some shelves and a desk but the best chair in the building, collapse there but leave the door open to hear Nan and Searle running on so differently, so equally, hear the baby giggle; but, please, no tears. On and on this way through the afternoon when a knocking came at the door.

Almost night. Melody was trying to explain to the two babies—Nan and Pushka—that either they eat the abbles or starve. She had just returned from taking Dok to the drainroom, then Chas, who insisted on being alone there. ("Certain, Chas?" "Certain.") Somehow he managed to get out of and back into his clothing, prop himself upright with the skinniest limbs, and later knock for Melody to retrieve him.

"Sorry you have to carry . . .," he began, unable to

say "me," unable to speak further, breathing okay, but as for strength: no strength whatsoever.

"As long as I don't have to do it when you're big again," Melody smiled.

"Whe—" he tried.

"When? As soon as possible. We'll be back to normal as soon as possible, Chas," she promised, trying to be convincing, but Melody wasn't fooled.

She dragged the pastor's gigantic chair into the sanctuary near the cookroom-hallway juncture, placing Chas there, for he preferred to be near his friends rather than alone. Even with Nan's babbling? Ye—

And a knocking at the door. The front, double doors.

Melody's alarm was minor; she guessed the oddies would not knock. Running to the window and peering out onto the walkway, there she saw a pack of residents; that is, citizens. A pack of fine citizens dressed in their best attire, perhaps every woman in town —no longer tremendous fatties—each with a man, fine bonnets and crisp jackets, Melody realizing the situation, but not wanting to think about it as she opened the door.

Smiling uncertainly, Melody greeted them.

"Good evening."

"Ooo-eee, it's the little foreign alien," someone called out from the back, someone Melody ignored.

"And what can I do for you folks?" she tried.

The nearest woman—not much older than Melody, but even post-bomb much bulkier—replied for the group.

"Why, we've come for evening services."

This was the concept Melody had avoided: now

that Ideatown had changed to fit the church, so had the people. But the human word artist had something to say.

"Oh, didn't the pastor tell you? He took his family and left because of a desperate and ungodly situation at his folks' home and won't be back today and has rescheduled services and it was so sudden and desperate he probably didn't have time to tell you all everything."

"He rescheduled services?" someone from the pack's middle inquired.

"I believe so," Melody answered.

"He rescheduled *Sonday*?"

She had no reply for that one, the next query coming before Melody could form a decent pause.

"And who is it you may be?"

"We're a poor family from out of town the Telaks took in to help with Xian aid, and we're trying to maintain the building until they return."

There were so many citizens that as a whole they did not need to think, someone always ready with a response.

"Where's the rest of your family?"

"They're inside and everyone's sick."

"I'm a doctor," a man offered, "maybe I should look at them."

"We have no monies."

"Maybe tomorrow."

They did not believe her. On and on the conversation went until Melody opened the doors wide and told everyone to come on in as she backed inside.

"Look around all you want," she said unpleasantly. "Go ahead, accuse an Xian girl of lying." Then she stomped off to the cookroom as though upset, returning with a backache and Pushka in her arms.

The citizens were about to infiltrate the premises until they saw tiny Melody carrying the big woman who was blubbering and spitting from her two-year-old mouth. Then they backed off.

"I don't know what my sister has, but I hope the doktor can tell me it's not spreading. Yes, Doktor?"

Reverse for the entire pack, away from the door, some saying nicely they'd be back when the pastor returned, one broad whispering to another, "The devil is in that girl!" Melody wondering which girl she meant.

Down with Pushka to the floor, Melody telling her about this new game: dragging baby by the armpits back to the dineroom and Nanny, Pushka loving it, Melody not so pleased because the baby needed changing again, and Nan was first to notice, notice also that Melody was a terrible mother, had no right with a child or—

On with this routine until nightfall, Melody thankful for mild weather, not having to battle heat spells or cold fronts. She was not so grateful for darkness, however, because Ideatown had changed, Melody noticing flickering lights in buildings down the street; but the church was still concept-powered, all the little tubes empty, the building too close to the idea expressed around it to have changed but superficially. Melody inferred trouble here, what with her people used to being awake a bit into the night. But her people were no longer the same, were they? Melody presuming Nan would fuss at the terrible mother's having no illumination, Chas not minding, Dok too busy on his own, and the baby—who knows? Only real babies go to bed early.

Her difficulties with the darkness were not so pervasive, however, Melody going upsteps to resting Chas and buzzing Searle to see a sight in the hall which frightened her: something on fire in their room, something electronically ablaze as seen in the no-longer-dark corridor. A cool product, fearful Melody moving into the restroom to see that bright Searle was making a light of his own.

# CHAPTER 17:
## A Service for Her Person

She wanted to watch the program, but it was coming too fast to comprehend, exactly as fast as Searle's words, exactly equal; for now on the ceiling were scenes to match his speaking, visual images—as though video—projected through his eyes.

The effect was bizarre, Melody looking down to Dok, whose face was seen in the halation from his eyes' projection. This dim illumination—visible only in total darkness—revealed buzzing lips Melody could hear, the subtly strangest eyes she had ever seen: fully open pupils, irises like mineral, all normal but for the lighting, the projected rays, thus completely strange.

Searle seemed rested, relaxed as possible considering his metabolism, and Melody wondered whether he was enjoying the show, rapid scenes flashed one to the next: architecture, the edge of the Powerhouse with people moving to—, a smaller, metal-coated room with two people removing—, MELODIES lined along a wall, erect in their uniforms as they listened to—, huge devices in a low-ceilinged;

217

lonnnng hall with crackling mechanics that—, and on and on.

Melody's neck was breaking. She had entered just as Searle was settling, his eyes projecting through the doorway. He was still now, supine on the bed, face aimed at the ceiling. But having to crane her head up to view the show was crippling Melody, though she had sat on the bed's edge. Rubbing the back of her neck, she turned to Searle and requested:

"Dok, can you look at the wall so I can see better?"

As Searle began to shift his shoulders, Melody could tell he needed help, and moved nearer to adjust his pillow. Then Dok seemed comfortable again, and his "vision" was broadcast against the wall. Until he settled, his paired projections flashing around the room were an eerie sight, as though visual spies searching in the dark for the proper surface to examine.

Just as Melody relaxed on the bed's edge next to Searle, she heard the baby crying. Carefully downsteps without breaking the sore neck or spitting from exasperation. Earlier, Melody had opened all the window blinds to allow the light of Phoebe and Desmond to enter, enough moon illumination to afford safe passage once downsteps and out of the windowless upper corridor. Soothe the baby —"Scared, dark . . ."—change her everwet bottom blind, stumble against the table, wash her hands once, Melody hitting her head on the cupboard, not enough moonlight after all for a busy mother, Nan all the while turning every wall switch on and off, off and on, then going through each drawer and compartment in the church, looking for candles, matches, handlights

—anything, anything to drive Melody insane since each new search through the latest drawer was accompanied by complaints and queries which Melody tried but failed to ignore.

Carry the huge baby upsteps, and this was nearly Melody's demise, broken everything, every muscle and bone, drop her and the doll between Dok and depleted Chas, now-happy Pushka cuddling against the latter with difficulty since he was a stick, thrilled nonetheless at the light scenes, adequate Chas unconcerned with the program.

Melody may have forgotten something, but she wasn't certain, wasn't worried. Since a sliver of space her size was available between the bed's edge and Dok, there she lay, head on a pillow. She tried to watch Searle's transmissions, hoping for vital revelations, but Melody fell asleep. Just before the sore, exhausted girl lost consciousness, some realization about specific, paining scenes struck her, but the awareness was lost in sleep. Woke minutes later from some old lady poking her with a terribly stiff finger.

". . . Won't even turn the lights on for me? You know I don't see well, but you leave me in the dark by myself. Well, can't you answer? Can't you answer, girl? I would like you to explain why you're up here having fun but didn't invite me. I called and called but you wouldn't even help me up the steps. I don't know how long it took me to get—"

"Will you please shut up!" Melody shouted, going stiff as a stick, limbs rigid as she hollered at the old biddy. "Nan, I want you to go over there and sit down or lie down or something and *be quiet, please*!"

Melody assumed she would have looked odd to a

normal person viewing this, snapping out orders as her legs flailed, an arm thrown left to point the direction, still flat as stitching on the spread. But there was no one normal to notice. Only Nan, and she complied, sitting primly in a chair by the bedside, unimpressed with Melody's display.

The baby was whining. Frightened by Melody's big mouth. Now Melody scowled more quietly.

"Nan, you better find some way to shut that baby up. She's a thirty-year-old man with tids who whimpers and pees on the floor, and I'm tired of it for a while. And Chas, don't you say a word about trying to be nice—because I am not nice," she snarled, and threw her arms across her chest, her quaking ended again.

Since Melody was still half asleep, she proceeded to awaken before doing any further screaming. Nan was talking nicely to the baby, who had calmed, enjoying the show with Granny. Smart Chas was doing nothing but resting. Realizing she had done her people wrong, bad-tempered Melody apologized.

"I'm sorry, everyone—dammit," she grumbled, then went silent again.

For a long moment thereafter, Melody enjoyed being settled, enjoyed hearing and feeling her deep, regular breathing, as though her lungs were fine instruments performing a vital service for her person. Then the images on the wall became important once more, Melody trying to focus, to understand. This was difficult, however, for the images were again unsteady.

So was the bed, this shaking due to Searle's heavy pointing toward his mouth; and now, his elbow bumping Melody. Just when she was figuring the plot. And, yes, this was exactly the case, Melody recalling her impressions before falling asleep, recalling significance.

People. People seated around a tiny table, their knees perhaps touching below. A table in a well-lit room which Melody had seen before in selective darkness. The Board table, the Board of Marzian Energy Limited. This was the scene Melody had almost noticed before falling asleep. She noticed now. And Melody knew that if the Board were in session, then Hagen was present.

Another awareness: the visual images were not in natural time, for Melody had seen daylight scenes alternately with those of dusk or dawn. Concentrating on the whole experience now, leaning close to Searle to listen, Melody determined that his speaking did fit the images, and thus had been changed by the bomb. His voice had literally changed from the pre-bomb era, for now it matched whoever was speaking in the projected scenes; and when there was no speech, Searle was imitating the ambient sounds: machines, vehicles, sliding doors, shuffling feet, silent spaces. Dok was no longer conveying received communiqués as before. Now he was intercepting experience; for there was no kamera work involved, Searle relaying the sights of other people, projecting on the wall exactly what MEL employees saw with their own eyes. And Melody was aware this was not just one person's sights, for the locales were too disparate—who could be everywhere? But she was having a problem here, trying to study and think while being jostled by Searle. Displeased Melody described her position.

"Dok, if you don't quit stabbing me with that thing, I'm going to let you starve," she hissed, trying to localize her anger, her voice, trying to keep it on her side of the bed, Melody twitching with stiff limbs again.

Then she changed. Relaxing in her body but not the mind, Melody turned to Searle, who still rumbled, still pointed to his mouth. And Melody decided to try a new tactic which was either psichology or cruelty.

"No, Doktor, I am going to let you starve. Everybody is a baby around here, but Chas is the only one who's trying. Pushka can't help it, but I'm about to smack Nan. And I am going to let you starve."

Agitated Searle began throwing his conical projections from corner to floor, all that pointing.

"I think you can do something except eat and pee," Melody continued. "I know it's hard with all that krap running through your head, but I think it's about time you did something for the group besides eat all our abbles."

She could sense his skin go clammy. His breathing became proper for the baby beside him. Now that Melody had thrown him into the raging torrent, she dangled the rope of salvation nearby.

"Look, Dok, I have these wonderful, ripe peeches standing at the ready, but you have to cooperate. You have to show me something better. I want to see on that wall something to get us out of these predicaments. I want to see the Em Ee El scientists doing whatever we need to get ourselves changed back, or something about Hagen and his next moves —anything except the stupid oddies changing shifts and the refrigeration units at the Powerhouse. Your clanking machinery imitations are the worst I've ever heard. I want to see something that will tell us where to go and how. And I think you can do it, if you only try hard enough. Or I think you can starve," and she turned away, staring at the wall, waiting.

Searle tried. His projections settled but for a slight trembling from his effort, his intensity. Then the images began flickering faster until they were a blur. Like some machine seen earlier, Searle huffed little vibratory breaths in and out, faster, his lips spitting nothing Melody could understand, light brighter, faster, Melody becoming worried, hoping Dok would not explode, hoping she had not gone too far, not forced him into newrosis, rapid Searle increasing all his rates, increasing everywhere until . . .

The projection stabilized. Searle no longer buzzed, steady himself, powerful, slowwww breathing, his sound effects the slightest breeze, for the scene was outside. An ore patch, huge, not unlike the one Melody had appeared in. The crop was shorter here, earlier in the growing season, and early in the day, the sun low; long, soft shadows of the ore crop's stalks. The view was a farmer's, evidently; for the vision was down, toward the crop, back and forth, row to row, Searle doing poorly with the sound of the man's feet plodding on the moist soil.

The farmer walked on, his examination cursory. Then, a peripheral catch, a sight at the edge of his vision, the farmer looking up and over to see . . . a ghost. A ghost rows away, a ghost turning solid. There before his eyes was a man appearing, a nude man, Searle imitating the farmer's rapid, frightened breathing as he watched a creature turn from ephemeral ghost to solid person. A person certainly as frightened as this farmer, the ghost solidifying to look around, look directly at the farmer with dread. And the farmer stared back, stared fearfully at the solid ghost before turning to run from future Prime Chairhume Josef Hagen.

# CHAPTER 18:
## *Bright Demise*

Dumbfounded Melody stared at the wall as the image thereupon began shaking again. She began shaking again, for Searle was coming out of his reverie, back to mouth-pointing and Melody-elbowing. Before Dok could become established in his insistent requesting, Melody left her own reverie, closing her mouth and looking away from the running farmer. She turned to Searle and promised:

"One more good one. Come on, Dok. That was only a few seconds. One more good show to help us all and I go for the abbles. Juicy peeches just one show away," and she turned from him, looking toward the wall, determined to ignore his begging.

After one giant twitch of either anger or frustration, Searle returned to his previous routine of rapid, choppy breaths, projections increasing in rate to a blur, the doktor finally settling along with his broadcast, depicting a new scene. This was an odd sight, for the view was of a person watching a vid viewer. The see-screen displayed the interior of a different room. Sophisticated devices there, measuring gear, illumination, other instruments. Looked medikal to Melody. The kamera's view was of a reclining woman, a patient evidently, what with the instruments near and/or connected to her, a woman familiar to Melody for two reasons: because she was known from another Marz, and because she behaved like Searle.

Since both were witches, Melody had a warm feeling for this fem even before gaining recognition. Hair brown here but greying blond on Melody's Marz, middle-aged, short—the Management person who had virtually attacked the Sueedes: Dr. Deign. And here was another sensitive changed conceptually. Pushka, regardless of her normal maleness on other worlds, certainly made an extraordinary girl. And this woman seemed quite successful as a human communication device, Melody recognizing her uneven-eyed expression, lax face with fast-talking lips characteristic of Searle in his average altered state. In her room, Dr. Deign was alone; but in the room of the see-screen were at least two persons; for the viewer was speaking, Melody catching the end of a sentence, Searle imitating an unknown voice.

". . . entire reversal, so that the communications received are only those chosen by us. And more important, that they be processed by the brain's intent-centers of desperation and become not information, but orders, as though of survival. Without exterior evidence, we have been processing this appearee as she lies. To even a close observer, her conceptually altered nature is as before, when in fact we have been bombarding the mind with data whose special rechanneling is allowed only because that brain was idea-modified beforehand. Since the subject is adequately prepared, I will now demonstrate using one of our people who remains uninformed so as not to render the experiment invalid."

By then a second person had entered Dr. Deign's room, a young man, evidently an attendant in that he proceeded to check gauges, examine the patient, talk nicely. Then the viewer turned away from the screen, looking to more total tech gear on a table. He next spoke to some device there.

"Without delay, leap over to strangle the person nearest you dead."

Without delay, Dr. Deign jumped from the bed, dragging wires and tubes, to throw herself against the attendant. Her force was so great, her move so rapid, that Deign allowed her victim no opportunity for reaction, for defense. At once she had an arm hooked about the man's throat, pulling with deadly force, her other hand locking that stranglehold on the victim. Such activity should not come from any type of doktor.

Melody's view was interrupted not by Searle or the subjects shown, but by the real Marz about her. She was wrenched from her total absorption by a bright light coming through the now unclad window which overcame Searle's projection. Melody last saw the attendant turning colorless, gasping not for air, but for survival. Then her attention was again in Ideatown, and was more than visual; for accompanying the flickering, irregular light was a sound, a noise: people, people hollering unpleasantly. And the light was that of a fire.

"What in the world have you done now?" Nan began, but Melody ignored her, rushing at once from the room, downsteps and to the appropriate window.

She was glad to get away, even if it meant facing fire, for Searle's show had been devastating. Not upsetting:

fictional depictions of murder are upsetting, but Searle was showing reality, real death, and Melody could not bear the experience. With Deign's first grasp of the attendant, Melody had literally looked for an ending to the display or a savior for the man; but she had found only genuine revelation, a program of killing that seemed enough to kill. She was glad to run away.

Not bothering to even glance through an upsteps window, Melody had hurried down to be closer to the cause of this new problem, to be away from Searle and his horror. On the ground floor, she saw bright lights coming through every pane, the voices louder, Melody looking out to see hundreds of people carrying torches—organic matter burning on sticks' ends. And the sound was tactile, having a depth and thickness to give it spacial substance, the sound of scores of angry individuals. As the crowd neared, some of their words became discernible, certain phrases, chants to Gahd about giving strength, about burning the devil out, burn the witches . . .

This last was enough to paralyze her. As though in a second life, Melody relived the feelings on the ore farms when she had nearly been burned as a witch, felt the terror, smelled the flames. And she was stricken cold and hot and lifeless a moment before she could begin breathing again, begin thinking, wishing for Searle's displayed phenomenon of death rather than her own experience.

Doors locked? Yes, she had checked this before nightfall. Would that stop them? With the first bomb, the windows had turned to glass, breakable glass, and now the building was sheathed in genuine wood, no longer a plastick imitation. The citizens' anger pressed through the windows like light, Melody peering out to realize she would soon discover what would stop them, how far they would go. Melody was about to experience their anger, not watch it on some wall.

Of course she had to act. She knew that waiting for the conflagration was unacceptable. If Melody had the ability to act, then she had the need to act—and what a choice: waiting for the flames or attacking them.

The mob had collected by the church's entrance. Without further deliberation, Melody walked to the front doors. The small, empty sanctuary seemed huge to her, then instantly tiny, the distance to be crossed nothing, one step, one breath required. And then size seemed nonexistent, all the flames and shouts outside convincing Melody—eyes and mind—that there was no space, no separation, that she was amongst the crowd; and though she was walking, she was not walking toward them or away, but with them to her funeral pyre.

This no-space feeling proved correct, for without evident duration, Melody was at the door. And then she seemed detached from her body, observing her moves as though one of Searle's projections, looking down at this foolish person standing at the door through choice, a ridiculous hand reaching for the latch intentionally. But in a complete conceptual change as though mandated by AM influence, as soon as the door opened, Melody's body was instantly filled with her consciousness, and there she was, inches from the flames again.

A wave of silence moved from person to person as each noted her. Somewhere the impression, the implication existed that Melody would be the wide-eyed innocent before them, the little girl come to plead her

moral case. But as she opened the door, Melody
—whole with her body again—became certain of this
person and certain of her move, stepping out with a
slow and eerie firmness, the idea of her expression
—that trace of a smile—one the crowd could not
comprehend.

As though looking at each of them, yet looking to
none, Melody spoke, voice as odd as her demeanor,
no longer a hint of humor within a universe of her life.

"You cannot burn the devil," she averred with a
small tone, the size of each flame before her and
equally hot, "but you can burn his house. Burn this
house, if you will, and have the devil move. Have him
move into your children and your bellies. Leave the
devil here, or I promise you will take him along."

Then she turned, reentering the church, and left the
door open. Walking steadily inside, steadily away, her
pace was a lie, her manner deception, the only honesty within her a prayer for none of the super-religious
outdoors.

"Please, God, please don't let them burn my
friends . . ."

As though hearing her silent thoughts, a voice from
the crowd—as though the voice of the crowd
—screamed out behind her.

"Don't burn the church, no! Burn that *gahddamn*
witch!"

And the crowd exploded, erupting in the fire of
impassioned hatred, every one of these devil's friends
moving toward the door, one hand of each pair
reaching out for Melody, the second holding her
bright demise. And then the world about her burst
into light.

Cold light. Quiet light. Ideatown's constant lights

again blazed outside, the horseboys within now returned to residents, each torch a handlight that would burn nothing. And the residents were silent for a moment, standing still in their ugly clothes to look between their bodies and the building, look at the handlight each held, trying to justify the combination. And quickly the one unacceptable oddity of this scene overcame them, again a single voice crying out for the entire crowd.

"Who dragged us into this *church*, you persons?!" And out the crowd went, hoots and hollers of a peaceable Town, most lights dropped, such a rush they were in, and Melody was alone.

Calmly she closed the door behind, not a glance for Ideatown returned to normalcy. Within the church, a dozen handlights illuminated the floor, crisscrossing patterns Melody stooped for, turning off one, then the next, another, initiating a sequence that would not end until every light within was extinguished and Melody's tertiary world was back to normal, having lost the first of Erth, the second of her original Marz. And as she bent and stepped and touched, her only thoughts were: Thanks, I'll remember this one, too.

The event initiated was not to end until each light ended, but after a handful, the memory of a vision on the wall came back to her, Melody grabbing one of the lights and running like heill to the restroom.

She got as far as the hallway's end where Dok was crawling. Unable to reach or find food in the dark cookroom, he had come after Melody. Searle still projected, his dim illumination, lost in the multiple handlights, inferior to the previous flames, the latter a vision Dok may have witnessed, may not have understood.

"I'm sorry, Doktor," Melody said as she helped him stand. "I really didn't forget you on purpose, but the whole town was trying to burn us—did you see . . . ?" and Melody shut up. Take your friend for food without excuses.

He ate all the fruit, but seemed satisfied. She led him to the drainroom next, and Melody was pleased to aid—not happy with those hidden portions she had to smell and see and handle, but pleased for the cool lack of flames, pleased to once again be back to normal, regardless of the scene's total strangeness.

Up the steps and Melody was thinking: The trok I stole, the leak—those effects wore off, and so did Ideatown's change. How about the changes to Nan and them? Will they be permanent? and if not, will they end at the proper interval, after a time equal to that between the two bombs? Or was the Town's return triggered by the horseboy-residents' entering the rather unaltered building? Or, or—or what?

Up the steps and into the restroom with Searle. Chas was so weak he could not stay awake. The baby was in her girly slumberland, curled next to Chas, who seemed the infant when their girths were compared. With them Dok formed a tight triptych on the bed. Beside them in a chair, half-awake Nan wanted to sleep but wanted to complain, so kept one eye open and grumbled wordlessly.

Melody had to collapse next to Dok, fitting in that previous sliver. And there were the random images which had accompanied them up the steps, clear now but coming too fast to make good sense of, Melody too exhausted to try, and certainly she could not ask Searle for specifics.

Then, the opportunity left. Minutes after settling, feeling beaten, Melody simultaneously felt an unplaceable thump on the bed—as though a weight had dropped from no distance—and blinked both eyes shut and open because of the bright lights inside, the normal lights of the church's interior.

Still flat on her back, Melody swiveled her head, seeing Chas with his normal size for this Marz, seeing a very crowded bed. And Nan: middle-aged, not ancient; Pushka awake now with the look of a child, not an infant.

"What happened?" Pushka asked everyone for everyone.

Turning to Searle, Melody saw and heard that the sound effects were gone, back to stolen communications, his eyes just eyes, not projectors.

"Is everyone all right?" Melody asked, looking over to her friends, to all her friends.

"Oh, I feel incredibly bizarre, but I think I'm . . . adequate," Nan moaned as she sat upright.

"Okay here," Chas said with his strong voice returned, a genuine pleasure for Melody to hear. But only for an instant.

She leapt to her feet, but not in pleasure—in anger or exasperation . . . or enormous relief.

"Nan, you are the worst old woman ever to exist in the galaxy!" she yelped, then turned to stalk toward the door. There she stopped, throwing herself about to again confront these people.

"I am going to bed and I don't want anyone bothering me until morning, and I don't care if Marz splits open right through this church, you people better handle it on your own!" And off she went, throwing herself about, into the hallway, having one final comment.

"I hate you I love you—dammit!" she cried, literally cried. But when later her friends looked in on sleeping Melody, they were quite correct to infer relief, and wholly sensible in predicting peace.

# CHAPTER 19:
## Elastic Thighs

Melody woke late to a world once again normal in its peculiarity. Immediately her friends began hounding her for stories, details—What of all these handlights? —and with a minimum of hyperbole, she told them.

The last part with the torches was such a shocker that even Nan had to stare at Melody with utter astonishment. And when she looked to the young woman, Nan saw in Melody not just the fact of her honesty, but the intensity of her truth, saw a tremendous combination of sadness and salvation, saw that the fires never touching her had still left their mark. And Nan had to hold her, had to embrace Melody and thank her, thank her, thank her for being Melody, for *still* being Melody, their Melody.

After she pulled herself away from Nan and Pushka, after running past Chas to the drainroom to wash her face and dry her eyes and again breathe like an adult person, Melody rejoined her friends to cheerfully demand their own stories.

Chas remembered, but had never experienced much, not with his weakness, total weakness, body

and brain. He recalled his size, though, recalled Nan's
and Pushka's ages, recalled Melody being mother to
them all. The big baby had the memory of an infant.
Previously senile Nan, however, remembered enough
to make her experience real, to make her experience
some guilt in the morning. Searle had been examined
only through his recordings, Nan waiting for Melody's awakening before calming Dok with chems and
speaking to the man, not the communiqué receptor.
More important than the bleeders' real experiences
—except sleeping Melody's—were Searle's recordings, but they were only verbal. Thus Melody had rich
descriptions of Dok's abilities to project scenes. Astounded Nan then asked what Melody had seen to
clarify a conversation wherein strangulation was ordered.

Anxious Melody made certain no bleeder but Nan
heard her story as the two fems stood before the
pantry factingrate. Nan's face was all intensity as she
listened. Suffering again from her illness of optimism,
Melody concluded by saying she did not believe that
Hagen could make Searle do such a thing, not their
Doktor.

Nan believed. Without a word to Melody, she ran
off, placed the doktor, then found Chas, telling him
the entire story, telling him to never ever leave Searle
alone with Pushka again. And, of course, Chas never
would.

Sick Melody was truly ill now, ill with dejection,
Nan telling her she needed to watch out for Searle, not
necessarily to worry; but Melody had not recovered
enough from the world of the concept bombs to be
objective on demand.

On with the stories. Although no longer in the

mood for enthralling Nan, Melody had that most important tale of the ore crop, the farmer, and bleeder Hagen.

Nan nearly dropped her spleen.

"Melody, this fact is so intrinsic to our situation that however we proceed must be based upon the datum. It might be the lever we need to have the Board oust Hagen."

"But what if they already know about it?" Melody offered. "They're mostly crazy, anyway."

"Some of them are nonsane," Nan corrected her, "but Hagen is mad *and* ambitious. Certainly Second Chair Gleeson is concerned with the problem of AM seepage and abuse. Hagen, however, is the abuser."

Melody agreed, looking for eats as Nan again examined the strangulation conversation. Thereafter, the morning turned largely normal: Chas out for food, making connections without kash (disguising the doktor and carrying him literally, effortlessly along), Pushka playing, Nan perspiring before the data integrator. Only Melody was without function, lost because no longer did she have to go everywhere doing everything for everyone.

Eventually Nan had a plan: she was going out to communicate with the Anti hierarch, learn of the Telaks, the Antis' response to the concept bombing and additional facts thereof, tell them what the bleeders had learned of Hagen (though not of Searle the destroyer). Her plan was to begin devising future dealings, but the bases remained the same: get Hagen off the Board, and return the bleeders to their original planets. Before leaving, Nan had a final instruction.

"Mel, I want you to promise me that this time you will not follow. You and I do not need the excitement that accompanies you. Do I have your promise?"

"No, you don't," Melody told her, and turned to walk away.

"I didn't think so," Nan said loudly, and left. Alone.

This time, Melody did not care to follow. She wanted fresh excitement no more than Nan. After trying to consume some of the terrible jarred food-stuffs Chas had brought (pasty, processed carbos he claimed to be "Good for overactive, too mean girl"), Melody resorted to playing with Pushka.

"Melody, because you didn't let us all get burned up and everything, you can play with my dolly all you want. Except when she wets herself. Then you better let me take care of her, because you didn't take care of everybody real good because the drainroom still stinks and even Chas couldn't get it clean."

Melody stared back as though she had been slapped. For a moment she was certain that again she had the wrong planet, another wrong planet. Perhaps she was right.

"Well, looks like I have to follow Nan," she sighed, and—to the protests of Chas and Pushka—threw on a half-fast disguise and hit the alleys.

She did not find Nan, but then, she really wasn't looking. Melody just wanted to be out, away from the church; and, yes, away from her friends for a time. The first thing she noticed upon leaving the building was how noisy Ideatown was in reality, the comparison with Ideahorseboytown still clear in her memory. Noisy with people blocks away and yards away and kars and karts skidding and screeching and sliding, noisy with projected sounds when she got too close. And—yes, yes, yes—visually noisy with the abrupt angles and filthy kurbs and horrendous colors and throwaway clothing. She missed the good clean dust of the bombed town, the broad and quiet expanses of the streets, the hand-constructed buildings. But in this real Ideatown, regardless of the hollering and begging for her to "please, well-loved lady, feed your empty face with my eats or I AM OUT OF WORK ON-TO THE STREETS!; still, no one laughed at her, leered at her, or came at her with fire. What a terrible world, she thought, when it's reasonable to prefer this town to others.

In a rush she thought of her previous, dull Marz, her absolutely perfect Erth—and Mom and Dad and her parents and her folks and hand mining and work forcing and all her other friends and home, her real Erth home that she would never, ever . . .

Melody stopped thinking. No optimism-illness here, just plain homesickness. The concept of her being separated from her true universe was an idea she could not bear at the time, not with all those other ideas expressed about her, the ones she had to avoid merely to survive. The idea of Home was beyond her; so Melody thought of Here, and turned back, walking directly to the church. Already she had a special fondness for Ideatown, for the wild, ever-working, harmless folk, but the fondness was not yet love. Melody returned to her friends.

"So, the girl who tortures people, you're keeping her?" Searle asked Nan. After returning from her journey of communication with the Antis, Nan nulled the doktor in order to compare her findings with his experience. As soon as he came around, however, Searle looked about for a specific person, for Melody.

"Gee, Dok, I was just trying to bring out the best in you," she offered sheepishly, not certain how to respond, Searle so strange now that he looked directly to people and spoke normally, with average words at an understandable rate. Dok just stared at her a moment, his expression difficult to read; for although he was largely back to normal, this normalcy was chem-induced, strange in itself. And though Melody expected tension to ensue after the doktor's final words, every-busy Nan obviated their anxiety.

"What do you remember, Doktor?" she asked with a scientific tone.

"Apart from the little witch torturing me, not much, I tell you," Searle maintained, and looked to Melody blankly.

Now she had nothing to say. She could not discern his attitude, and was not about to make pronouncements such as, "I did it for the good of the community." Uniquely, Melody kept quiet.

"Don't look so sad, small bleeder," Dok then told her. "I'm sure you had some fine cause, perhaps for the community's good—no?"

"Perhaps," she mumbled, and looked to Nan for salvation.

"Dok, you say you don't remember anything of what you saw, or how you showed Melody?"

"Of this, I remember little. That I was like some light, yes, but what I saw . . . ? This I can't say. Normal vision I had, however, if only a little. But enough to see the witch here and her crowd. Had she fed me, I would have missed this."

Dok was neutral as water, but Melody had to swallow something. Nan glanced to her, to unaffected Searle, and continued with the great communicator, describing the recordings of his displays, asking Melody for clarification. Businesslike Melody supplied details plainly, trying to be a recorder herself. Remember facts, not feelings, was her goal. Through Nan and Melody, Searle was told all that occurred, all of his projected stories, except for that final scene. No mention was made of Searle's being a potential killer.

Soon Dok was up walking on his own, taking a turn about the church with Chas and Pushka, the latter delighted by his condition, unable to look away from his again-normal face. This lasted for minutes, until Melody heard childish shouts from the sanctuary.

"Stop calling her a witch! And I don't care if you are only kidding—it-is-not-fun-ny!"

"Back to normal," Nan sighed to Melody, the former back at the factingrate telling Melody of the latest.

The Telaks had disappeared, as per their deal with Hagen. Ideological exile would be the results of their returning to the Antis. Though no real damage had been caused by the concept bombs, the Antis also judged this to be a desperate move, and feared that Hagen was ready for more desperation. Searle's intercepted communiqués and recordings revealed that the Board, in its inferred humanity, was placing increased pressure on Hagen to moderate his use of the Powerhouse's AM energy. Hagen insisted that Marz must reach a peak of growth before cutting back on energy expenditures, else the planet would languish as just another farming state. What Searle had not nonconsciously learned, however, was of Hagen's most secretive plans: nowhere in his recordings was there any inkling of the concept bombing, and nothing of the experiments with Dr. Deign as a killer at a distance. Nan had an interpretation.

"The two areas are in conjunction," she told Melody. "Likely, Hagen's experiments with Dr. Deign allowing him to control a communication bleeder at a distance also revealed how to limit Searle's reception abilities. Either Hagen can now block specific communications, or else he's being more careful in keeping them quiet."

"All they have to do is write notes to each other."

"Of course they discovered that early: Searle can only receive electromagnetically transmitted data —unless he's concept-bombed. But this type of communication is difficult to avoid in a modern business organization. All along, of course, we've managed to learn of MEL's intents by piecing tiny bits together, not by simply learning of a significant conversation. Now these bits are becoming harder to find."

"Could they be feeding Dok false stuff?" Melody wondered.

"Oh, I've always noted conflicting data—falsified data—but since Dok receives nearly everything communicated within the Powerhouse complex, the false data are only a minute percentage of the whole. All I can say now is that we have to be more careful in applying what they say. But this puts us and the Antis in a quandary: we have to take time in making our next move, but the more time we take, the more Hagen will be able to nullify Searle."

"Oh, not more time, Nan," Melody moaned. "I want to get back to *my* lousy Marz. I hate this one."

"But of course, Melody," Nan added wisely, "you've been here shorter than anyone else."

"Yeah, but I've been burned more often," Melody

grumbled, and Nan could not disagree. "Let's not mention surgery," concluded the younger quasi-ghost.

Since the most profound story had not been mentioned by Nan, Melody asked of Em Ee El's number one bleeder.

"We are assuming the Board does not know that Hagen is an appearee," Nan replied, "so we are going to inform them—but how can we prove it? And we're going to let Hagen know we've learned of his background. Perhaps he'll be more cooperative with us thereafter, since we could be so valuable in his returning home."

"Maybe he doesn't want to go home," Melody offered. "Maybe he's just a petty businesshume on his Marz, but he's the number one entrepreneur here."

"All we can do is use this new datum as best we can against Hagen and wait for a response," Nan shrugged.

Since Nan needed to speak with Searle again, Melody needed to be elsewhere. Regardless of his name-calling's being ultimately more humorous than accusatory, Melody was uncomfortable around him. Deep down, no one likes being a torturer. But before she could escape, a strange chiming from the corridor was heard, a sound Melody should have been able to place, but could not.

"What's that?" she asked anyone.

Nan was already running to the hallway, Melody watching her pass as Chas answered.

"Phone," he said, "the tellaphone."

Melody replied, "I didn't think it worked; no one uses it."

"Emergencies," Chas said, "emergencies only."

And then Nan was back in the cookroom, excited and speaking.

"That was from a viewer on the Town's edge. Hagen has sent the oddies in—all of them. We're leaving, and there's no coming back. Everyone to her hideout. I'll call you. Go!"

Melody was nearly lost, but not quite. She knew enough to cooperate when Nan pulled her along, upsteps, disguises for everyone, out the back and side doors in three directions. Chas took Searle who had not yet returned to buzzing. The bleeders moved efficiently, only Pushka balking.

"I want to take Melody to my spot," she pleaded to Nan.

"Pushka, you worry about Pushka alone," Nan stated firmly, and virtually shoved her out the door, Pushka going one way, Nan and Melody another, Dok and Chas out of sight.

Along building edges, beneath overhangers, through porticoes, past mad businesses, moving quickly but not running, trying to look residential. And there were the oddies, Nan slowing whenever they were seen, trying to blend in with the busy folk around them.

Soon Nan guided Melody into the fore door of an eatery. Eye contact with the waiter d'. Nan and Melody into the back, off with the disguises, on with long, full pantingloons, hairpieces, demi-helmets, all of an ugly pucia. These were the uniforms of the eatery's servers, Nan and Melody the latest. Both looked rather male. Quick words to Melody: You don't know what to do; so sit there and nibble; you're on your break. Nan then went to the huge front room's far side and began serving. As soon as the meals were slid out on siramic trays from the cookroom, Nan found the purchaser and led him to the food, telling the customer to eat and be out, too crowded.

Melody did no nibbling. The food was complicated —all these textures and smells—but nothing before her seemed developed originally for human consumption. Looking at the waiter next, Melody saw a fake. This man was no resident, Melody recalling Nan's comment about certain people being unaffected by idea power, about the Antis' having stationed some in the Town. And she wondered what kind of generosity would allow a person to endure such madness instead of going about his normal life, just in case his associates needed help.

Selfish Melody felt gratitude, but said nothing. Examining their location, she looked through the window to discover the significance of this site. Nan had led her indirectly to an excellent view; for straight down the facing street was the church, part of the building's front visible. And then there were oddies, a row of blue vehicles before the white structure. This was no coincidence: one kar checking the church, yes, but a horde? And Melody could only think, How did they learn? If Telak had told, why not send oddies to the church earlier, and thus avoid bombing the entire city? Then she recalled Dr. Deign displayed on the wall, controlled. And what now of Searle?

Nan was also looking, from yards away sharing a glance with Melody. Between and around people on the street, Melody looked toward the church, the kars and oddies there. But then she saw people nearby who demanded her attention. Astonished, Melody noticed silhouettes, postures which she recognized at once. And there, a couple, a farming couple passing and gone, a pair Melody recognized above all other people, for these were her parents.

No odds outside. Run to the window: parents to the left, no constables in the vicinity. Run to the back, not looking at Nan, off with the uniform and on with her disguise, to the front door and out, not looking at Nan, who moved toward her then, but Melody was gone.

Traffic ahead, all these people walking, projected ads everywhere; and there, her parents. Looking about, no odds, Melody removing her beard and nose until her face was natural. Then she ran ahead, through the crowd and around her parents, breathlessly watching them as they approached. And, yes, God of heaven, there were her mother and father walking toward her, Mom and Dad stepping to Melody, looking at her, directly at her, then walking past, no recognition—none—in their faces. And they were gone.

Slowly Melody moved from the edgewalk, into a shop where men begged her to spend monies on WHATEVER *was to be* HAD! but she could not hear them. Still with sense enough to don her disguise, Melody apart from that was senseless. Perfect sense, though, and so simple, Melody stepping back onto the walk with the understanding that on this Marz, her parents had no children. At least no Melody. Had this been the case, she would have never appeared here, for she would already be present.

With no pause, she moved back to the eatery, feeling nothing, absolutely nothing, and seeing little else. Inside the building, Melody's perceptions improved, for at once she noticed that Nan was not there.

Completely, then, she forgot her parents, looking everywhere for her friend, but no Nan. Melody knew where to turn, however; for the waiter d', though completely still, had a frantic look which drew her. And when she was inches away, he spoke so quickly that Melody could barely hear, but there was no mistaking his ideas.

"Chaeung was here. Searle went wild; Chaeung went wild back, learned Searle told the MEL of these sites with his head. Chaeung left him and came here for Flamini. Run, you better run."

Immediately Melody returned to the front door. No oddies. Outside, moving quickly. Look around coolly, no danger, keep going, not running—that's too obvious. Think as you move. And Melody continued for seconds until through the crowd she saw a man lying on a stretcher as though the victim of an accident. But he did not seem to be injured, eyes open, lips moving quickly as was usual for Dr. Searle.

Searle.

Melody forced herself not to panic, not to look at Searle or look around everywhere for oddies. But she moved to one side of the edgewalk so that Searle could not see her, would not identify her. But he did not need to. Three more steps and it seemed every person on the walk was a constable. They had come from the nearest buildings, no kars. They all looked at Melody exactly as they had when she was in the stolen trok. Melody stopped. The oddies stepped near, and one began speaking.

"Good day, Mizz Preece," he smiled as though Melody were a valued customer in his salon, "this way, please," and he and several other odds led her to Searle.

He seemed unchanged. Lips buzzing, one eye looking here, one there. One at Melody. Then his buzzing stopped, his lips going still. When Searle next spoke, his voice was different, Melody recalling the imitations Dok had performed when projecting on the wall. But this was no imitation, for the voice was exactly that of Josef Hagen.

The street continued. Miners around them looked, but were pressed away by the oddies. Residents left and right were prepared to ignore this scene, and did not care to listen to the improper, too real voice from Searle.

"Welcome back, fine Mizz Preece," the doktor said clearly with Hagen's cultivated tone. "It will be so satisfying to have you again in our surrounds. I am so looking forward to concluding our incomplete dealings. Before you leave Ideatown, however, our people must be certain to obviate interference. If you will excuse me . . . ," and Searle's one focused eye turned to the nearest oddie.

"Enforce her," Hagen ordered with Searle's mouth, "so that our fine appearee will not be walking away."

Without acknowledgment, the oddie motioned over his shoulder; and past him stepped another officer, this one with the special accouterments of the Ideatown force: that bag, those bracelets.

Quick as a crime, the oddie reached for the latter;

and Melody saw firsthand how they worked, saw how elastic they were regarding size, saw how easily they fit above her knees, and clicked around her thighs. Then her view became poor, shocked Melody rushing past these oddies as she fell to the walk, fell roughly on her backside past her still-vertical disconnected legs.

# CHAPTER 20:
## *Prey to a Cordially Pieced Creature*

How fine to hear old music, classic themes soothing the very air, so it seemed, no Ideatown screeches or screams, no anxious speeches from friends. No tears from children or the injured. Forever Melody lay before determining that she was on her front, but all along she knew she felt . . . odd. No better term. Odd, but warm, and comfortable with the music, nothing unpleasant exactly, only a trace of impropriety, the possibility that something might be wrong or might have been wrong. For a time she held this feeling, Melody unable to determine the interval; but, then, she was not questioning.

Minutes, maybe. Excessive seconds. Soon or eventually Melody opened her eyes, and intentionally tried to look around. Trouble with focusing her eyes, so she focused her feelings. Prone, yes, on a bed, head on a narrow pillow—clean and medikal yellow —smelling this fabric surface, feeling these smooth materials immediately about her. And beyond, seeing better now in the bright light, a wall, a high wall extending an unknown distance to either side, for Melody's ability to turn her neck was limited. A broad but closed door there painful to see, her head not fully responding when she wished to move, Melody unaware of the problem, the imperfection, not feeling groggy exactly, yet not feeling aware, Melody recognizing the remnants of a medikal sleep, a precise, chemical unconsciousness.

Turning her head, chin on the pillow, was easier to her left, Melody's view here filled with equipment, nothing visible beyond multi-level tables with orgotronic machines, clear biological tubings for fluids, opaque cables for electrons, tiny pipes for a negative-yellow flow, all arranged like neat bristles, flexible bristles growing toward her, their goal unseen. This working girl knew some of these devices, certain of the adjacent instruments for measuring: graphed displays, adjustment knobbees, and functioning lights. Others were a mystery. Furniture for work here, equipment for medikal use. Immediately recognized, however, was the monolithic machine which blocked her vision, Melody not likely to forget the concept surgeon regardless of dull consciousness.

Turning her slow-acting neck, Melody was thinking of looking to her opposite side; but directly before her was the sight to study: a small see-screen at the bed's end. Difficulty focusing here, with the screen so low and near, Melody grasping pieces of a scene before comprehending the whole: sheets the same pus yellow as hers, a skin-like area where the bristle machines' snakes ended, more sheet color; and at one side of the screen what could have been the rear of a half-shaven head, for wasn't that witch-colored hair above a sheet-covered back?

Melody was able to think better now, to ask questions if not answer them. Why this program? No fun that she could see, Melody almost thinking that the hair was her texture, her length where not chopped; but wouldn't that make the skin-colored area a body being repaired? Nothing moving on the screen. Looking closer now: weren't those covered shapes legs, feet with heels up? Melody so brilliant as to twitch her left leg which responded in kind on the screen, but why so sore? as though crushed. As though . . .

Now she remembered, recalling the neatest dream: both her legs cut off precisely as this recollection, Melody looking at the screen, turning her right ankle —seeing the screen's move—then her left, left calf, the right, watching the screen's identical actions, twist the right knee, left foot, both, do everything, repeat; for Melody was recalling better, recalling that the amputation was no dream.

Her heart was loud now and Melody was awake, fully awake. The only feeling or intent within her was to turn around, to look at her legs without electronic intermediary, but she could not raise her body, Melody feeling a strap on each shoulder. Still, she managed to pull her neck around and kick high, high as possible, kick painfully. And, yes, she could see the sheet jump, could feel it settle, Melody finally convinced that her limbs were attached. And because she was whole again, Melody no longer had to recall that dream, the horror, that truth. But before she could fully calm, Melody had to look again, had to study the screen to see what else was missing.

Tubes were taped to her back and multiple wires and the skin was pink. No cuts, no staples, no wounds—had she hurt herself when falling? after that oddie . . . Something was wrong, but how can you tell with modern medicine, with a concept surgeon available? Perhaps that man would know, the one Melody saw moving in the vid. Yes, perhaps Hagen would know.

Not since their sharing brunch had she met so suave a person. Neither his chiffon apparel nor perfectly groomed face made this man, however: his singular attitude—from carriage to gesture—marked Hagen as special. Not necessarily good, perhaps unnecessarily evil, and certainly different from his reserved demeanor on Melody's Erth. But this was not her Erth, her planet. It belonged to Hagen.

"I wanted you to see me first," he told her cordially, and moved into Melody's direct sight, not far, but not too near. "After all, you personally have caused me more distress on this planet than any other individual. I thought it only fitting to return the honor, and manifest my impression of proper treatment for you. Please understand that since you left, this notion has become an obligation, a matter of pride."

Gracious, seemingly gracious, but perhaps Melody was in no condition to judge his mood. Neither did she understand the gesture he next made. Regardless, the door slid open and a medikal person entered —with a sterile-pus outfit—pushing an important-looking kart holding a thin, semi-rigid container, the kind used for shipping artificial limbs. The kart was placed near Hagen, who gave another gesture, sending the physician away without ever having looked at him. All the while Hagen had been looking at Melody. And slowly he lost his courtesy.

He gained a look of tremendous potential which Melody recognized: the same expression Hagen had held on Erth the moment before he turned furious and . . .

"I owe you," he told her, his voice cold, face still neutral—too neutral, as though dead or about to die. "I owe you this," and he opened the container's end, pulling forth a long skeletal part, pulling out a backbone.

Dry, clicking like a rhythm box as he removed it, held it out like a necktie, a human spinal column, all these vertebrae, all of them Melody's.

"Yours," he reported, voice as composed as a concept bomb, "herewith returned as promised."

And he broke it, crushing his hands together with a grimace that was hate, crushed and twisted the spine till it snapped, crackled like kindling, Hagen continuing to contort his face and the backbone, but only the latter lost small white pieces which snapped away. Only the bone was left twisted and misshapen. Human bone is hard, as proven by Hagen's effort; but Hagen was determined, as proven by his results. In the end, silent Hagen was calm, no smile, no excitement. Hagen was quiet, but the backbone was a racket, graceless, useless, and once again Melody's; for Hagen casually tossed the pieced creature onto her back, Melody watching his moves with no panic, no pain. The Prime Chair then turned and walked away, his fulfillment enough to ease through his skin like an odor. And she emulated his motion, her head falling to the pillow just as Hagen flowed from the room, movements equal in instance and grace, her eyes moving past that pale skin and bone pile on the see-screen, Melody instantly unconscious, prey to an impossibly deep sleep which claimed her.

# CHAPTER 21:
## *Heart in the Hospital*

Melody became awake because she had no cause for sleeping: not tired, not dregged off, slept too long regardless, regardless of circumstance. The sweet music had not disturbed her, no true thinking going on, and Melody was certain those quiet words would not be waking anyone, those . . .

What quiet words? This speaking from behind her. No way she could turn around. Look up to the see-screen with a horror story, the same static terror as before; and Melody jumped to knock it from her sight, but could move one inch, a stiff inch with those straps, that reduced body. Then she had the clearest thought in an era, recalling that this positioning of see-screens for flattened patients was not unusual, Melody in her youth having worked in hospitals, having worked everywhere; and where was the chin adjustment? Stabbing her pillow, she found the padded plate, and lunged down to elicit a click, the kamera angle changing, Melody seeing all her head, wrong way, reverse, back to the back, the goddamn broken back, past, past the covered legs/feet to the end of the bed, more furniture and equipment, spares, and there: another bed. On it lay a man, properly supine, an unwilling traitor she called friend, Dr. Searle speaking beneath the palest blue light.

A second concept surgeon flashing low-level negative yellow on him, off, on. But something else before settling on Dok, something on the wall behind. Chin the plate for a wider view, Melody panning up, autofocus on dark windows, another known sight, auditorium windows now with no audience behind them, no one to be seen but down, down to the doktor, the speaking doktor. Twisting her chin, Melody found no volume control, and she did want to hear him speak, for what else was there to do? Oh, well, narrow the acceptance angle and read his lips, Melody having worked with the communicative sub-abled. And, strangely enough, she could understand him; for no longer were Searle's lips aflutter. He was not speaking with perfect clarity, but by listening and looking, Melody understood him to say that, "By listening and looking, I'll get what he says."

"What?" she said distinctly to herself, and watched the doktor say "What?" simultaneously.

"He can't be reading my mind," Melody thought, exactly as Dok said the same, the pale neg-yellow going off and on.

Aware that people commonly sub-vocalize when thinking, Melody carefully, consciously thought with no movement in her throat, concentrating not on a word, but a . . . color.

"Blue," Searle muttered.

"Aqua; you were close," she and he said as one.

For a time thereafter, Melody continued to experiment with Searle's capabilities; and, yes, it seemed he could read her thoughts, but imperfectly. She surmised the concept surgeon was creating and/or improving his abilities therein, but Melody was having difficulties with her own abilities therein, with thinking and concentrating. Luckily this weakness aided her, preventing tormented thoughts of Hagen and his bones, of her back she could not feel, not feel the heap out of place.

"Tired," Melody thought, Searle mocking her. "Strength not regained from the work done on me." And she relaxed her strained thinking, no more viewing the see-screen, Melody comfortable in her fading consciousness, but not happy, not pleased, not on this Marz.

Sometime, sometime later, people entered. Medikal personnel. No faces half-awake Melody knew. And she was able to ignore them; for after speaking soothingly to her, all they did was read the machines, empty some bottles connected to her side, adjust something here, and flip the cee-surgeon on a moment. Melody felt nothing from the latter, very little from any of the former, felt nearly satisfied to have company, people who at least seemed kind. Minutes and they were gone, smiling and telling her to feel better, progressing nicely, relax, Mizz Preece; and didn't Searle mumble the same words?

A great length of sleeping this time. Wake to look at Searle on the screen, Melody's thoughts still dull, med personnel returned, removing bad fluids and installing good ones, nutrients, friendly, neg-yellow awhile, people gone, Dok's mumbling stopped. Medfolk again, but these for Searle, one man familiar, but she didn't know how, uncertain of recognizing the face or the brace; for whom did she know with an injured neck? One of Searle's meds was her doktor, too, seen before at her bedside, seemingly in charge. Some speaking by them and two left, two remaining, machines manipulated around Dok's face, Melody presuming therapy. This procedure thereafter occurred often.

No way to tell day from night, but some of these came and went: one of each, a pair, perhaps, Melody in a lethargic routine which unfortunately was ending.

Pain, she awoke and every part of her was uncomfortable. No torture here, just discomfort. New, unrecognized medfolk came and went, Melody aware she was coming around because their friendliness made her sick at first sight; and though able to speak, she refused to. And later, anxiety, Melody finding herself nervous and not liking it. She wanted to do something, wanted the scene to change, wanted most to get out. Then Melody began scanning the room with the kamera, trying to gain a view of something different. But what she found was an old story nearly forgotten, Melody spying this flat body with exposed flesh supporting a white pile. She found that her backbone had been ripped out and crushed to pieces, and something stopped within her. One good look at the screen and her heart stopped or her mind but certainly her sanity; for that bone heap was a creature eating her, killing her; and she had to get it off, had to fling it away. And she tried, leaping and bucking with every muscle, every remaining bone as she hissed and grunted no-words which Searle repeated as Melody tore at the restraints, tore at her own skeleton, but she could not rid herself of the horror. And deep within she knew that the bones' location would have no effect on this riddance, but at least she had to get that sick thing away before she LOST HER MIND. And she tried, Melody an insane, frightening sight of convulsions and frothing to the man who ran into the room and adjusted a small device until she calmed, until she slept. But even unconscious she seemed in a fit, her expression one more of defeat than repose. And though he guessed the cause of her hysteria, the man knew better than to move that heap, because certainly he wanted to keep his own intact.

". . . Got to get her away from that thing, or she won't consider me worth . . ."

". . . more hours to get . . . credit this . . . end . . ."

". . . running low on . . . as though food, enough to make a . . . person out . . ."

". . . biggest one I ever saw; glad I didn't have to . . . it."

She had not thought for hours. Hours before, she had found a goal, something to concentrate on so that she would not be able to concentrate on herself. Melody was listening to Searle, trying to find anything familiar, trying to place the people whose minds he read. Consistent pieces about medicine, the word "hospital," other terms to fit these two concepts, all placed the thinkers as nearby, as medfolk. Much therapy for Searle, these specialists evidently changing his abilities, Melody determining this not by their actions, but by their results; for Dok's speaking became even more partial, a word at a time, then two, finally proper terms to capture Melody with their profound syllables. First, "Anti" was spoken. Later, Melody heard "Nan." The latter provided new life for her, Melody acutely feeling alien again, realizing she was on the wrong world, away from the familiarity —the family—of her friends.

After a day or days, after further therapy, Searle was able to convey parts of conversations as well as thoughts. Soon he relayed whole sentences, and was able to imitate not the sound of voices, but their emotional content. Imperfectly, yes, but Melody could tell that the speaker was upset when saying, ". . . Please, Nan, please—God—*please* we have to get our Melody back . . ."

No heart in the hospital broke with this phrase. Melody presumed all of Searle's words were being recorded, and she seemed equally mechanical, recognizing Pushka as the doktor's source, but no weeping, no destruction within her, Melody in no position to be pitying either Pushka or herself. In this bed, Melody was alone and was busy, concentrating on the facts Searle conveyed, not the feelings he intercepted. Soon Melody was certain that Dok read only conversations now, and only those of the bleeders. No more mind reading, but perhaps distance was involved, Melody wondering how far you can think. The conversations Searle relayed were partial, pieces Melody connected into an increasingly clear intent, the flat doktor speaking the words of the nearest witch as she thought to herself one bed removed.

"God, they're coming to get me."

"Yes, they are, Melody," Hagen told her.

No words from Searle here, for Hagen was in this room, speaking for himself. Taken by her own thoughts, Melody could not tell whether Hagen had just entered, or had been present for . . . forever.

He stepped before her where she could see, for certainly Melody did not turn her head, did not aim the kamera. She had shown no reaction with his speaking, and now had none for his move, not looking away as he stood before the bed. But since their levels were unequal, Melody saw only his chest, and sought no better view as Hagen continued.

"As you of course deduce with your fine intelligence, my child, the remaining appearees have strong intents regarding your position. What you may not have discerned from listening to the good doktor here is the intensity of your associates' activity. What a tremendous lure you are, Mizz Preece, to have so activated your people. You must be a wonderful cook."

Hagen laughed mildly at his own humor, a sound ended by Melody's tiny burp, an intended noise for which she had no apology. Moved by her lack of manners, Hagen ceased his laughter. Standing calm and quite erect in his chiffon, he continued.

"Dr. Searle was found to progress more rapidly while in your vicinity. The idea expressed, we believe, is satisfaction at being with one's own kind. Perhaps the remaining appearees will show improvement in their attitude toward Marzian Energy once they are near you two again. The situation can only get worse, you understand. The only thing left in the relation between myself and you bleeders is violence. And no one wants violence."

He paused, waiting for Melody's rejoinder, some word from her. She had only a stifled yawn. Hagen saw this, but now had learned of Melody's etiquette, and was showing nothing.

"They are coming shortly, and since we know exactly how and when, of course they shall be captured. My colleagues and I can only hope that once you people are finally shown to be completely under our control, you will be disposed toward cooperating in order to solve our mutual problems. If not, I am afraid there is nothing left but violence. And no one wants violence."

No waiting for her rudeness now, Hagen having turned to leave with his final phrase. No reaction from Melody regardless: no depression or pain, no quick thinking of her choices to determine how best to aid herself and her friends. Melody was not thinking how to leave, to escape, for she was going nowhere. The day she had rioted on her bed to toss that bone off was Melody's best effort with her body. Irrespective of straps, Melody knew she would remain. Were more nulling chems within her? Regardless, she was not together and feared that pulling away from these machines would mean pulling away from her life. Melody was going nowhere.

For another day she hurt everywhere, the dull ache so pervasive it stole her concentration, Melody sleeping more, no longer having to fight her condition in order to distinguish Searle's words, for Hagen had silenced him. After that one-sided conversation, medfolk arrived with a translucent box which they placed over Searle's head. Air came in, but not a sound left, the box of a distorting material which precluded Melody's reading Searle's lips. Clearly she was to be uninformed as to the specifics of her rescue. Since Hagen's visit, Melody had done no worrying, only waiting. Regardless of calming chems, Melody was not anxious about the other bleeders, about the nature of Hagen's certain trap. She only waited for her friends, however, whenever they would come. There was to be no surprise, however, for Hagen told her in advance.

He entered within her vision this instance, through the broad door, a snatch of active people in the corridor, their sound. At once Melody realized the closest she had come to feeling pleasure lately was simply being apart from Hagen. The only emotion she had for him was the desire to be away, never again near for any cause, not to see his execution or his assured entry into Hades. Heaven for Melody would be separation from Hagen forever.

"I just stopped by to mention that you and I have only one day and a half to wait," he told her cheerfully, "for then the appearees will be here with our stolen refractor and many Antis. Their plan is to attempt a coup as before when your services were taken from me. Their intent is to again succeed with surprise, by attacking without warning, but now using many Antis, more than have ever been gathered before. Several details in this planning show great imagination, a tribute to Mizz Flamini, you might be sure. Fortunately, since we know all the details that the appearees know, we can capture them peacefully. Most of the hospital staff will be replaced by disguised constables. These men will be armed so as to obviate any violence on the part of the bleeders. No one wants violence."

He left. Melody waited. No anxiety within her, no true hopefulness or foreboding. Only waiting, soft music about her, Searle constant within his box. But hours or a half day later, Melody found a new aspect of her situation: insanity. The bone heap on her back was itching her, a mild irritation she could not reach, Melody twitching about first in discomfort, then aggravation, ultimately in torment. She tried to reach, but her shoulders were secured, her arms seemingly attached to the bed. With great compression here, stretching there, she managed to reach her rib cage, but not her back, not that itching, that torment. Melody continued to twitch and roll those several degrees she was able, but did herself no good, longing for the next medfolk to enter. And this future scene of relief was one she lived in advance for hours, Melody as she waited envisioning the exact devices of aid, seeing professional hands scratch at her with medicinal fingernails, simple manipulation to bring her certain joy.

The most excitement she felt in days was from the entrance of that single attendant, one seen before or not—who knows?—Melody finally anxious for salvation, the salvation of fingertips rubbing her skin.

After a croak necessitated by days of speechlessness, Melody managed to tell the woman, "Please scratch my back, it's killing me . . ."

"Certainly, Melody," Nan told her. "Where does it itch?" but all her fingers went to the right spot without searching.

Nan told her.

Nan's fingers.

Nan's voice. Non-hopeful Melody knew that voice.

Non-deluded Melody recognized that tone, that speaking, and aimed the kamera at the woman's face as she scratched, first moving the bone heap. Melody thought she just tossed it, but heard no sound, and did not see the pile leave. But she saw those fingers and felt them exquisite, saw them move about the tubes and wires, the woman bending over Melody having no known face. This med caused the expected joy with her hands, unexpected, additional joy with her identity which was explained by the one silent word spoken not to the kamera, but to Melody as she looked into her face.

"Refractor," those lips pronounced.

Melody was in heaven only for seconds before the other medfolk arrived. Two men pushing a kart with a pile of instruments and storage units. New faces again, but she could guess the people behind them: a slim man who made no skinny lady, a tall Oryental whose complexion was actually dark.

"We killed all their listening," the Oryental with Chas' voice told Nan. "They see what we want."

"Good," Nan said, scratching Melody's back with only one hand now. The other was pulling and plugging tubes. Soon both were on Melody's straps until the girl was loose on her bed.

The other medfolk were also pulling, busy at their pile of supplies and equipment until it was revealed to be a single unit disguised as pieces. But first an interruption, the slim man sliding in a rush to Melody to bend and kiss her forehead. "Oh, Melody," Pushka's sad voice pronounced, and the man returned to work.

They swung the front of the false pile open as a

whole to reveal an unsegmented interior, reveal its temporary contents: a body. Melody's body. The kissing man pulled this nude form out, a lightweight figure of expanded plas, Melody recalling Pushka's doll, this one no more comforting as it flopped in the bleeder's hand. Nothing special was seen in this action; yet still there came applause. Applause from the balcony.

Lights came on there revealing Hagen before a crowd of oddies. Only he was seated, but after a moment rose to give the appearees a standing ovation. The odds remained silent and staring, only the Prime Chair with a smile.

"Isn't this remarkable," Hagen exclaimed with true enthusiasm. "We were certain you knew of our reading your conversations via Dr. Searle, thus knew you were lying outrageously. So we used common, human agents to discover the truth via infiltrating the Antis. Only today did we learn of your true schedule, but time enough. And here we are, all together again. But I think, Mizz Flamini, that I arrived first."

And the lights went out. Immediately several oddies moved through the lower doorway. Each held an unfamiliar tube object at the ready, pointed toward the sensitives. A too brief moment later, Hagen entered behind them, and the door closed.

He seemed so pleased, as though joining a party. A dull party with no one speaking but him, no one moving, looks pulled so tightly between the bleeders and oddies that their eyes seemed to be projecting as Searle's had that evening. Smiling Hagen held out his hands, gesturing for peace, as the party ensued.

"Please, no moving," he purred, looking in turn to

each standing sensitive, each grim, unmoving bleeder. "What wonderful disguises you three have achieved. I am told that if I wait long enough, they will fade to nothing. Then, perhaps, I'll be able to tell if I've captured appearees, or just three internurses," and he laughed lightly. "But, no, I of course know Mr. Chaeung here, our unique Pushka, and the redoubtable Mizz Flamini," and he faced in turn the appropriate bleeder.

As Hagen spoke, he stepped closer as though daring the sensitives to move. The oddies moved, carefully stepping in kind so that neither Hagen nor another odd was in line with the brandished weapons.

"You can scarcely imagine my satisfaction in again being with you," he told the appearees. "Only this reunion can cleanse me of the foolishness I displayed by so underestimating you originally that you escaped my jurisdiction. My thinking then was that you would not be so absurd as to leave the site which literally contained your best chance to regain your homes. But, no, you were so selfish as to become thieves, so thoughtless as to reject my aid. And inadvertently, I allowed this."

Then Hagen changed, displaying a sadness fit a betrayed leader.

"I have always been too . . . kind," he said. "Perhaps I've learned better by now."

His smile was lost with those last phrases, his humor completely dissolved. Then his introspection vanished as a noise came to the broad doorway, the sound of a struggle. Loud speaking as the door opened partially, then fully, many oddies outside; but only one man entered, a member of the Board, the small-

est. Hagen greeted him with a calm expression that
was in fact strain.

"Mr. Second Gleeson, you are here in conflict with
my instructions."

"Mr. Prime," Gleeson replied with a smug smile, "I
might point out that your order is in conflict with my
position. I am not your servant, and not a sensitive."

"Very well," Hagen intoned, "but you will join us
regardless, and take a place as special as these sensitives'. For I order now, Mr. Second, that if you
interfere, the nearest officer will shoot you."

With the faintest gesture of one finger, Hagen
directed an oddie to swivel toward Gleeson, to aim
his tube exclusively toward the Second.

Now Gleeson had no smile, no false humor; for
nothing but shock was on his face as he stared first at
the tube, then at Hagen.

"Not a word, sir," Hagen told him quietly, then
turned to the bleeders.

"Let us begin," he pronounced, gesturing broadly
with outstretched arms, "by moving away from Mizz
Preece. She must be reconnected with our instruments in order to heal properly. Certainly we do not
want her ill."

With small waves he pointed for Nan to move here,
Pushka there, and Chas away. Cautiously they complied, the oddies locked on their every move. Only
Chas found difficulty, taking one short stride before
stepping on some refuse, misplaced debris that
cracked beneath his weight, Chas looking down to
discern the interference, looking down to part of
Melody.

He went motionless, staring at his feet. Hagen was

saying, "Please continue, Mr. Chaeung," but Chas was captured by that sight as surely as though he were caught in a net. He stared down to his shoes as though the sight, the fact, were a total surprise, then looked up to Melody, down to the floor, Hagen becoming anxious because Chas ignored him, Melody only thinking that he must have known, must have known all along. Perhaps, but he had never seen, never seen exactly how Melody had been shredded.

Look to his feet, look to Melody, the Prime Chair becoming firm, more false smiling, and finally Chas looked up to Hagen. Then he provided the Chairhume with his ultimate underestimation.

Great force in a small mass enables remarkable acceleration. Such is the principle of racing vehicles, athletes, and bullets. Chas, the altered bleeder, seemed more an example of the latter than any sort of human, seemed more a magician in his ability to astound than a mere, incomparable athlete. Chas looked up to Hagen, finally up to Hagen, his expression as tight as his changed muscles, conceptual muscles which exploded like bullets, like a concept bomb, manifesting the idea in Chas' person that he would leap twelve feet to Hagen quicker than human reflex and duplicate those bones, breaking Hagen into pieces before the first odd could re-aim.

As though a film at double speed, Chas flew across the floor to grab Hagen's head and crack it backward, then forward, all in the space of a blink. The angle he formed between head and spine was perpendicular, was freakish, Hagen's eyes pointed up, though he stood perfectly vertical, then exactly at his own chest, though he was perfectly dead.

Finally the quick-moving oddies caught up with Chas and were able to aim; but they hesitated, for any expert—any fool—knew that Hagen was dead. Apart from trained response, good soldiers live by orders, kill by orders; and finally they received one before deciding on their own, the new First Chair shouting out quick as any shot.

"No!" was his only word. And the oddies paused, ready at any moment, still, to send Chas to Hagen's new world.

But, no, Chas would never gain that locale. He dropped Hagen, who hit the floor with Gleeson's shout, a heap as lifeless as Melody's spine. And then the former Chair began leaving again: having left his life forcibly, he now left this Marz gradually, for Hagen was fading away.

"Hold, hold," Gleeson uttered as though about to choke, and stared with everyone else at the ghost forming at their feet.

Melody had to strain to see past the screen, but missed nothing. Hagen with his neck at a revolting angle was disappearing. His clothes dissolved, and then his body, every bleeder familiar with that sight, a ghost vision seen by each, and experienced.

Just as he was fading from sight, Hagen astonished them all by moving. Moving. He straightened his neck to a normal angle, looked about, then began to stand unsteadily. And, yes, they could see his face, although transparent, and discern his expression, Hagen as surprised as they as he stood, returned their stare, and vanished.

They continued to look, astounded, all continued to stare at nothing. Then slowly they raised their heads as had Hagen, and stared at one another. Not a word was spoken, the only sound Gleeson's eventual laughter.

He was shaking his head side to side, Melody expecting hysteria; but, no, his response was irony, as proven by his words.

"If only I had known before," he told himself, Gleeson seeming to be alone in the room.

"You didn't know he was a bleeder?" Nan offered clearly, no longer astonished, and never amused.

"Of course I knew he was a 'bleeder,'" Gleeson returned loudly, "but I didn't know he would regain his world by dying. If I had known that, I would have killed him years ago. How perfect that would have been," he sighed. "Of course, I could not have *killed* him—not even Hagen ever *killed* anyone. Yet it would not have been death, but a paradoxical return to proper place. Oh, great Gahd, if only I had known . . .," and he covered his face, appearing exhausted, Gleeson now mourning an unmatchable loss, a loss of opportunity, a loss of time.

Finally there came more speaking, unpleasant words from another source, just the one croak to get her throat going again.

"Hey, Glieson," Melody declared, her tone unkind, "tell these jerks to put their gons away—what are you going to do, kill us?" and she snorted one small, disrespectful laugh.

The implication petrified them all. The oddies kept their aim, but even they seemed uncertain. As though a true leader, however, Gleeson continued with assured words.

"Of course," he countered, looking first to Melody,

then to all the bleeders. "You have killed a man. Regardless of the victim's position, murder on any moral world is typically punished with execution."

"Kill us and we're home," Chas said.

"Are you certain?" Gleeson replied. "You have only the single example. Are your lives worth Hagen's wager?"

"I'm certain," unhappy Melody retorted.

"We have time," Nan told them all fervently. "We have time to study the phenomenon using ourselves and the concept surgeons."

"You have *some* time," Gleeson corrected her. "But even I, the First Chair, might not be able to keep you alive for long. I will not have the power over the Board that Hagen did. And understand, an acceptable execution might coincide with their style, for these people are not completely sane."

A fervid Nan then urged, "Whatever time we have can be used to better understand AM and aid you in solving the problem of the power's misuse." But Gleeson disagreed.

"No, Flamini, moderation is the key here. The problem was Hagen, and he is . . . solved."

More slowly, Nan added, "Then . . . then we can use the time to return to our original states before you, before you . . ." But she could not say, "Before you kill us."

"Why bother?" Chas said. "Hagen was broken but he returned to normal. He was dead."

Nan was not normal. Her condition was worsening, changing from certainty to thoughtfulness, now approaching either ignorance or confusion. But apart from the mental, she was altering bodily; for Melody could recognize her: the refractor's influence was wearing off, Chas growing darker, silent Pushka feminine again.

"Melody," Nan stated, not looking to the strangely displeased girl. "We can help Melody . . . heal."

Gleeson looked to her, looked to Melody, who stared back with a nearly angry expression, seeing Nan in the same manner.

"I'm afraid not," Gleeson intoned with political neutrality. "We've been working with the concept surgeon on her steadily. The doktors here had the idea of truly healing her without Hagen's knowledge, but there has been no progress, not even with a concept surgeon on a sensitive. Because, you see, that's how Hagen kept her alive: because she is a sensitive, because the concept surgeon is her home. I am afraid that on this world, she will never be the same."

Allowing no one pause for great sadness, Melody sternly told the world, this improper world, "I want to go home," and that was no child speaking. Pushka was the child, the baby, as she spoke, trying not to whimper.

"Me too. I want to go home."

"Me too," Chas said, and that seemed an order.

"Let's not be rash," Nan with more confidence called out. "What's the hurry if we're going to die regardless?"

"That's the hurry," Chas said, and pointed to Melody's back, his stiff arm like stone.

No reply here. And since Chas was about to out-think Nan, he continued, turning to Gleeson.

"Second, get us a doktor."

Gleeson stared back at him, took the time for a

single blink, then tipped his head to one side, the nearest odd complying with this order: out the door, back in seconds with a man in med yellow.

The bleeders' doktor, the one Melody considered in charge, the one giving more instructions than therapy. As he stepped inside, the doktor looked about, trying to understand the scene. As though arriving at an accident site, he seemed to be determining where to start. He would start by killing people.

"Tell him to bring chemamps with his best poison. Quick and no pain," Chas said to Gleeson.

The same response as before from the current Chairhume. A blink, a thought, and he pushed his hands flat to the floor. All the oddies lowered their weapons. Then Gleeson turned to the doktor.

"Do precisely as he says," he ordered. "They need five."

The doktor paused. Gleeson nodded, and the same officer responded, taking the man by the arm, leading him out the door. After a wordless minute, the two men returned.

Something in the medik's hand, something ordered. Without pause, Chas stepped to him and took a single chemamp.

"We need a volunteer," he said, and popped it into his neck.

Only Nan gasped, and she gasped completely, her face a disaster. But she made no further sound, for Chas was speaking, looking only to Nan.

"I love you all," he said harshly, and tried to smile, but Chas was not good at smiling. Besides, he was dead.

Not enough time for Nan to begin breathing again

before Chas dropped to the floor, plopping on his backside like a child. Smoothly he slumped forward, already translucent, and lay in an awkward pose as he faded, clothes and body. His last expression as he fell was open-eyed and unaffected, the same old Chas —exactly the person who looked up to them; for as he faded, he also grew dark and large until he was the Chas everyone knew. And when huge and nearly transparent, he looked up, met Nan's eyes, and smiled. A dull smile, but certainly the most gorgeous any sensitive had ever seen. As he raised his hand to wave, Chas was gone.

Nan was weeping, not a sound, but she had thrown her face down to her upraised hands as Chas vanished, and her shoulders heaved. Hard, hard she pressed her hands against her face, Melody looking at her once, then to astonished Pushka, finally to Gleeson.

"Dr. Deign," she stated clearly, voice as firm as her gaze. "What of Dr. Deign?"

Not averting his eyes, Gleeson informed her, "She is in terrible condition," and shook his head. "Hagen went too far with Deign. This death will be so good for her."

"You promise?" Melody asked him.

"Yes, I do."

"Hagen was no liar," she declared; and with total honesty, Gleeson stepped closer, bending to look into her eyes.

"Melody," he said firmly, "I so promise."

She looked past him. Nan was no longer weeping, but seemed frozen, hands wrapped on her face, no movement. Pushka wanted to run to someone, but there was another bleeder to see.

"Our Doktor," Melody whispered, "we have to do our Doktor."

As he straightened, Gleeson looked toward the MEL physician. "Inject this man," he ordered casually.

The medik looked to him as though he had ordered suicide instead of murder. "I won't kill my patient," he shuddered, not concealing his horror.

"You saw what has happened here," Gleeson confronted him.

"I don't know *what* I saw," the shaken physician proclaimed, "but I am not killing a patient."

Melody was looking at that oddie, the one who knew gestures. "You," she said, and Gleeson agreed.

The Chairhume took the physician's remaining chemamps, and handed one to the constable. "Inject that man," he ordered casually.

Melody saw the slightest pause in the odd before he reached for the ampule, and took it. She saw the briefest hesitation as he stepped past her to Dr. Searle. But he bent without difficulty. Only then did he balk, and only because of ignorance.

"How do I do it?" he asked, looking up first to Gleeson, then over to the med; but the doktor would not tell him, slowly, slowly shaking his head, looking awful, about to change his state himself, about to faint or scream or vomit. The doktor would not tell him. So Melody did.

"Stick the point into his neck, and squeeze the part you're holding," she said, and the oddie complied, his move as certain as Melody's speaking. A moment later, Searle was gone. All they saw was this uncertain lifting of his head as he looked around, then vanished.

This MEL physician was no sensitive; why then did he appear the same as Nan, both their faces sagging, bodies weak, their minds only part functioning?

Melody looked to the odd. He appeared as though he had just killed someone, a soldier who had murdered: acceptable, but not the sort of order a decent man should have to follow.

She looked at Nan who weakly returned her gaze, but a different sort of vision, Nan unable to be confused or aware or . . .

"You want to, Nan?" Melody asked, voice as kind and concerned as any doktor, any friend could be. "I love you enough to kill you."

Nan stared, only stared, until weak Melody spoke those final words, and raised her hand for Nan to join her.

Not stumbling, not running, Nan moved in some awkward manner to Melody, who lifted her arm, the women embracing, and neither of them wept.

"You were the best, Nan," Melody whispered, "the best old lady in the world," and Nan could nearly smile, face against Melody's. Nearly smile, but not quite.

Unaltered Melody read her mind. As though manifesting an idea known only to similars, Melody sensed her friend's emotion, her deepest thoughts. Then she raised her hand to Gleeson for him to bring that death, to bring her life.

As though he had practiced the move, Gleeson placed the amp onto Melody's palm, the older woman with an arm around her friend, fingers lightly moving against the girl's head.

"Nan, my Nan, I'll see you in my world," and she slipped the point into her neck, that slightest squeeze to kill her.

With Nan's first slump, Gleeson gave a gesture, the oddies running to grasp her and keep her from collapsing against Melody. Gently they lowered her to the floor, kneeling beside the dead woman. But soon they held nothing, a half-gone Nan looking up sharply to meet Melody's eyes as though surprised. After lifting her hand to her face, young-again Nan stared up to the bed, and then disappeared.

Melody had to hurry. She could feel it coming, and was not about to torture Pushka. Trembling, she raised her shaking hand to Gleeson, anxiously waving her fingers for another amp, another bleeder.

"Pushka, Pushka," she said with a breaking voice, and the woman/girl did not hesitate, rushing to Melody to hold her and weep, hold her and weep as Melody gave her eulogy.

"I'm finding you on my world, and you better find me on yours. You can never have too many friends, too many perfect friends," and into her neck went the chemamp, Pushka stunned for an instant, then hurrying to kiss Melody good-bye, to tell of her leaving.

"I'll find you, Melody, I'll find you and tell you every—" then Pushka could no longer speak. She could no longer stand. The oddies, experts now in dying, held the girl without requiring orders, held her away from Melody, who for a moment would not release her. For a second too many she held her friend, held her dying friend near, not because Pushka was the best, but because she was the last.

Pushka would not go down. She was the slowest to

leave, looking to the oddies holding her, looking to Melody, looking pitiful as she faded. Then she slipped through the officers' hands, the oddies feeling a sensation, a freakish state, they would never likely seek, never volunteer to experience. Pushka slipped from their hands, and they held nothing. She was still genuine, but not on a single world, split and spread between the two Marzes. On her side as though sleeping, her clothing gone, Pushka next lost her gender, growing as she faded to become a man, become a man upon dying. No waving, no smile before or after, Melody recognizing that face regardless of transparency, irrespective of sex, Pushka looking up with her reestablished life to find Melody and stare, that striking visage now masculine, his intense gaze all for Melody, then gone, Pushka gone, and Melody was alone.

Too late, too late, Melody tried to reach for that final amp, her own injection, but could not, could not reach or speak or decide to die. Too many friends had passed away for Melody to remain courageous. Too many friends had Melody killed for her to refrain from breaking down; and since the one remaining seemed somehow least important, she found it acceptable to collapse in her mind and body and cry, completely, weep effortlessly but as though all the effort of her life were in this weeping. And she dropped her hand and her head and her heart and sobbed, absolutely, the tears enough to blind her; but she could not see regardless, for there is no vision in a mind given to misery.

This is what she had saved Pushka from, saved for herself. Melody had felt the collapse coming, and did not want Pushka to have to wait before leaving. Pushka, after all, had been there so long compared to Melody, had been there as a child. But Melody had never been a child on Marz, despite her social status. Weeping absolutely was in no way immature, as proven by the fact that she stopped, wanted to stop, so that she might continue.

A moment, an endless moment, and she calmed, but the calmness was nearly one of unconsciousness. Breathing through a wet mouth, wet nostrils, Melody was exhausted, eyes still a flood, but she could see, could see Gleeson bending near, bending near and speaking. Even with her poor vision, Melody discerned his condition, could tell by his sound that Gleeson had surprised himself.

"I, I think I can do it," he told her with dismay; but, of course, he could not.

"No," she whispered, the best sound she could make that was not a groan, "I'm the only killer here," and with depression as deep as her recent losses, she reached for the ampule, her hand so weak, but no longer shaking.

His was. Gleeson's fingers were so unsteady he nearly dropped the injection. Now he resembled the medik and Nan, still the important Chairhume, but also an affected person. With tremors in his wrist he gave Melody her ampule, gave the device as though handing her death instead of salvation.

Too weak, too weak to hold it, Melody dropped the chemamp—right into her neck, finding enough strength to squeeze, all those tears precluding her vacillation. "Oh . . . ," she said, no poetry, a boring breath as this Marz finally found a way to kill her.

Someone was screeching. Something had gone wrong and Nan was back and gasping again. And yes, yes, it had gone wrong; for just as Melody fell into an obliterating sleep, she saw Gleeson's Marz fade to nothingness; but in its stead was not her own appearing, Melody aware that with her there had been a departure, thinking of her friends dead, then returned with odd expressions, looks which ultimately seemed satisfactory. Now she experienced the strangeness, and knew her expression was most unusual of all; for Melody had not been returned to her true world, not via the needless intermediary that was Marz, those undesired million miles, Melody waking nude in bed, her bed—her home—as proven by her mother in the doorway shrieking. Having manifested great desire via unreal death, suicidal Melody reached without moving to ideas made actual, made substantial from a matrix of love.

Looking at her slighted ceiling, smelling an area as personal as her history, Melody began to sit, feeling strong, began to turn to the sound just as her mother ran to her, fell to the bed, and grasped her daughter's shoulders. Then they looked to one another, inches away but completely together, looked as deep as family blood, as deep as mended bone, searching for identity, praying that this fantasy was true. And there was no mistake in their findings, for here was the only mother, and there her only girl, more real than the world around them. "Hi, Mom," she said, Melody boring again, having nothing more to say, nothing better to do than weep, now with her mother, now with total joy, such satisfaction not even a human word artist could express. Certainly not Melody, speechless Melody, the child—the adult—shown ultimately to be no expert in words, but an artist of humanity.